Hold Me Fast

A Twist Upon a Regency Tale
Book 8

By Jude Knight

ARE YOU SIGNED UP FOR DRAGONBLADE'S BLOG?

You'll get the latest news and information on exclusive giveaways, exclusive excerpts, coming releases, sales, free books, cover reveals and more.

Check out our complete list of authors, too!

No spam, no junk. That's a promise!

Sign Up Here

www.dragonbladepublishing.com

Dearest Reader;

Thank you for your support of a small press. At Dragonblade Publishing, we strive to bring you the highest quality Historical Romance from some of the best authors in the business. Without your support, there is no 'us', so we sincerely hope you adore these stories and find some new favorite authors along the way.

Happy Reading!

CEO, Dragonblade Publishing

About the Book

Childhood sweethearts Tamsyn Roskilly and Jowan Trethewey are ripped apart when her mother and his father conspire to sell Tamsyn to a music-loving earl. He promises to make her a famous singer and to keep her from Jowan.

Hold Me Fast starts seven years later, when Tamsyn has become Tammie Lind, a sensational singing success. Jowan, now baronet in his father's place, hears she has returned to England after a lengthy and successful tour of Europe and beyond. He travels to London to speak to her, but the earl continues to stand in their way.

However, Jowan discovers that Tamsyn has become addicted to drugs and alcohol, supplied by the earl who has seduced, debased, and abused her. Their childhood romance may be over, but now he owes her a rescue.

As he and his friends nurse her through withdrawal and help her make a new life in their home village, Jowan and Tamsyn fall in love all over again. But Tamsyn does not believe she is worthy of love, or that Jowan can truly overlook her past. And the wicked earl is determined to take her back.

It will take the help of their friends and their entire community for Jowan and Tamsyn to finally prevail.

DEDICATION

This book is dedicated to those women I have known and loved whose preferences or circumstances led them down a dark path, and who made the choice to walk away from the substances that gave them relief from their pain. One, sadly, failed and left her two beloved children to be raised by others. One succeeded and built a beautiful life for herself and her family. Bev and Debbie, I am in awe of your determination and your courage. This one is for you.

Prologue

1813, Cornwall

"IT WILL NOT be for long," Tamsyn Roskilly told her beloved. "Mother says I must go, and I can come back when I have learned what his lordship can teach me."

Mother was afraid for her position, and rightly so. Sir Carlyon Trethewey had threatened to dismiss her and to throw her and her daughter off the estate if Tamsyn continued, as he put it, "to sniff around my son."

"I know." Jowan Trethewey took her hand in his own. Her right hand. The one that wore the ring he had given Tamsyn on their sixteenth birthday. The ring she had given him glinted on his own right hand. "They won't part us for long," Jowan promised. "I can bring Father around, or if I cannot, we can run away to be married. I'm his only heir. He will have to forgive me once it is done."

He pressed his lips to her right hand. "I cannot wait to give you a ring for the other hand."

Tamsyn shook her head. The chances of Sir Carlyon changing his mind were somewhere on the same level as the moon falling or the sea turning sweet. Or her mother putting Tamsyn's wants and desires ahead of her own. "When we are twenty-one, we can do as we please," she commented.

It didn't comfort her. Their twenty-first birthday was nearly five long years away. An eternity.

"I will miss you so much," Jowan told her, and pulled her into his arms, ignoring the Earl of Coombe, who stood tapping an impatient foot beside his carriage, and the man's driver, footmen, and outriders.

"I will write to you every day, and I will send the letter every week," Tamsyn promised, burrowing into his chest, taking a deep breath of the unique smell that said 'Jowan' to her. She couldn't speak about missing him, or she would cry. "Lord Coombe says he will frank my letters."

"I will do the same," he promised, dropping a kiss on her hair.

"I hate to break up this touching scene," Lord Coombe drawled, "but we really must get on the road."

Jowan cast him a glance seething with anger and impatience. Jowan didn't trust the earl and had made such a fuss about Tamsyn going with him that Sir Carlyon had paid Dorwa from the village to go with Tamsyn as her maid. Just for a few weeks, until Lord Coombe could hire her a London girl because Tamsyn was going to be a singer in far-off London and would need a maid who understood the demands of the stage.

"I have to go," she whispered to Jowan. Part of her wanted to go. To be able to make her living with her music. To be away from her mother and her mother's constant criticism. To be safe from Sir Carlyon and his threats towards her and her mother. To be valued for her singing and her beauty, the very things that drew her mother's anger and Sir Carlyon's scorn.

"I know," Jowan said. He set her free from his arms with the greatest of reluctance, and she had to fight not to clutch at him again. The larger part of her didn't want to go. The part that had belonged to Jowan since she was five years of age and had first come to Inneford House, to be scowled at by the baronet and welcomed by his son.

She took a step back and then another and another. Jowan

stood, his gaze a caress and a farewell. Lord Coombe took her by the shoulders and turned her to face the carriage and she climbed aboard.

She took one last glance before sitting down next to Dorwa, in the backward-facing seats.

"You will soon forget this godforsaken place," Lord Coombe predicted, as he, too, sat down, spreading his knees and resting his hands on the seat so he spread across the whole of his side of the carriage. "You will find there is too much to do for homesickness."

Dorwa had her ticket to get back home safe in her bag. Tamsyn had one, too, but no one knew about it except her and Jowan. Jowan said if things were not as Lord Coombe promised, she was to write to let him know. He would meet her in Falmouth, and they would catch a boat to Scotland. She gave Lord Coombe a non-committal nod. If it proved to be unbearable, she would simply come home, for wherever Jowan was, that would always be home.

Chapter One

1820, seven years later, Inneford House, Cornwall

J OWAN'S BROTHER BRAN was already at the table when he came down for breakfast. A newspaper sat at Jowan's place. It had been folded open to one of the center pages, and an article had been circled with a heavy pencil line.

Jowan met Bran's eyes. "Something you wanted me to see?"

"Something I thought you would want to see," Bran replied. He was using his English voice this morning, Jowan noted. Branoc Hughes was a chameleon, able to mingle with country-folk and quality alike.

The day before, when they had been out with the shearers wrangling sheep, his speech had been laced with Cornish words and spoken in the West-country lilt he'd learned from his mother's people, who were fisher-folk.

Their father had insisted that, if the bastard son who suddenly appeared on his doorstep was going to stay, he would at least learn to talk like a civilized being. Bran had never told him his mother had arranged for him to be tutored by a vicar who was the son of a duke and could speak even more like the loftiest of the upper classes than Sir Carlyon himself. Bran was always careful to speak broadly when their father was about, and Jowan was certainly not going to let the man in on the joke.

Jowan poured himself a cup of strong black tea and added milk and sugar before taking his place at the table and picking up the newspaper. He lifted his cup to his mouth as he began to read and a moment later his cup dropped from suddenly nerveless hands. The oath with which he colored the air had as much to do with what he read as with the hot liquid soaking through his trousers.

Without comment, Bran handed Jowan a napkin, and he blotted absently at the mess while rereading the article.

"Tamsyn is back in England," he said, more to himself than to his brother, testing the words out loud as if hearing them would make them truer. She was still separated from him, as much by her chosen lifestyle as by three hundred and fifty miles and seven years. But she was, at least, in the same country.

"You should go to London," Bran said. "Find out why she stopped writing. Find out why she didn't come home."

She'd stopped loving him. The thought cut the way it always did, lacerating his heart yet again. But what else could it be? She'd had a ticket she could have used at any time. The Earl of Coombe might have stopped franking her letters, but he did keep his promise to make her famous. She had just been on her second tour through Europe for crying out loud. She must have money to burn, plenty to buy her own tickets, frank her own letters.

Her silence was her message to Jowan, and the more fool him for the hope that lingered, somewhere in the remote corners of his mind and heart.

"I must assume she changed her mind," he said and if his jaw was set and his foot tapped with the tension in his frame, his voice was commendably even.

"Or she thinks you did," argued Bran. "Look, Jowan, the girl you told me about isn't one who would cut you without a word."

Why was Bran pressing this? Couldn't he see how much it hurt? "She changed," Jowan pointed out. "Or I was wrong."

Bran shook his head. "You are not wrong about people. You

recognized me right off. In any case, you haven't let her go. If you're right, this is your chance to dig out the last of your hope and start to heal. If I'm right, the lady might need to be rescued."

Jowan was still thinking about the pain of losing all his hope, and Bran's last few words took a moment to make sense. "Rescued?"

"If she wants to come home and can't? For whatever reason? Yes. Rescued."

Jowan shook his head. "How can I leave? We haven't finished the shearing and then it will be planting time. I've the plans to sign off for the new mine." He shrugged. "You know the list as well as I."

"And how to make it all happen," Bran pointed out.

Jowan put his knife and fork down while he thought about that. Bran was right. He could stay here with Jowan's authority and do everything Jowan would do himself. "I could go to London," he said, testing the words on his tongue.

He'd been there before but with Bran at his side. Their father had agreed for him to go to Oxford, and Bran had gone—theoretically as his servant, but they had looked after one another and Bran had been his shadow, attending lectures and tutorials even though only Jowan was enrolled.

Jowan always introduced Bran as his brother, and people became used to the arrangement and behaved towards Bran as they did to Jowan. They had friends with homes in London and had stayed with them during long weekends and holidays.

The tutors soon realized that Bran was learning more than Jowan, and he had just been offered a scholarship when word came that Sir Carlyon had died. Jowan was now the baronet. Bran had insisted on coming home to Cornwall, leaving the scholarship behind, and while Jowan felt guilty that Bran had given up a potential academic career for him, he was also grateful, for Sir Carlyon had made as much of a mess of the family's finances as he had of his personal relationships with his wife, his mistresses, and his sons.

Bran had worked as hard as Jowan on the recovery and knew as much as Jowan about what needed to be done. "I could go to London," Jowan repeated.

"You could," Bran agreed. "You should. You could go and see the man with whom Sir Carlyon apparently invested. He hasn't answered any of our letters, but you might get some answers if you are there in person. We need to check up, too, on the agent who is handling the investors in our mine, who keeps promising but failing to deliver. You could do all that and work out where you are with your Tamsyn."

Jowan thumped the papers. "Tammie Lind, the Devon songbird." He growled his displeasure. "Even the name is a lie. Is Tamsyn still there, inside?"

"You won't know unless you go to find out," Bran said.

EVERY SO OFTEN, Tammie Lind was struck by a sudden moment of clarity—a step into reality, as it were. Moments when she saw the company she was with, and her own behavior, through the eyes of Tamsyn Roskilly. It was a sort of haunting, for Tamsyn had been killed long ago, strangled by Guy's manipulations and Tammie's own weaknesses.

Today, Tamsyn gazed with scorn at the fellow denizens of the laughing gas party. Ether was the drug of choice today. Tammie herself was as high as a kite, floating well above such mundane concerns as tomorrow's rehearsal and the foolish fellow pawing at her. He was a peer of some sort. A boy with pretensions to being a songwriter. Guy would own him within a few weeks, and Tammie was part of his bait.

The boy was far too drunk on ether to do more than squeeze and prod. Tamsyn was indignant on her behalf. Silly Tamsyn. Tammie had not owned her own body in more years than she could, at the moment, count. She tried it anyway, numbering the years on her fingers, but she became lost in the mystery of whether a thumb counted as a finger and forgot the question.

She was vaguely aware that Guy was free from Tamsyn's scorn. Tamsyn avoided looking at him. Wise Tamsyn. As usual, Guy sat a little apart, the untouchable Earl of Coombe, amused at the havoc he had caused. He seldom indulged in more than a taste of the various substances he supplied to his sycophants and the people he owned, as he owned Tammie.

Tamsyn despised them all, and she hated Guy. Reality was overrated. Tammie no longer bothered with such emotions. She lined up for another turn at the gas, to nail Tamsyn's soul back in the coffin of her imagination, but Guy stopped her with a word to the attendant.

"No more for Miss Lind. She has a rehearsal tomorrow. Tammie, time for bed."

Tammie wanted to whine and howl. Instead, she turned obediently towards the stairs, but the sudden movement set her off balance, and as she steadied herself, she saw Guy nod towards the boy, who followed her to her room.

Tamsyn had made a mistake years ago, when she was still a girl, and followed it up with several more. Ever since then, Tammie had paid and paid and paid. The boy was making a mistake now. Tammie felt a distant pity for him, but in the end, she would do as Guy ordered.

She took his hand. At least tonight was only the seeming of the thing. He would sleep off the ether and by the time he awoke, she would be at rehearsal. Everyone would believe he had been favored by the Devon Songbird. Perhaps he would believe it himself.

Sooner or later, it would be true. Guy had used her that way before and she knew how it went. Blackmail material or bribery or simply yet another way to soften the boy's resistance and break his spirit until he was putty in Guy's hands.

Tammie was desperately trying to claw her way back to the floating sensation, but the harder she tried, the further it receded.

She needed a shot of the gin she had hidden in her room. Guy had taken the last of her secret laudanum.

The boy threw himself at her as soon as she closed her bedchamber door. He clawed at her gown, increasingly frantic as the buttons refused to open for him. "Patience, my lord," she soothed. "Lie down on the bed, and I shall prepare myself for you."

He blinked at her, swaying on his feet, his surge of energy draining away.

"Lie down on the bed, my lord," she repeated. She would sleep in the dressing room tonight. It would not be the first time.

She found the gin where she had hidden it, in a bag concealed within the folds of the new gown Guy had chosen for her to wear for a command performance at one of Society's balls. Thank whatever deity looked after harlots and drunkards for this season's fuller gowns.

She rinsed out the mug that held her toothbrush and poured the gin. Just a couple of fingers. She would be watched more closely now that he had her booked for so many performances. This would have to last until she could bribe or blackmail someone into supplying her with another bottle.

Without it, she would be dependent on Guy for each dose. He knew she needed a small drink of laudanum before a performance—on stage or in a drawing room. Just enough to quiet the jitters. Then, afterward, if he was pleased with her performance, there would be something more powerful as a reward.

Tamsyn had tried to give up the substances that Guy insisted Tammie needed. More times than Tammie could count. Twice, she refused until he forced it down her throat. Once, she managed to evade her minders and hide until the craving turned to cramps and nausea, then vomiting as pain seized her whole body, then bad dreams so bizarre they exceeded anything that she'd experienced while under the influence.

In one of those, the monsters that invaded the refuge she'd

found proved to have been sent by Guy. Or perhaps the monsters were unreal, and Guy's men retrieved her while she was unconscious.

Whichever it was, Tammie woke up in the house Guy was renting at the time, in the half-floating, half-dreaming state that said he had already given her something.

Tammie never allowed Tamsyn to run away again. Giving up opium and alcohol was hard enough, but worse was being brought back when she'd thought she was free.

It hurt too much to think about it. Tammie poured another two fingers. "You have had more than enough today," Tamsyn scolded. "You will pass out if you drink that, too."

"Fair point," Tammie conceded.

She slid open the door. The boy was sound asleep on the bed, flat on his back, snoring. Tammie moved him so he lay on his side, with a pillow behind his back to keep him from rolling. There. If he vomited, it would go on the sheets instead of drowning him. She patted his cheek. "Run as fast as you can, my lord," she whispered. "The Earl of Coombe is not your friend. He is not anyone's friend."

Even if he had heard, he would not listen. She returned to the dressing room, tossed down the gin, stretched out on the maid's pallet, and waited for oblivion.

THE REHEARSAL WENT terribly. Tammie blamed Guy, for the dose of laudanum he gave her, while the usual size, must have been adulterated, for it was not enough to stop the jitters. Guy, though, blamed Tammie. The screaming fight that ensued was a mistake Tammie would not have made had she been in what passed for her normal mind, for it ended in the usual way.

As had happened so often in the past, Guy found her anger exhilarating. He locked her dressing room door, subdued her, and took her, laughing at her attempts to resist him. Afterward, he handed her to one of his followers. "Take her home and lock her in her bedchamber," he commanded. "You can have her if you like. But don't give in to her demands for opium or alcohol or anything else. She doesn't deserve it after that rehearsal and that tantrum."

It was Fergie, which was some sort of good fortune. Some of the others enjoyed a display of strength to the point of violence even more than Guy—yes, and over the edge, too. But Fergie was a straightforward sort of a lover. A quick tup and he would leave her alone.

Sure enough, he took her straight home, marched her up to her bed chamber, stripped her, and enjoyed her, though he wasn't best pleased with Tammie's refusals to respond.

"Give me opium and I'll give you the best time you've ever had," she told him, but Fergie was a loyal acolyte to Guy and would not agree. He finished, left her naked in her bed, and shut the door behind him.

Tammie lay there for a while, feeling sicker and sicker. She needed a dose of something. There must be something she could do. After a while, it occurred to her she had not heard the rattle of the key in the lock. A cautious test, and she found that Fergie had forgotten to lock the door.

Almost, she slipped out then and there, but a stray breeze reminded her she had no clothes on. She dressed, some instinct prompting her to wear the drabbest clothes she could find. Out of habit, she slipped the ring Jowan had once given her into the tiny pocket that she sewed into the side seams of all her gowns.

Money. She would need money to buy alcohol or—if she could find it—opium.

With opium and oblivion as her goal, she found the strength to sneak quietly into Guy's chambers. He would not be home for hours, but there was always a risk his valet might be within. Marco frightened her even more than Guy. He had an affinity for pain—giving, not receiving, and on the two occasions Guy had given Tammie into his hands, she had been frightened into silent obedience for months.

Her good fortune held. Not only was Guy's room empty, but he had left a small fortune in coins scattered across his dressing table. She stuffed as much as she could into her reticule. "It isn't theft," she muttered. "He never gives me my share of what I earn." He said it all went into a savings account for her, and into investments. But Tammie doubted he intended her to ever see a penny of it.

Looked at from a certain light, all the money on the dressing table and more was hers.

She met no one as she crept down the stairs. The butler was in the front hall. She had to wait for him to be called elsewhere before she could hurry across the tiles and out the door. The risk of being stopped lessened once she was down the steps and walking along the footpath, just another lady, anonymous in her bonnet.

She wouldn't find what she craved here in Mayfair. She needed the docks. She needed one of the places she had heard Guy's acolytes speak of. If she understood correctly, she had quite a walk ahead of her. A hack would be faster, but it would also be a risk—someone to question who might bring Guy upon her.

She did not know the going rate for opium, but perhaps she had enough. She could only hope. And walk.

Chapter Two

EVEN AFTER JOWAN had agreed to go to London, he kept finding reasons to put off the journey. After the shearing finished, he met with all his farmers to discuss the planting, and with the mining engineer to sign off the plans for the new mine. Then he couldn't go until the first sod had been turned, for they were having a ceremony, and he was to give a speech. After that, he insisted that he couldn't leave before Mrs. Dunstone's eightieth birthday party.

Bran sighed but did not openly accuse his brother of procrastination. However, he became an avid reader of the London papers, searching for the little bits of news they published about Miss Lind, the Devon Songbird, and sharing them with Jowan.

One morning, some five weeks after Bran ringed the first article, he double-ringed another.

"Miss Lind, the Devon Songbird, has been taken ill and is to be replaced in the performance of *Le Nossi de Figaro* by Miss Stephens, who is no stranger to London audiences, and will, we are certain, sing a wonderful Susana. We are sure our readers will join with us in wishing Miss Lind a swift recovery from her illness."

Jowan unfolded the paper so that he could find the date. "This was two weeks ago," he complained. He put down the paper and went to the door, calling for the butler. "Ask my valet to step into the breakfast room and tell the stable master that I'll be leaving for London in two hours. He's to have my horse ready at the door."

"And mine," said Bran. "Jowan, I am coming with you." He set his chin, ready for an argument, but in truth, Jowan felt nothing but relief. One or both had put in motion all the major projects planned for the early summer. The people in charge of each piece of work could carry on without one of the brothers leaning over their shoulders.

Also, they still hadn't had the first payment of capital needed for the mine works. The man in London had come highly recommended, but all Jowan had got from him were excuses.

"I'm glad to have your company, Bran," he said. "I need to send my apologies to the Dunstones, see the land steward and the mines' overseer, and write a note to the engineer letting him know that the overseer will be reporting to me by letter every week. Anything else?"

Bran mentioned a couple of other social engagements and offered to send for the steward and the overseer while Jowan dealt with the correspondence. The valet knocked on the door and was invited to enter.

They left two hours and ten minutes later, heading for Exeter, which was a six or seven hour ride away. The mail coach traveled both day and night and completed the journey from Exeter to London in thirty-two hours. On horseback or in a private or hired coach, Jowan and Bran couldn't expect to cover the same distance in less than two and half days, and possibly more.

"Collect the horses from the Arundel Arms in Lifton after giving them a day to rest," Bran ordered the stable master.

"Send any questions or reports to Bran or me, care of Fladongs Hotel on Oxford Street," Jowan told the butler, the steward, and the mines' overseer.

It was a hard day's ride, up and down hills, skirting the high moorland, and keeping to the coach roads. They didn't try for more than fifteen miles in a post, carefully checking the horses offered for the next stage before they paid the fee and took off again.

The day was fair, and they received few checks. Bran put the toll fees for each stage into a handy coat pocket, so they needed to stop only long enough to hand over the money and wait for the toll gate to open sufficiently for them to ride through in single file.

At Okehampton, they grabbed a pie and a jug of ale. It was half an hour past noon, and they were just over halfway, but the road ahead was more down than up. If they wasted no time, they would easily make today's mail coach, which left Exeter at four in the afternoon, come hell or high water.

They changed for the last time at Crockernwell, at the Golden Lion, the same place used by the man who brought the news of the Battle of Trafalgar from the Mediterranean to the Admiralty in London.

For old times' sake, they stood for a moment to look at the plaque commemorating that historic moment. They had heard the story for the first time when they stopped at the Golden Lion to change horses on their way to their first year in Oxford.

But they had no time to reminisce. It was nearly two o'clock and they had perhaps as much as twenty miles to go. Two good horses and a clear run. They should be able to do it easily.

"If we miss the coach," Jowan said, "We will lose twenty-four hours."

"Then we had better not miss the coach," Bran told him.

Those were the last words they spoke for some time. They stopped only for the toll house at Cheriton Bishop, and they arrived at Exeter with twenty minutes to spare. The inside seats were all sold, but they secured two seats on the top, and Bran went to find food while Jowan secured a couple of bottles of light ale each.

The mail didn't stop for the convenience of its passengers and the inns had changing a team down to a fine art. They'd have to eat and drink whatever was available when the coach took one of its brief pauses, and the same with any other needs of their bodies.

They left Exeter holding on to their seats with one hand while eating meat and potato-filled pasties with the other. It would do. Bran had also brought them an apple each for dessert, which, Jowan told him, elevated the meal to a feast.

They were grateful for their greatcoats to protect them from the bitter wind, but as the hours passed and the sun came out, the trip was not unpleasant. They bought bread from a peddler at one stop, and yet more pies at another. When they reached Bath in the early evening, two of the inside passengers ended their trip. The brothers were able to take those inside seats and sleep the rest of the way to London.

They shouldered the bags that had traveled the distance in the coach's baskets, and, not wanting to search for their hotel in the dark, went inside the Swan with Two Necks Inn, where they were able to secure a room for what remained of the night.

London was no less of an assault on the senses than the last time they visited. A quiet moorlands village in Cornwall was no preparation for the noise, the smell, the sheer number of people. They'd been recommended to try Fladongs Hotel, on Oxford Street, which was almost an hour's walk away, but the vicar, who had stayed there himself, said it was very pleasant, and not at all noisy.

Oxford Street proved to be a major thoroughfare, but they reserved judgment and secured a room, anyway. The place was supposed to be comfortable and was on the outskirts of the upper-class areas of the city, as well as being nicely placed for the theatre district. Until Jowan had done a little research, he had no idea whether Tamsyn was living close to where she worked, perhaps with other performers, in the household of the Earl of Coombe in Mayfair, or somewhere else he had not yet considered.

The hotel was also, apparently, popular with naval officers. They thronged the public rooms and Bran and Jowan saw even more coming down the stairs as they went up.

"Let's just drop our bags and call on Coombe," Bran proposed.

"People like Coombe won't be awake at this time of the morning," Jowan protested. Now that it came to it, he was afraid of what he might find. She had forgotten him, it was clear. In favor of Coombe? It seemed all too likely, though from what he'd read of Coombe, the man was unlikely to be satisfied with just one female at a time, or with any woman for the length of time Tamsyn had been in his clutches.

Bran had an answer for that, too. "All the better if he is asleep. Or still out at some party. We can ask after your Tamsyn."

Jowan told himself to stop prevaricating. He had agreed to this trip, after all. Either Tamsyn needed him, or she didn't. And if she didn't, he had to deal with it. Bran was right. Better to know.

"You're right," he told Bran.

On their way out after freshening up in their room, they asked the doorman how to get to Brackington Street, where Coombe had his townhouse. It was a short walk, but into a different world than the parts of London they had seen so far. Wider streets, more elegant buildings, fewer carts, and less bustle altogether.

At each crossing, a child with a broom hurried to clear their path and said "Thankee" while catching the coppers Bran tossed in reward. Two streets across and five along, the doorman had said, and here they were.

It hadn't changed since the last time they came. In their first year at Oxford, they had taken a leave of absence for a weekend and hitched a ride with a carter to come to London. But when they found the townhouse belonging to the Earl of Coombe, the knocker was off the door. Someone was within, though. Smells of cooking had drifted up the area steps from the kitchen.

They had knocked on the kitchen door and charmed the cook

into telling them that Coombe and all his entourage had gone to Europe. "A tour for the Devon Songbird," the cook had explained. "Such a nice girl. I hope she does well."

In five years, Tamsyn had toured the whole of Europe twice, spending months in each of the major capitals. She'd also performed in Russia, Alexandria, and Constantinople. Jowan had followed her through the reports in the newspaper, several times hearing about a lightning trip to England after she had already been and gone.

This time, five years later, the knocker was on the door, but the place was otherwise the same, and delicious smells still wafted up from the basement kitchen.

"Up? Or down?" Bran asked.

"Up," Jowan decided. "We're not dressed for down." Or, rather, they were dressed for up—in the gentlemen's attire they wore to church, or on the rare occasions they accepted an invitation for an afternoon with the neighboring nobility.

Twelve steps took them to the red-painted door. Bran plied the knocker. After a short wait, the door opened. "Lord Coombe is not receiving," the footman who answered the door declared.

"Sir Jowan Trethewey and Mr. Branoc Hughes. I will leave a card," Jowan declared, stepping forward. The footman responded to the note of command and fell back.

Jowan appropriated a corner of a hall table to write a brief note on the back of his card and handed it to the footman. "Please see that Miss Roskilly—Miss Lind, I suppose I should say— receives this. She and I were childhood friends." He handed the footman a second card, "And do let the Earl of Coombe know that Mr. Hughes and I called."

"I will, Sir Jowan," the footman assured him. "When Lord Coombe is awake." He hesitated, with an anxious frown, and added, "Lord Coombe sees all of Miss Lind's mail, of course. To keep her from being bothered by her public. Men, you know, who do not have proper respect. But I am sure he will be happy to pass on a card from an old childhood friend."

"I would be grateful," Jowan replied.

"Sir Jowan and I are in London for a short time," Bran added. "Visiting from Cornwall."

"Ah, yes," said the footman, his anxious expression clearing. "Miss Lind is from Cornwall. I am sure a visit from an old friend would cheer her up."

"We heard she had been ill," Jowan commented.

"Ill. Yes," the footman repeated. "She is better now, but still very low." He bit his lip, frowning. "A childhood friend, you say?"

"Indeed. We met when we were five," Jowan told him. "We used to play together as children—we took our lessons together, in fact. Her mother was my father's housekeeper." *And my father's mistress*, he did not add.

"Sir," said the footman. He looked over his shoulder before he continued, "I shall try to slip her your card." His brow and mouth shifted, and he shuffled his feet before he added, "His lordship is very protective, sir."

"It is to his credit, no doubt," Bran said.

The footman looked uncertain. "Yes. Of course."

"Thank you," Jowan said. "I would be grateful if you make sure she gets the card on which I wrote a note."

"Would you be on door duty at this time the day after tomorrow?" Bran asked. "We could return to see if the lady has an answer for us."

That fetched a smile from the footman. "Yes, sir. I am always on at this time. The butler serves at my lord's parties, you see. He is not awake before ten o'clock." He glanced at the large clock that graced the hall. "In fact, he shall be here soon, I expect, if you wish to talk to him. His lordship and his guests, they sleep until the afternoon. The ladies, too. Miss Lind and the others."

"In that case, we will be on our way," Jowan said. "If either Miss Lind or Lord Coombe wishes us to call, a message at Fladongs Hotel will reach us." He passed the footman a crown. "Thank you. You have been very helpful."

Out on the street again, Bran commented, "A half-crown

might have done well enough."

"A crown makes him feel he owes us something and may be enough to ensure that Tamsyn gets the note I wrote on my card," Jowan replied. "It sounds as if he didn't think Coombe would pass on the message."

"Yes. That was my impression," Bran agreed. He changed the subject. "What do you want to do now?"

Wait outside to see if Tamsyn got his message, but that wouldn't serve. There was no way of knowing when she would wake, or when the footman would get a chance to pass the note. Or even if the man would do so.

"Let's drop into the agent's office," he suggested. "Even if he isn't there, we can make a time."

"Better to surprise him," Bran grumbled. "Less time for him to hide things."

※ ⟫⟪ ※

TAMMIE HAD NOT spoken to Guy or been close enough to do so since the day of the rehearsal. It had been him who retrieved her from the opium den, or so said the two maids who took turns nursing her. She had only the vaguest memories of the den, and none at all of Guy coming for her.

No doubt he was furious. She had nearly escaped him in the only way left to her. Daisy, one of the maids, told her that a physician had sat with her all through the first night and that Guy had been beside himself with worry.

Tammie believed the first statement, but not the second. Guy was not immune to all human emotions. He felt lust and anger and a sort of fierce joy that had fascinated her before she realized it fed off the subjugation of others. But he had no ability to worry.

Unless he was concerned he might lose her ability to earn for him. She would be worth nothing to him if she was dead. Perhaps that was why he had approved a measured amount of laudanum to be given to her every six hours.

She was much improved. At first, she had been so weak the maids had had to help her even with the basest of needs. Now she could spend much of the day sitting by her window or pacing her room. Yesterday, she had begun her voice exercises again, and by the end of the week, she was sure she could once again take her place on the stage.

But when she sent a note to Guy, telling him that she was better and able to sing again, his valet Marco delivered the response.

"*Il Conte* will tell *Signorina* Lind when she is to sing again." He leered at her, leaning against the doorframe as if to show off his lean physique. He was handsome enough, with his dark curly hair and his large brown eyes, but Tammie always saw him through a haze of remembered pain.

She knew better than to show her fear, though. She nodded to indicate she had heard and understood the message. The earl was still angry with her. Angry she had run away. Angry she had tried to escape him permanently into the dreams. Angry she had been too ill for him to punish.

Daisy, whose turn it was to watch her, said, sharply, "You have delivered your message, Mr. Ricci." Tammie managed to keep her shudder until after Marco had sniffed his contempt and left. "Do not annoy Marco Ricci, Daisy," she warned. "He is mean when he is annoyed."

"He should not treat you with such disrespect, Miss," replied the maid, her tone and expression showing her indignation.

Tammie was touched. How long had it been since someone stood up for her? It was futile, though. "I do not mind, Daisy. How Marco treats me tells me where I stand with the earl. At the moment, he is angry with me. When I am back in favor, Marco will be most respectful. You watch."

If she was allowed to find her way back into the earl's favor. He had no other singer of her caliber, which was to her advantage. Guy collected musicians, and kept some of them—those without friends and family to make trouble for him. At the moment, he had a violinist, a virtuoso on the pianoforte, a promising alto, and several lesser voices. But Tammie was a star attraction and opened doors that the scandal surrounding him would otherwise shut in his face.

Sometimes, when he was in a temper, he would forget that fact. She could think of several musicians who had simply disappeared when they offended him or were no longer useful.

But he had had time since her rebellion to calm down, had he not?

Marco had said "when." "When she is to sing again." So, if he had not forgiven her yet, he planned to do so. Come to think of it, the regular and measured doses of laudanum were another sign that he had plans for her. Not enough to completely subdue the cravings, but enough for her to get from one minute to the next, especially when she lost herself in song.

The next sign that Guy still had a use for her was in the afternoon when she was ordered to put on a riding habit and join the weekly ride. When she reached the mews, her usual horse was ready for her, but she was directed to the rear of the group of acolytes, dependents, grooms, and invited guests who would make up the procession of horses and glitteringly dressed riders who would display Guy's wealth and influence to London's fashionable crowd in Hyde Park. His new violinist, Miss Tempest, took the place by his side.

Guy had organized these processions in London, Paris, Rome, Venice, Vienna, and a dozen other cities of Europe and the Middle East over the years Tammie had been with him, and for most of those years, she had ridden at his side or close behind him.

It was a statement about power. The time and place were carefully chosen to impress those who held local power. The position in the procession spoke of the internal politics of the group Guy had gathered around him.

Her position at the back displayed to all and sundry that she was out of favor. It was also a relief, taking her out from under Guy's shrewd eye and allowing her to pay attention to the park and the rich and powerful who gathered there to show off to their peers.

Of course, Guy and his riders drew every eye, as was intended.

Fergie, who had left the door to her room unlocked, was not in the vanguard with Guy. He was nowhere in the procession. In fact, she had not seen him since she recovered enough to move around the house. Had he suffered for his mistake? Of course, he had. She hoped he had merely been sent away. She would not think about the alternative.

It was pleasant to ride again. When she was back in Guy's favor, Tammie would ask permission to take a ride each morning, when one's horse could move at more than a walk. As it was, unused muscles complained bitterly an hour later when she dismounted.

Once more in her room, she asked Daisy to order a bath. "Miss," said Daisy. "One of the footmen gave me a message for you. It arrived this morning, Miss, and I wasn't sure if I should give it to you, for the earl has said we are not to let you be bothered but to give all messages to him, and he will let you have those he approves."

Tammie grimaced. She was not surprised.

"But Hen...*the footman* said it was a childhood friend, Miss. Oh dear. I hope I am doing the right thing." She pulled a little pasteboard rectangle from the pocket of her apron and brought it to Tammie, where she sat by the fire.

"I will burn it when I have read it, and never tell a soul you gave it to me," Tammie promised, folding her hand around the card. *Jowan*. It could be no one else. Was that hope she felt? No! Hope was not allowed. Hope would only be squashed and leave her more miserable than ever. She should throw the card into the fire immediately and forget she ever saw it.

But she could not resist opening her fingers. "Sir Jowan

Trethewey," she read out loud. "Yes, I knew him when I was a child."

So, the old baronet was dead. Good. He had sent for Guy, knowing the man's predilection for musicians. Guy himself had told her that the baronet and Tamsyn's mother had sold her to the earl, and Tammie believed him. Whether Mother had conspired with Sir Carlyon, or whether he had truly threatened to turn Mother out with Tamsyn, Tammie didn't know. But Sir Carlyon objected to her relationship with Jowan and had wanted her gone. She was certain of that.

The fingers of her free hand crept down the hem of her riding skirt and rubbed across the outline of the ring, safely in its tiny pocket. She had nearly lost it. Guy had ordered her maid to burn the clothes she wore to the opium den, but the girl had found the ring hidden in the hem, retrieved it, kept it a secret, and returned it to Tammie when she recovered her senses.

It was her last connection with Jowan and Tamsyn. She would have hated to have lost it.

Dear Jowan. She wished she could see him, but Guy would never allow it. And perhaps it was for the best, for it was Tamsyn that Jowan remembered, and Tamsyn had died long ago.

"There is a message on the other side, Miss," prompted Daisy.

Almost against her will, Tammie's fingers turned the card over. "In London. When can I see you? Answer via footman."

Dangerous words. She truly had better burn the card before the footman got into trouble—"Henry" Daisy had nearly said. Tammie had always made it her practice to learn the names of the servants in any house where Guy stayed, and her with him. Guy mocked her for it, but she found it brought her better service. Besides, it made her feel as if she was not entirely without allies, even if they were as helpless as she was.

"Daisy, if I give you a message, will you give it to the footman?" *Henry.* It must be. Daisy was nodding. Tammie crossed the room to her little desk. It had been years since she discovered that the letters she had been faithfully writing to Jowan, despite the silence from his end, had been read and burnt by Guy. Jowan's to her, too.

Guy had told her of his perfidy one night when somewhat more under the influence than usual. She had stopped taking her letters to him for franking after that, but from habit, she continued to write every day, using notebooks in a sort of a diary.

She was certain Guy read it, and she took a childish delight in writing into her diary things she would never say to his face.

Would he notice if she tore out a page? She would have to risk it. She tore the partner page from the other side of the stitching. Unless someone counted the pages, they would never know.

"Daisy," she said, when she had written her message, "tell the footman to be careful. The earl is very possessive. My message is merely to tell Sir Jowan to leave me alone. You can read it if you want to check. But I do not want the earl to cause trouble for my old friend or the footman. Do you understand?"

Daisy nodded, her eyes wide with apprehension. "We will both be careful, Miss." She bit her lip, her frown deepening. "Couldn't this Sir Jowan help you, Miss? Take you away from all of this?"

Poor innocent child, but it was sweet of her to be concerned. "Daisy," Tammie told her sadly, "no one can help me. Lord Coombe is too powerful."

But oh, how sweet and seductive it was to hope.

Chapter Three

THE AGENT WAS a solicitor by the name of Thatcher, and he took a bit of finding. The address on his letterhead—the address to which Jowan had been sending correspondence—proved to be the office of somebody else—someone called Beckleston. The clerk there was not disposed to give them any information, and Beckleston was away at present. Or so the clerk said. He was a young man—still a boy, Jowan would have said, short and slender, except that the stubble on his cheeks and something about his eyes suggested he was older than he looked, as did the way his brown hair was already thinning away from his forehead.

When the clerk deliberately turned back to his work after making the last claim, Jowan leaned over the desk, resting both hands on the documents scattered across the surface. "Bran," he said. "Fetch a constable. It is clear that Thatcher is a fraudster, and this man, or his employer, or both, is Thatcher's accomplice. I'll stay here and make sure this man does not escape."

After that, the clerk had a change of heart. Mr. Thatcher was merely a client of Mr. Beckleston's. They allowed him to use the address for correspondence out of kindness, for Mr. Thatcher had experienced some bad luck. The clerk did not know where Mr. Thatcher lived or work—he always called for his correspondence once a week, on a Thursday.

"Not good enough," Jowan decided. "Fetch a constable, Bran. We shall let them find Thatcher, and the courts can decide who is guilty and who is not."

"Who are you, bullying my poor clerk?" said a voice from the doorway.

"Beckleston, I presume," Jowan commented.

The man nodded. "I am. State your business."

Jowan straightened. "Excellent. I am Sir Jowan Trethewey. This is my colleague, Mr. Hughes. I was given this address as the place of business of Mr. Silas Thatcher."

From the corner of his eye, Jowan could see the clerk open his mouth and Bran put a finger in front of it.

Beckleston eyed Bran's move and then turned his attention back to Jowan. "I suppose my man has told you that Thatcher is a client who uses my address because he currently is between premises."

"I need to see him as a matter of urgency. Where might I find him?"

Beckleston shrugged. "I am afraid I cannot help you," he said, jutting out his chin.

Jowan resisted the urge to bop him on it. "I take it, then, that you are a party to his fraud and embezzlement. Bran, you had better fetch those constables."

Beckleston put up a hand. "Wait! Those are serious charges. Thatcher is a gentleman I will have you know."

Jowan laughed. "In Cornwall, we find that gentlemen thieves, when shot, are just as dead as those from lower levels of Society. I daresay the same applies to hanging. I have other matters to attend to while I am in London. If I cannot meet with Thatcher and find out what he has done with my money, I shall let the constables sort it out."

Beckleston paced to and fro, saying, "Wait a minute. Wait a minute." He stopped, having clearly made a decision. "I might be able to get a message to him. Might. I can guarantee nothing."

"Not good enough," Jowan replied. He nodded to Bran, who began to move towards the door.

"Wait," Beckleston begged, again, and went back to pacing. "I know where he is boarding," he admitted after a few seconds. "If he is home, I can have him here in under an hour."

"We shall save you the trouble," Bran said sweetly. "The address, and we shall be out of your hair. Unless Thatcher implicates you in his schemes."

"I am certain you are mistaken," said Beckleston, drawing himself upright. "Mr. Thatcher is a respected member of London's legal community, and the trusted London agent of a number of country gentlemen."

"I am aware of how Thatcher presents himself to country gentlemen," Jowan commented, dryly. "Being myself one of those country gentlemen. At the very least, Thatcher is guilty of gross incompetence. Given his repeated failure to respond to my increasingly urgent missives, I strongly suspect that his sole goal from the beginning has been to separate me and my investors from our money. You must decide, Mr. Beckleston. Are you confident of his innocence? Then give me his address and allow me to investigate. Or are you his co-conspirator?"

"You are possibly being unfair to Mr. Beckleston," Bran suggested. "He might have been as taken in by Thatcher as we were. Perhaps Mr. Beckleston is in this up to his neck, and perhaps he is just a poor naive fool."

"I do not think so," Jowan argued with Bran. "Mr. Beckleston would be as keen to find out the truth as we are if he was innocent. I think Mr. Beckleston is in this with Thatcher."

"I am not," Beckleston protested. "I am sure you are mistaken. Let me give you the address. Paper and pen, Oliver!" The last was addressed to the clerk, who hurriedly provided the required items.

"There." Beckleston handed a sheet of paper to Jowan. "I will thank you to leave my office, Sir Jowan. *If* that is who you are."

"I will leave for the moment," Jowan replied. "If you are

implicated, I will be back."

They strolled out of the room and down the stairs and then, with no more than an exchange of looks and a nod, separated to cover the doors, Jowan to the front and Bran to race around the row of buildings to the rear.

After ten or so minutes, Bran returned, dragging the clerk, Oliver, by the upper arm. "Sent with a message to Thatcher," he reported to Jowan.

Oliver was white and shaking. "I know nothing," he kept repeating.

Jowan pulled out his purse and abstracted a guinea. "This is for showing us to Thatcher's place, then going to a coffee house for a while before returning to your employment. Though, if you are wise, you might start looking for another position."

"Unless he is part of it, too," Bran growled.

Oliver must have decided that his own skin was more valuable to him than that of his employer. "I am guilty of looking the other way," he admitted. "But what was I to do? Who would have believed me if I said anything? Beckleston is the master mind. Thatcher is the man who sells the idea. Beckleston gives references to Thatcher, and forges references from some of his clients. Were you taken in by the find-an-investor scheme? Or one of the canal schemes?"

"Investors," Bran replied, though Jowan was still wondering whether the man's change of sides was genuine.

"Ah. That's a clever one. They do a good and genuine job for around half of the projects. Then they use those projects as references for other opportunities." He sounded impressed. Jowan was more convinced than ever that Oliver was in deeper than he admitted. Still. The man could be useful.

"If you are prepared to be a witness to what the others have done, we will put in a word for you," he offered.

Oliver shook his head. "If you can keep me out of it, I am your man," he countered.

He was still pale and trembly, but his jaw was set. There'd be no shifting him today, and in any case, Jowan was interested in bigger fish.

"Show us to Thatcher's address," he said, without committing himself.

"It isn't the one Beckleston wrote down," Oliver confided. "This way."

Jowan stayed alert. His instincts told him that Oliver couldn't be trusted. But he proved reliable in this instance, at least. He led them to a street of run-down but still solid townhouses. When they knocked on the door he pointed out and asked for Thatcher, the woman who answered the door directed them up four flights of stairs and to the room at the back of the house.

The door to the room was open. Jowan stepped inside and stopped. Either someone had ransacked the room, or Thatcher had been warned and had packed in a hurry and escaped. Bran pushed him out of the way and rushed to the window. "He's getting away," he said.

Sure enough, a man was clambering over the back fence. He dropped to the other side and took off along the mews, pausing to look back over his shoulder at the window where they stood. They couldn't see his expression, but they could see the rude gesture he made with his free hand.

"I'll get after him," Bran said.

"Too late," Jowan told him. "Look."

The miscreant had a horse. How he'd managed to have it ready in time to escape, Jowan couldn't guess, but he swung aboard, and kicked it into a trot, balancing the bag he had been carrying in front of him.

"Damn," Bran commented.

THEY HAD A stroke of luck after that. They were just trying to persuade the landlady to give them permission to search the room when several other men arrived, two of them obviously constables, and two of the men were familiar. The gentleman who led the way took one look at Jowan and Bran and greeted them.

"Trethewey and Hughes! I take it you are on the same mission as we are. Where is Thatcher?" It was Lord Andrew Winderfield, who had been tutoring in Central Asian History at Oxford when they were students. Lord Andrew had been the first to see Bran's potential as a scholar.

"Thatcher is on a fast horse to somewhere else," Bran said. "We arrived just in time to see him mount up and ride."

"His landlady was just considering whether to let us search his room," Jowan added.

"Madam," said Lord Andrew. "These gentlemen have a warrant. Please show it to the good lady," he added, to one of the constables. The man produced the warrant, and then two constables followed the landlady up the stairs, followed by two of the other men. Central Asian servants of Lord Andrew's by the look of them.

He had had several of them following him around Oxford, too, one of whom was sometime valet, sometime partner, always friend. Jamir was as close to Lord Andrew as Bran was to Jowan and was even now at Lord Andrew's shoulder. Jowan nodded to him in recognition.

"We think a man called Beckleston is in it, too," Jowan said.

"He should be under arrest by now," Lord Andrew told them. "Unless he, too, got nervous and ran. I wonder what tipped Thatcher off." His eyes fixed on Oliver. "You are Beckleston's clerk," he commented.

"It wasn't me, sir," Oliver assured him. "Mr. Beckleston sent me to Mr. Thatcher after these two gentlemen called, but I agreed to help them after I left the building."

"I stopped him in the back lane, and he switched sides," Bran explained, "but I would not trust him as far as I can throw him."

Oliver cast him a hurt look.

"We frightened them," Jowan realized. "I am sorry, my lord. We spoiled your arrests."

"Call me 'Drew'," said Lord Andrew. "Not to worry. We had men watching them both. They won't get away, and they may lead us to others involved in the schemes they were running." He paused before adding, "I hope they didn't take you for much."

Jowan groaned. "Only the future of the new mine that means security for my people, plus whatever it is going to take to pay off the investors they trapped," he admitted. It was an impossibility. If he'd had the money to fund the venture, he'd not have sought investors in the first place.

Bran clasped his shoulder. "We'll work it out."

Drew was grinning. "It might not be as bad as you think," he said. "The group of investors I belong to became suspicious of this pair a while ago, and have been gathering evidence to arrest them. Can I ask if the mine you're talking about is the Wheal St Tetha?"

Jowan nodded.

"We agreed to invest to draw them out. We were to hand the money over today," Drew told him. He shook his head. "It would have been the last nail in their coffin, but we have enough evidence without it. And it does mean you still have 90% of your investors, Trethewey. You'll have to meet my group, of course, and convince them of the value of the proposition. We did our due diligence on what Thatcher had to say, but the vote was a foregone conclusion since we never intended Thatcher and his colleagues to still be in business to steal our money."

From despair to elation in a moment. Jowan's head was spinning. "Call me 'Jowan', Drew," he managed.

"Bran," his brother offered, even as he shot out a hand to stop Oliver, who was edging towards the door.

"Jowan and Bran, then. Do you have plans for Beckleston's clerk?"

With one eye on the clerk, Jowan said, "He is, at the very least, a witness. Possibly a co-conspirator. He has, though, been very helpful since he agreed to abandon his employer. Not an arrest, I think. Is there a way to detain him without actually arresting him?"

"You could trust me to come when you ask?" Oliver sounded hopeful. "I only did what my employer told me. I am not a criminal, Sir Jowan, my lord."

He sounded sincere, but Jowan was not such a fool as to believe him without proof.

"Good idea, Jowan," Drew said. "We can manage a detainment, can we not, Jamir?"

Jamir bared his teeth in a shark's smile. "Come along, Beckleston's clerk."

"I would rather not," Oliver replied, but Jamir's smile only broadened, and Oliver, his shoulders slumped, walked in the direction Jamir indicated, Jamir at his shoulder in case he changed his mind. One of the other men fell into step behind them.

"Shall we see what Thatcher's room can tell us?" Drew asked. "Then, if you are not otherwise occupied, perhaps you would care to come with me to meet my two colleagues. Between them, they have been supervising the search of Beckleston's premises— one at his office and one at his home."

The brothers exchanged a glance and confirmed they were of one mind. Jowan spoke for them both. "We would love to."

Chapter Four

THE FOLLOWING MORNING, Guy sent for Tammie to attend him in his study. Tammie hid her relief at the venue. It might, in any case, be premature. A meeting in the study might yet involve duties Tammie did not like to perform. Even so, Guy's bedchamber would have been worse. And the room he referred to as his "playroom" would have been much worse.

"Sing for me," he demanded as soon as she stepped into the room. She took a couple of deep breaths and began the aria from *Figaro* that Susanna sings, purportedly to another man, to tease her husband Figaro.

He listened in silence, then said, "You shall be singing at a private gathering tomorrow evening. Prepare three songs, one a duet with Evan Davies. No. Five. You shall need two encores. Write me a list of the songs you have chosen and bring it to me before dinner. We have guests for dinner, Tammie. Are you well enough to be my hostess?"

Only one answer would be acceptable. "Yes, Guy."

"Good. We shall discuss your rebellion, but not at this time."

Thank goodness for that. And thank you, too, to the hostess who had decided she must have Miss Lind to entertain her guests. Usually, one of Guy's "discussions" would leave Tammie unable to perform for several days. The lady must be important, or he would not have put off Tammie's discipline.

"Yes, Guy. Thank you." That was the required response. Now to distract him. "What can you tell me about the gathering? The more I know, the better I can choose a program to delight the hostess." Pleasing the gathering would reflect well on Guy as the person who had discovered Tammie and promoted her to those who appreciated music.

Guy frowned, as if he suspected her of some nefarious scheme. "The Duchess of Winshire is holding another of her infernal fundraising events. This one is a *musicale* but with professional musicians rather than half-trained and untalented members of the ton."

"What is the event to benefit?" Tammie asked. "If I can pick songs that fit the theme, and play on people's heart strings…"

That pleased her capricious master. He smiled. "Yes. Good. More money for the duchess's charity." His mood changed again. "Kneel," he ordered.

Tammie dropped to her knees in front of his chair. He took her chin in one hand and forced her to meet his eyes, his grip tight enough to bruise. "You are mine, Tammie Lind. Say it."

"I am yours," she parroted, obediently.

"You are mine and everything you do, everything you say, especially everything you eat or drink or breathe in, is at my pleasure." He shook her again. "Do you understand me?"

"Yes, Guy. I am yours."

"You are mine." This time, it was a snarl. "Whether you live or whether you die, I choose. I do!" He pushed her away with the hand that held her chin, and she fell backward onto the floor.

Another lightning change of mood. His tone turned mournful and his voice lyrical. "I could have lost you in that den. I nearly did lose you, Tammie Lind. How could you do that to me? Haven't I loved you? Haven't I made you famous? Haven't I kept you as my prima soprano for seven years? My mistress for much of that time? Don't you love me anymore?"

Trick question. Tammie was beginning to lose the brief lucidity that she enjoyed between when her dose of laudanum began to wear off and when the cravings for another dominated her mind, but she was still alert enough to return a duplicitous answer to a trick question.

"I love you just as much as I ever have, Guy."

He narrowed his eyes at her, but her tone must have satisfied him she was sincere, for his suspicion faded into lust. "You are still beautiful. It is because of me you are still beautiful. Left to yourself, you would have shriveled into ugly old age, like those other miserable creatures at the den. I have looked after you, Tammie. I give you what you need but stop you from taking too much of it. You should be grateful."

"Thank you, Guy," Tammie said. *Thank you for introducing me to a poison that has gripped my soul and will not let me go. Thank you for using that poison to put me on a leash—to force me to be your whore, and to go with whomever you order whenever you order. Thank you for ruining me and dragging me down into hell.*

Perhaps she failed to keep her thoughts hidden, for anger rode in his voice as much as lust when he pointed to his groin and ordered, "Pleasure me." Then, letting his voice turn persuasive, he said the words she could never refuse. "Pleasure me, and I shall let you have the pipe."

Tammie crept forward on her knees and reached for the buttons of his fall. She didn't know who disgusted her most. Guy, for his pleasure in her degradation, or herself for being all too willing to be degraded if the reward was the seductive pleasure of the dreams.

THE SMOKE, WHEN she had earned it, wiped away the memories and carried her into dreams. But the dreams turned sour, as they sometimes did. At first, everything was wonderful. She was back in St Tetha, walking the moor with Jowan. They stopped to kiss—a tender, innocent touching of lips that had once seemed so daring and still felt more meaningful than any of the far more carnal kisses she had learned since they were parted.

Even as the thought came to her, the kiss changed, becoming consuming, forceful, a declaration of dominance demanding her submission. She tore herself away to confirm what she had already deduced: Jowan had become Guy.

Tamsyn ran—in this dream, she was Tamsyn again—but Guy pursued her on a ghost horse, a fearsome creature, all black with red, burning eyes and clashing teeth. Tamsyn knew Bodmin Moor as well as anybody and fled down paths Guy could not have known, but the ghost horse stayed on her trail, avoiding the mine shafts and pits, mires, and bogs, never quite catching up but never losing her, either.

In a sudden shift, like a scene change at the opera, she was on the shore, running on the sand, the pursuit still on her heels. Jowan called out to her from a rowboat. He was a few feet from the tide mark, using his oars to stay in place on the waves. "Quickly, Tamsyn. It is a witch horse and won't follow you into the water!"

Did the sea count as running water? Tamsyn could not remember, but she dashed into the waves and waded out to the boat. The horse pulled up short of the foam, gnashing its teeth, and Tamsyn laughed even as the waves splashed up, soaking her to the waist. She caught the gunwale of the boat, smiling up at Jowan.

"You came for me," she said.

"Of course," Jowan replied, even as his eyes turned red, his teeth grew longer, and his legs fused into a tail. It was not Jowan at all, but a *bucca*—a Cornish water spirit. He leaped for Tamsyn with a flick of his powerful tail, wrapping his arms around her and sweeping her out to sea.

Just before they plunged into the water, she smelled the cologne that Guy always wore. She could not escape the devil, even in her nightmares.

They lingered, the nightmares. At dinner, she was called to

stand with Guy and welcome his guests, a sign that she was back in his favor. The guests were all followers of his, most of them nobles and all of them as dangerous as snakes, including the smattering of ladies. Some of them were accompanied by members of the demi-monde. One of the noble ladies brought with her the actor she currently had in her keeping.

To Tammie's eyes, they seemed otherworldly, eldritch. Perhaps it was just the whiff of nightmares still drifting through her mind or the small dose of laudanum that kept her jitters under control. But as the evening progressed and the diners' behavior regressed, she looked at Guy slouched in his chair, watching the bawdy behavior around him with amused contempt, and thought again, *He is a devil. No. He is the elf king, and this is his court.*

THE VISIT TO Coombe's house gave Jowan food for thought. The footman handed over a note—a single sheet of lined paper torn on one side, neatly folded, and held together by a dab of wax. It had his name written on it in an untutored hand, but when he opened it, the paper that fell out was of a far higher quality, and the writing was also very different, precise and elegant in an understated sort of a way.

He unfolded the paper and looked at the foot of the page. "Tamsyn!"

Now to read from the beginning. His eyes did not want to obey. He was afraid, he realized. Afraid of what he might read. Afraid she would reject him, that she no longer cared for the country boy she had left behind. Why would she, when she had spent the last seven years surrounded by the handsomest and most sophisticated men in Europe?

"What does she say?" Bran asked.

Jowan forced his gaze to the top of the page.

"Dear Sir Jowan," he read.

"First, let me offer my condolences. Your father was an ass, but he was still your father. And I daresay you didn't want to be baronet. Or not so soon, in any case. I am sorry, Jowan. I hope it has not been too difficult.

"You ask to see me. My answer is 'no'. Let us leave the past in the past, my dear. You are my sweetest memory, but I am no longer the girl you once knew. Please remember me as I was. It will give me comfort to know that someone still thinks of me as 'Tamsyn.'"

He handed the missive to Bran, watching his hand extend the piece of paper to his brother. How could his hand still grasp, his arm extend, when his heart had ceased at Tamsyn's rejection? The pain hadn't hit him yet.

He'd been trapped in a mine, once, halfway under a rockfall. This was like that. He didn't feel a thing, but just as he'd known the bloody great rock on his leg must have crushed flesh and broken bones, he knew Tamsyn's words had killed his heart, and how could a man live without his heart?

"Sir?" said the friendly footman. "Sir, the maid, Daisy, who took the note to Miss Lind? She says that Miss Lind said she didn't want the earl causing any trouble for you. Daisy says that Miss Lind cried when she wrote the note, sir."

"She didn't want to write it?" Jowan asked.

The footman shrugged. "I only know what Daisy said. But his lordship is mean, sir, I can tell you that. And Daisy worries about Miss Lind."

"Will you take her another note?" Jowan asked, but the footman stepped away, shaking his head. "It's as much as my job is worth if I'm caught, sir. And the lady did say to leave her alone."

It hit him then, shutting down his throat and squeezing his chest so he could not breathe. He'd been wrong before. This was real pain. Pain like he'd never known. Had it not been for Bran, he'd not have been able to leave the house, but his brother took his arm, gave the footman a half-crown, and escorted Jowan to the pavement.

"She says no," he managed to croak.

"She didn't want to," Bran pointed out. "She cried."

Jowan thought about that as they walked back to the hotel. "I don't know whether to be hopeful or not."

"We need to know more," Bran agreed. "That letter was all about you, and she cried. The girl still loves you, Jowan."

Jowan shook his head. "Then why won't she see me?"

"She thinks you won't love her anymore. Not as she is now," Bran said. "Read it again."

Jowan wanted to run all the way back to Cornwall, but he stopped on the street and forced himself to take the paper that Bran thrust at him.

"First paragraph, she is worried about you. She still cares. Second paragraph. She wants you to remember her as she was. She is ashamed of who she is now, from the sound of it."

Bran stabbed at the page. "There's nothing there about not wanting you, about having outgrown you. 'You are my sweetest memory.' 'Please remember me.' Up to you to change her 'no' to a 'yes', I would say. If you want to. Maybe she is right, and she has changed too much for you to swallow."

"Never," Jowan replied, fervently.

"We need to find out what has happened to her," Bran mused. "Treat it like the rest. We've solved the problem of Thatcher and the investors, or nearly. We'll look for your father's solicitor tomorrow and figure out whether we can recover anything there. This is just one more problem to solve. What has become of Tamsyn Roskilly, and does she need a knight in shining armor, or to be left alone?"

Jowan took a breath and then another. Perhaps the letter hadn't killed him, after all. And Bran had made a good point. Several in fact. "We don't have enough information," he said. "I wonder what Drew knows about the Earl of Coombe?"

"Or his friends," Bran commented. "If you don't mind involving them."

"A barrister and a viscount," Jowan mused. "They could be

useful, but I have no claim on them, Bran." Drew had taken them to his meeting with Mr. Fullerton and Lord Snowden after they left Thatcher's rooms. Drew's men had found nothing incriminating, but Beckleston had been less careful. Both Fullerton, who had overseen the search of the office, and Snowden, whose group had searched Beckleston's home, arrived at the meeting very pleased with what they had found.

"I'd be better pleased," Snowden had complained, "if we had also found our miscreants."

Drew had introduced Jowan and Bran as former students and possibly future partners. "Trethewey owns the mine Thatcher sucked us into, and he and his brother are in London to find out why the money Thatcher was collecting has not yet arrived."

"I let them think we were only in London to investigate Thatcher," Jowan said to Bran now, referring to Drew's friends.

"Drew told them that," Bran pointed out. "Or implied it, at least. And we *are* here for that purpose, at least in part. It can't hurt to raise the topic of Miss Lind and Coombe."

"When? When we are presenting our credentials and the progress on the mine to persuade their investment group to give us their money despite my poor judgment in agents?"

"Perhaps not," Bran acknowledged, but I daresay we can find an opportunity."

Shortly after the brothers arrived back at their rooms in the hotel, the manager brought Jowan a small pile of mail.

"We have been invited to a *musicale* tomorrow night," Jowan told Bran. "Invitation only. For the benefit of a hospital apparently. The hostess is the Duchess of Winshire. Isn't the Duke of Winshire Drew's father? I thought he was a widower."

Bran, who had a far greater interest in the London news than Jowan, knew the answer. "He married again several years ago—to the widow of the Duke of Haverford. According to the papers, the pair were sweethearts before they both married elsewhere. I imagine we have Drew to thank for the invitation."

Jowan nodded. "We had better go, then." He could not find

any enthusiasm for the evening. The last thing he wanted to do was meet a lot of aristocrats at a fancy party when all his heart wanted was to storm Coombe's house or alternately flee back to Cornwall and hide himself away.

Bran shrugged. "Perhaps the subject of your lady will come up tomorrow since music is the entertainment for the evening."

⟫⟫⟩⟨⟨⟪

THE NEXT DAY was frustrating. The solicitor their father had been dealing with was no longer at the address Jowan had for him. Their father's papers had been in such a mess that it had taken Jowan and Bran three months after they took over the office to realize certain irregular receipts were probably profits from investments handled by someone in London, and possibly connected to a couple of large payments that had left a substantial hole in the accounts a couple of years before the payments started to arrive.

Another three months had passed before they tracked down the name of the man, by which time the receipts had stopped and none of Jowan's letters received a reply. And now, they discovered, he was not where he was supposed to be anymore.

No one in the building knew where he had gone, either. They went from office to office seeking someone who might have been in the place for more than four years, but without success. "I suppose your letters finished up in somebody's bin," Bran said. They proceeded to visit the buildings on either side of the address, but no one they interviewed claimed any knowledge of the man.

They also called on the Earl of Coombe and were denied at the door.

"Let's go back to the hotel, and I shall buy you a drink before dinner," Bran said.

Jowan would prefer the drink without the dinner. He was

doing his best to remain positive, but the word "no" kept echoing in his mind and, somehow, in his gut, too.

Still, Bran wasn't about to let him stew in his own misery. Besides, Jowan knew he could not turn up drunk to the musicale. He owed it to his people to make a good impression on these Londoners, especially those who were going to decide whether the new mine went ahead.

They had brought evening wear with them—Jowan had Bran to thank for that, too. He had insisted they should be prepared for all eventualities. They had both been outfitted by a Plymouth tailor and were—or so the man had assured them—elegant enough for London Society.

Certainly, Bran looked good in his, and Jowan could have been his twin but for one inch more in height and hair that was a lighter shade of brown. They had both chosen black for breeches and coats. Jowan had a green waistcoat embroidered in copper and Bran's was blue with silver embroidery. The clocking on their stockings matched the embroidery, as did the buckles on their black shoes. A pin on their white cravats added another spot of color—green for Jowan and blue for Bran.

From what he'd seen on his way around London, Jowan wondered if many of the gentlemen would fill their garments to as much advantage. He and Bran both lived active lives, turning their hands to anything needed on the estate's farms, in the mines, or on the fishing fleet.

Perhaps London ladies preferred the weedy creatures he'd passed on Oxford Street. What did Tamsyn prefer now? And there he was again, thinking of her.

"Shall we take a hackney, Bran?"

"Will we get dirtier catching one of those flea and stink traps, or walking?" Bran wondered.

They walked.

Chapter Five

THE WINSHIRE MANSION was in one of the older squares of Mayfair. The largest building of any in the vicinity, it was lit from basement to attic, and so many carriages were attempting to access the front steps that the traffic was queued as far as the eye could see down the streets in every direction.

They bypassed the carriages and joined a second instance of traffic congestion on the footpath, as guests waited to ascend the steps of the house. This queue was short and swiftly moving. They soon reached the front door, where they showed their invitations to a footman. The entry hall was large enough to swallow the drawing room at Inneford House. The stairs rose up through the house, lit by a great chandelier, but the house was twice as high as Inneford House. Jowan could just make out a ceiling lantern high above.

They ascended the stairs step by step in the queue to the reception line on what in any less elegant house would have been the landing. If one could call a space as large as four tenant cottages a landing.

At last, it was their turn to be greeted by their hostess. The butler took their invitations and announced them to the Duke and Duchess of Winshire. The ducal couple were perhaps in their sixties but still vigorous. Jowan could see traces of Drew in the duke—or the other way around, he supposed. The duchess greeted them both with a smile. "You are Drew's guests," she said. "Go on into the drawing room, Sir Jowan, Mr. Hughes. Drew is waiting for you there."

The drawing room carried on the theme of the house. Jowan had seen assembly halls that were smaller, though to think of assembly halls in the same context as this richly appointed and elegant room seemed like a form of blasphemy.

"I'm feeling like a country mouse," whispered Bran.

"You are," Jowan pointed out, keeping his own voice low, "and so am I."

"There you are," Drew greeted them. He had a lady on his arm. "Margaret, may I make you known to friends of mine from my time at Oxford? Sir Jowan Trethewey and Branoc Hughes. Gentlemen, this lovely lady is Lady Snowden, wife to Snowy, whom you met yesterday. He is around here somewhere."

Lord Snowden came hurrying through the crowd, carrying an upright chair. "Here you are, my love," he said. "Oh, I see you have met our Cornishmen. Good evening, gentlemen."

"Hal," Lady Snowden protested. "Wherever did you steal that chair?"

"You needed an upright chair, darling," Lord Snowden said. "I found one." He placed it next to the arm of a small sofa. "Now sit down, please."

Lady Snowden laughed, but did as she was told, saying to Jowan and Bran, "I find it uncomfortable, at the moment, to use a low seat." Lord Snowden sat on the sofa at her elbow.

The poor lady. Jowan hoped it was nothing serious. Lord Snowden must have seen his concern, for he explained, "My wife is *enceinte*." His pride and affection warmed his voice, and sent a pang of jealousy through Jowan, even as his eyes registered that yes, the lady was not merely plump, as he had assumed, but rather more rotund than the flesh on her arms and face would suggest.

"Congratulations," Bran said. "Your first?"

Had Jowan's father and the Earl of Coombe not interfered, would he and Tamsyn have a house full of children by now? His mind's eye could see them. Joyous imps with her dark curls and her wonderful voice.

He should make an effort to join Lord and Lady Snowden's conversation with Bran. It moved from babies to Society's expectation that pregnant women should be least in sight. Jowan couldn't muster a single comment that did not touch on his own personal grief.

"I usually stay at home to avoid ruffling the feathers of the biddies," Lady Snowden said, "but when I heard the name of the singer who is to perform for us tonight, I had to come."

"Margaret had not yet come to London when the singer left to tour Europe," Lord Snowden explained. "We had tickets for the opera *Figaro*, but the understudy took the part instead."

"Then Aunt Eleanor sent a note saying she had secured Miss Lind for her musicale this evening," Lady Snowden confided. "Of course, I had to come."

Jowan struggled to believe his own ears. "Miss Tammie Lind?"

"Yes, the Devon Songbird, as they call her. Have you heard her sing, Sir Jowan? But no, you would not have been on the Town when she was last in London."

"Not in London, and not for seven long years," Jowan replied, hardly knowing what he was saying or where he was.

"She and Jowan grew up together," Bran explained. "Her mother and our father were acquainted." He took Jowan's arm in a firm grip. "Jowan, do you need to sit down?"

There was not enough air in the room, but otherwise, Jowan was fine. He waved his brother off.

"You did not know the lady was singing tonight?" Drew guessed. "The news has flown around Town with the wind since my stepmother changed the program to accommodate Miss Lind."

"We are in a hotel," Bran commented. "We are, I daresay,

handicapped in not having a housemaid whose aunt is the cook in a place where the lady's maid has a brother who is valet to an earl who employs a boot boy whose mother is housekeeper to a baron whose…"

God bless Bran. He was speaking nonsense to give Jowan time to recover his poise. Jowan continued in the same vein. "You are assuming that London is the same as our small village, where no one with any pretensions to gentility can do anything without a servant knowing and passing on the news, but only to their nearest and dearest, and in strictest confidence. And thus, gossip flies."

"It is the same here in London," Lady Snowden confirmed.

The tinkling of a bell attracted their attention. "Time to move through to the ballroom," Drew said. "Margaret, the chairs that have been set out for the concert are upright, so Snowy won't have to carry his stolen one for your comfort."

The lord so named stood to assist his wife to her feet. Jowan and Bran followed the pair through a wide-open double doorway, down a short flight of stairs, and into a cavernous ballroom that could easily have held a thousand guests and still left room for dancing.

Jowan gave the surroundings a glance, registering the quality of the appointments without paying them any attention. His attention was entirely focused on the stage that had been erected in the center of one long side of the room.

The stage held a piano, several rows of chairs arranged in a curve around a music stand, and a lectern. Long rows of chairs faced the stage, grouped into three columns by aisles that allowed easy access. Lord Snowden conducted his lady to a seat at one side of the middle column, in the middle of the third row back.

Drew followed, then Bran, with Jowan close behind. He was about to see Tamsyn! He could not focus on anything else. He held himself back from leaping to his feet and demanding to be taken to her. Her letter had said, "No". He couldn't forget that. But he would see her soon. He just had to wait.

And wait he did, though it was excruciating. First, people took their time coming to the ballroom and being seated. Lots of people. He wasn't going to count, though each group of seats was a score wide, so sixty in a row, and he'd guess at twenty rows.

When, at last, they were all seated, chattering away like a thousand monkeys or jackdaws rather than people, the duchess came up onto the stage. The noise diminished and then ceased when she tapped the lectern.

It was a formal welcome and an explanation of the charity hospital that the night was intended to benefit. They, the audience, would be helping the hospital through ticket sales, several raffles, and an auction.

In return, they would receive not just the pleasure of doing good—a comment that fetched a much bigger laugh than Jowan thought it deserved—but would also enjoy an evening of unparalleled musical excellence.

Jowan managed not to shout out an instruction to get on with it, but Bran must have guessed it was a possibility, for he put his hand back on his brother's arm.

The duchess was outlining the program for the evening, and doing so with a lot of description and a few jokes.

First, a pianist of whom even Jowan had heard. He had been mentioned quite a few times in the newspapers that made their way to Cornwall.

Next, a couple who must have been well-known in London. The audience's hum of appreciation indicated the couple was a popular choice, even if they weren't famous all the way to the western corner of south England. They would both sing while one of them played the harp-lute.

Following that, a short break would allow the assembly to see the items that were being raffled and to write their names and their donations on the paper by each item.

A gentleman whose name Jowan didn't catch would sing next, and would then sing a duet with Miss Lind before the pianist returned to accompany Miss Lind in further songs. Jowan sat up straighter.

Another short break would be followed by the last musical segment of the evening, this time all Miss Lind.

The duchess went on to talk about the auction that would end that part of the evening and the supper to follow, but Jowan now knew he was doomed to keep waiting. After seven years of waiting, another hour or so should not be a problem, but somehow it was.

He shifted in his seat, trying to make himself comfortable, and caught Bran watching him. His brother looked concerned. Jowan did his best to smile but must have failed, for Bran's worry deepened.

The duchess had finished speaking, for everyone began to clap, and Jowan joined in. A tall gentleman who looked remarkably like Drew offered his hand to help the duchess down the steps at one side of the stage, while another man bounced up the other side and took a seat at the piano.

He was good. Jowan had to give him that. If not for the anxious wait to see Tamsyn, Jowan might even have become lost in the music, as many of those around him were doing. Jowan did not recognize the two pieces he played, but the gentleman sitting just behind him named each one to the lady he was escorting.

The harp-lutist couple were good, too. The man's baritone voice complemented the contralto of his partner. Jowan knew what to call the voices because the helpful pundit behind him, who had obviously taken on the role of educating his lady, was speaking loudly enough to improve the knowledge of those around him.

Two songs for the harp-lutists, too. Ballads, and very pretty, though Jowan was hardly in the mood to hear about star-crossed love, betrayal, and dying lovers.

The applause for the harp-lutists was even more enthusiastic than for the pianist, poor man.

"We should buy a spot in a couple of the raffles," Bran murmured, as people around them began to get up and move along the rows to the aisles or the edges.

Jowan supposed Bran was right. He wanted to stay in his chair until Tamsyn sang, but he knew nothing he did would make the time go faster.

Footmen moved through the crowd with trays of drink and plates of tiny savory or sweet bite-sized treats. He ate something that tasted of salmon and Bran handed him a glass. Champagne. The wife of the viscount two villages over had it for her yearly harvest ball.

He put his name and his promise to pay against a raffle for a fine saddle, and Bran did the same for a twelve-place setting of fine china from Doulton, Jones, and Watt. "What?" he asked, when Jowan questioned the choice. "I'm sure it will be useful, and it is pretty. I like it."

Between them, they'd donated fifty pounds, but some of the other pledges were much higher. Without exchanging a word on the matter, Jowan and Bran headed back to the chairs where they had been sitting.

Lord and Lady Snowden were already there, and Lord Snowden must have been telling his lady about their need for investors in the new mine, for she asked, "Do you employ children in your mine, Sir Jowan?" The martial light in her eye hinted at her motive, but it wasn't a simple question.

"I don't allow children under the age of twelve below ground, my lady," Jowan told her. "I would like to see legislation to set the age at fourteen, but until we have that, all mines are competing under the same conditions. I have to let those twelve and over have jobs if their families demand them, or they will move to an employer who doesn't have the same rules and those children will end up below ground in the end."

And if that just lost him Lord Snowden as an investor, so be it. Jowan respected those who were against the use of children in mines and factories. He agreed, in principle. In fact, he'd prefer it if all children had only family chores, as happened in the wealthier working-class households, and were otherwise able to attend school.

The reality was that few turned up for the school he funded in St Tetha, both because their families saw no value in reading and writing and because their choice was not whether to work or to go to school, but whether to work or to starve.

Bran interrupted, leaning forward to look past Jowan and Lord Snowden so he could address the viscountess. "You cannot blame them, my lady. They need the money. And you can't blame Jowan. He pays as much as he can and still be competitive, and he gives work in the house and the stables to any family who does not have an adult breadwinner. Indeed, some of the locals have been most indignant that their ten and eleven-year-old children *cannot* work underground."

Lady Snowden was amused. "You are a good brother, Mr. Hughes. If I sounded critical, I apologize. I understand that child labor is not a simple question. You make a good point about legislation, Sir Jowan, does he not, Hal?" The last few words were addressed to her husband.

Lord Snowden said, "You shall have to come to dinner, gentlemen, so we can discuss this matter further." Like his wife, he appeared interested and sympathetic. Perhaps he would still invest after all.

He was interrupted by a rapid hammering sound from the lectern. The Duke of Winshire was calling the room to attention for the second segment of the entertainment.

Jowan leaned forward. Just one more act, and it would be Tamsyn's turn. The gentleman singer gave them an aria in Italian or a similar-sounding language. Since Jowan didn't understand Italian and knew nothing about Don Giovanni, the opera the aria was apparently from, all he could do was sit back and listen to the voice, which he enjoyed, even though in his own mind, he was just filling in time until Tamsyn appeared.

A round of applause for the singer, and at last she was there. Older, of course. More beautiful, too, though much thinner. He had wondered if the reported illness was true, or just an excuse to avoid him. He wondered no longer, for she was so thin he hurt for her. Her hair, though, was a dark cloud about her face, just as he remembered it.

He was close enough, too, to see her eyes—the dark grey he remembered so well. He had never seen that color in anyone else. The shape, too, was distinctive—an almost perfect almond.

Her gown was as rich and as fashionable as any in the room—a bright amethyst against which the fair skin of her throat and shoulders gleamed, creamy-white.

He waited, hardly breathing, as the duke introduced her and announced the next song. A duet from another opera written in Italian. This one was by Handel, whom Jowan had thought to be German. Or maybe English. Jowan was reasonably certain the man was buried at Westminster Cathedral, so why wasn't the song in German or English?

Jowan did his best to ignore the man in favor of allowing Tamsyn's voice to envelope him and carry him away, but beautiful though the sound was, he could not quite ignore the interaction of the couple. It was a love song, he supposed, from the way the male singer gazed fatuously into Tamsyn's eyes.

And she gazed back, but presumably, she was acting. Certainly, she showed no particular interest once the song was over, and the man turned away as soon as the final note was sung, to bat his eyelashes at the audience.

"I've no idea what the song was about," Jowan murmured as he clapped for Tamsyn.

Lady Snowden whispered, "It is called, *Vivo en te, mio caro bene.* I live for you, my dear heart."

As he thought. A love song.

Tamsyn now stood alone on the stage, smiling as her gaze skimmed over the audience. "I thought a change might be welcomed, Your Graces, my ladies, my lords, gentlemen. I wish to sing…" Her eyes caught on Jowan's and faltered, her voice stuttering to a stop. She recovered almost instantly, continuing, "to sing a folk song from the north of England. A simple story of former lovers, now at odds. First, the man."

She had been standing with her feet together and her hands folded at her waist, but as she finished her sentence, she changed her stance, legs astride, hands on hips, and chin lifted. Even as a half-trained girl, her voice had had exceptional voice range. As she sang, Jowan had no difficulty in seeing her as the youth who was demanding an impossible task from the girl who had once been his true love.

Once the lover had demanded a cambric shirt, made without needlework and washed in a dry well, Tamsyn changed both stance and voice to become the girl, asking for him to sow land below the high tide mark and to plow, seed, and reap with tools that would never work.

Her gaze had been moving over the audience as she sang, but on the last lines of the song, after the maiden had finished listing her demands, Tamsyn stared directly at Jowan.

"When he is done and finished his work," she caroled, "Ask him to come for his cambric shirt. Then, he'll be a true love of mine."

Was that a challenge? And if so, to do what? And why? Surely, she knew he would do anything for her? For old time's sake, if for no other reason, he owed her that.

After their separation in time, distance, and silence, he had no idea what else he owed this new Tamsyn. This stranger with Tamsyn's hair and eyes. His mind worried at the question as his body reacted to her loveliness and he joined the rest of the audience in showing his appreciation by standing and clapping.

Chapter Six

THE EVENING WAS going well. The music was excellent, the singer with whom she had had a duet was brilliant, and the audience—a glittering host that put her in mind of a fairy court—were darlings.

"Next song," hissed the conductor, recalling her to her duty. Guy had allowed her to smoke a pipe of opium in the carriage. It was a stronger batch than any she'd had recently—not just enough to smooth off the world's sharp edges, but sufficient to erase sharpness altogether and cloak her surroundings in a kindly mist, through which she saw only brief glimpses of detail.

Part of the mist was the light each person emitted. She could usually see that light, unique to each person and changing with their mood and their health, but it was always stronger and easier to perceive when she was drugged or drunk or both. Tonight, most of the people here were happy and relaxed.

Look at them standing and clapping, the man who looked like Jowan among them.

Tamsyn stole another look at him, the stranger who reminded her of Jowan. His light was largely a true green, with touches of sky blue and veins of gold. Good colors.

The orchestra played the introduction to her next song and Tammie's training took control, drawing her away from her thoughts and prompting the deep breath she needed for yet another aria, this one from a little-known opera by an English composer.

Caught up in the music, she ignored the audience, singing not for them but for Jowan. Wherever he was, and whatever he was doing.

The duet and two more songs before the break, she had been told. One more song after, and then two encores, if the audience asked for them, and they would. Tammie was in fine voice. She was untouchable, immortal, incomparable. Sure enough, they clapped, and they cheered. After her third number, they would not sit down until the duke, a handsome man despite his age, shouted to ask them to be seated.

Once he had the attention of the room, he held it. In the dream world that waited to engulf Tammie, he wore a crown, not unlike the one she often visualized on Guy, but emitting light where Guy's crown sucked light in. A king of light, with an aura of clean pure blue rather than a king of dark, whose red-black aura hurt the eyes.

They were both tall and broad-shouldered, but the duke was slim-waisted where Guy's indulgence of all his senses showed in his expanding paunch. The duke's hair was iron-dark tipped with frost and Guy's was sandy-fair and fading to white.

The duke was still talking but Tammie, since people were no longer paying her attention, let her slender grasp on reality drift. Perhaps she would not sing again tonight.

If she did, she would like to sing for Not-Jowan. The more she looked at him, the less certain she was about him being a stranger. Certainly, he smiled at her as if they were friends. He might be just a regular stage-door lecher, sure that every singer could be had for a price. But Tammie was an expert at detecting lust, and she was surely not deep enough in the opium dream to miss it if it was there.

It wasn't. Those eyes held something else. Curiosity? Concern? Those eyes so like the eyes of the boy who had been her dearest friend. Jowan would, she supposed, be twenty-three now. Yes. Twenty-three. She was twenty-three and so was Jowan. He would have grown taller and broader. This man was taller and broader, but he had Jowan's eyes.

People were moving, forming into queues. Was the concert over? She glanced at the duke, and he smiled back. "Would you care to have a seat, Miss Lind? We will not be long, and then they will expect their reward."

Reward? What kind of a reward? Tammie obediently sat in the chair the duke indicated and waited to find out. Her mind kept spiraling away. Soon, she would sleep. Sleep and dream. Perhaps of Cornwall, and at the thought, Bodmin Moor rose in her mind, and the children who used to play there, escaping from their lessons to ride the half-wild moor ponies.

When the duke touched her shoulder, she found it hard to let go of the dream.

"Miss Lind? It is time for your next song."

Guy materialized behind the man. "The duke said you would sing your encore pieces, Tammie, if enough people signed up for the raffles. You have your encores ready, do you not?"

Tammie could sing in her sleep, and perhaps she had sometimes done so. She nodded to the conductor, who had her music, and sang a lullaby that was all about the baby's father who had, as the song lamented, "gone for a soldier". The first encore was "Greensleeves", which was always a crowd-pleaser. She had prepared a third aria to finish the evening, but another idea occurred to her. A song for Jowan, if it was Jowan.

Guy glowered when she crossed to speak to the conductor, but Tammie ignored him. The dreams were crowding her now, the audience turning into mystical beasts before her eyes and the ballroom fading away as ivy and other creepers pulled down the walls to show castles and forests beyond.

One of the musicians carried a chair for her to the front of the stage and gave her his harp-lute. She played a brief introduction and launched into a ballad from home—one she had never before sung on stage, but that was as much a part of her as her bones.

It was a Cornish lament, about a girl who was lost on the moor, taken by the fair folk, and the miner boy who wandered the moors day in and day out, unwilling to give up searching for his beloved. Even in Cornwall, where few now spoke the old tongue, most people would not understand the words of the song, but the music carried the sentiments.

Jowan, if it was Jowan, learned the lament when she did. Could he see, as she did, the elf king rising up from the bog to pull the girl down, then trying and failing to do the same to her sweetheart?

The man was mouthing the words of the chorus as she sang them. It *was* Jowan! It must be. Her hands on the harp lute fell still and she repeated the chorus one more time, unaccompanied, the miner boy's lament for his stolen beloved floating out across the large room.

As her voice fell still, the assembled guests paid her that highest of all compliments from an audience. A moment of complete silence. And then they were on their feet, clapping and smiling. Probably-Jowan, too. Tammie kept her eyes on him as the duke spoke a few words of thanks and encouraged them to take their seats again for the auction.

Then Guy was at her side, taking her by the elbow. "Come along. I will introduce you to the duchess and then I am sending you home," he said.

"I would like to stay and meet the guests," Tammie protested.

"You are too tired," Guy declared. "I have already told the duchess as much. The song you sang last? It is not the one you prepared."

Tammie blinked at him. Was she tired? It was increasingly hard to think.

"Come along," Guy said again. "You may have a sip of laudanum before you meet the duchess, and then I will give instructions for another dose back at the house when you are ready for bed."

Another dose. Sweet oblivion. Tammie put Probably-Jowan from her mind and allowed herself to be escorted out to the room that had been set aside for her and Guy's other musicians.

"What was that last song?" Guy grumbled as he measured out the laudanum. "It was not on your list."

"They enjoyed 'Scarborough Fair' and 'Greensleeves'," Tammie told him. "I thought they would appreciate another simple song. And I was right, Guy, was I not?"

"What was the language?" he demanded. "Where did you learn it?"

Tammie shrugged. "Who knows? It might be Welsh. Or Gaelic, perhaps." She volunteered a little more, minding her words as if they were the gold coins of the old tales. Or knives. Didn't one of the folk tales tell of a girl who was cursed to spit knives with every word she spoke? For certain, if she was careless with what she said, Guy would find a way to turn her words against her.

He leaned over from his seat and grabbed her chin, forcing her to face him. "What is it about, Tammie?"

"A girl who drowns and is lost, and the boy who searches for her," she replied. "Or so I understand. It is a pretty tune, is it not?"

"Pathetic," he replied, examining her eyes as if a different answer might have been written there. "True love and all that nonsense." He must have been satisfied, for he pushed her face away from him, letting go as he did so.

"They enjoyed it," she repeated. "All the sad songs. The es-tranged lovers who demand impossible tasks as a sign of true love. The lover who bemoans the loss of his fickle mistress. The lad whose sweetheart is lost and gone." It was very sad.

She had made them sad, and they had loved it. All the bright and beautiful people, with their silk and lace and jewels. A host for the elf king. No, but they were not Guy's people. They were the duke's people. Was he, too, an elf king?

It made sense. Her *mamm wynn*, her grandmother, had spoken of the light elves and the dark elves. Guy was the dark king, so was the duke the light king? And if he was, could he save her? But no. The elf kingdoms avoided one another, if Mamm's tales were to be her guide, and would not risk war for a human girl who had wandered into Guy's clutches of her own free will.

Guy was still frowning, and his aura was even darker and muddier than usual. "Sir Jowan Trethewey is here," he said, abruptly. He was still holding the laudanum out of her reach.

"I wondered," Tammie replied, less interested in the conversation than in the glass of happiness he was withholding. "He was staring at me. I thought it could not be Jowan." Guy would not believe a complete lack of interest. "What would Jowan be doing here, in London, I asked myself. But he kept staring. Was it Jowan, then? The man with the dark curls in the third row, near the middle?"

Guy handed her the glass. "Possibly. He doesn't matter, Tammie."

Tammie downed the drink.

"Perhaps he will call," she suggested when Guy said nothing more.

"You will not see him," Guy commanded. "It is for the best, Tammie. You loved him once. You don't want him to see what you have done. What you have become."

"No," she replied, obediently, and added, "He loved Tamsyn. And Tamsyn died, long ago. Only Tammie remains."

Guy pulled her to her feet and offered her his elbow. "Just so." His voice was dark with satisfaction. "And Tammie is mine."

"Yes, Guy," Tammie agreed, keeping her eyes lowered lest Guy read the rebellion there. Tammie was Guy's, but Tamsyn stirred within her, not nearly as dead as she had believed. And Tamsyn had always been Jowan's, just as Jowan was Tamsyn's.

TAMSYN WAS ABSENT during the auction but appeared briefly at the start of the supper. Jowan recognized the man with her as the Earl of Coombe, but he had changed over the past seven years. Then, he had been a gentleman in his prime, elegant, and sophisticated but also handsome and charming. To the sixteen-year-old Jowan, he had represented the fashionable world—that circle of superior beings who sometimes passed through their village, pausing only long enough to look down their noses at the locals. Jowan had hated that he found the man impressive and somewhat intimidating.

From a distance, he looked much the same, but as Jowan worked his way through the crowd to approach, he realized how much the man had aged in the last seven years. The firm skin beneath his eyes had become bags, his neck had relaxed into jowls, his waist had expanded, and his hair had receded from his forehead.

He was moving from group to group, introducing Tamsyn and stopping to chat for a few minutes. Jowan placed himself in a group with Lord Andrew and several others, waiting for the man to reach them, but Coombe turned the other way and was soon lost in the crowd.

No matter. Jowan would follow as soon as he had finished the conversation he was having with Snowden about inquiry agents. But when he did, he found that Coombe was on his own.

Jowan, having concluded that Tamsyn was nowhere in the ballroom, asked Lord Andrew to introduce him to Coombe.

"Not a nice man," Lord Andrew warned him. "Aunt Eleanor decided to tolerate him for the sake of Miss Lind's singing, but he would not normally be invited to any of her entertainments."

"We met some years ago," Jowan explained. "Miss Lind was a childhood friend. I had hoped to speak to her."

Lord Andrew shrugged. "As long as you're warned," he said.

Coombe was holding forth to a group of men about his European tour. When Lord Andrew and Jowan approached, his eyes darted sideways, as if he was about to work another disappearance. He must have thought better of it, for he greeted Lord Andrew, saying, "Winderfield. I trust your belle-mere is happy with the performances this evening."

"I believe Her Grace is well satisfied," Lord Andrew replied. "Coombe, I wish to make known to you Sir Jowan Trethewey from Cornwall."

"Lord Coombe and I met long ago," Jowan said, with the minimum of polite bows. "You may remember your trip to Cornwall, my lord since you collected such a treasure there."

"You were no more than a gormless boy, Trethewey," Coombe replied. Up close, the signs of dissipation were even more obvious, from the threading of broken veins on his face and the discoloring of his eyes.

Obvious, too, was the hostility in those eyes.

Jowan ignored it. "Yes, and Miss Lind was no more than an innocent girl. I hoped to pay my respects to my old friend."

"Miss Lind was tired, and an associate has taken her home," said Coombe. "However, you are wasting your time, Trethewey. I can assure you that Miss Lind has no interest in revisiting her girlhood." His eyes narrowed and he shifted into a threatening stance, setting his shoulders, and leaning forward. "Leave her alone. That is my last word on the subject."

He turned his body to shut Jowan out, saying to Lord Andrew, "I do not wish to be rude, Winderfield, but I consider it my duty, as Miss Lind's protector and patron, to keep such annoyances from her. She has moved far beyond past acquaintances such as impoverished baronets from the remote corners of nowhere."

Jowan didn't bother to hide his grin at the lame attempt at an insult, and Lord Andrew, seeing his expression, rolled his eyes. "Lord Coombe, I am surprised to hear you insulting my friends under my father's roof," he said.

"Perhaps you might give Miss Lind my compliments on her performance," Jowan said to Coombe's back. "Drew, thank you for the introduction."

Bran was waiting within sight, and Lord Andrew walked with Jowan to join him. "I'm sorry that didn't work out as you hoped," he said. "Miss Lind is Cornish, is she? I wonder what she really thinks about meeting you again."

"You think Coombe was lying?" Jowan asked.

"I think he lies as easily as he breathes," said Lord Andrew. His eyes were alive with questions, but he had no chance to ask them before another of Her Grace's guests stopped to talk to him about the evening's cause. "Duty calls," said Lord Andrew, and left Jowan and Bran to talk.

Jowan told Bran what had happened. "That last song was for me," he said. "It's one her Granny used to sing to us both." But then why, having recognized him and sung to him, did she run off before they could meet?

"She can't have known you were going to be here," Bran argued.

That was true, and Jowan had followed Tamsyn and the village choir to enough festivals and competitions to know the next question to ask. "Are the musicians still here?"

They were, having a supper of their own in a little room off the ballroom, and someone soon pointed them to the conductor. "Miss Lind's last encore," Jowan asked him after he had introduced himself. "Was that unplanned, as far as you know?"

"It was, as a matter of fact," said the conductor. "We had the accompaniment for 'Say, Can You Deny Me', but at the last minute, she told me she was going to sing something else. I didn't know the tune. It was Welsh, was it? Sounded a bit like Welsh."

"Not Welsh," said the man who had sung the duet with Tamsyn. "Pretty, though."

"Very pretty," Jowan agreed. He thanked them for their music and left the conductor with a guinea to share with the others.

"That last one was for you," Bran conceded.

Before Jowan could comment, Lord Snowden found them. "Ah! There you are. I have a couple of people I want you to meet." Jowan dropped the topic and did his best to focus instead on the new mine and its benefits to potential investors. Still, at some level, his mind must have continued circling around Tamsyn and the lament.

"Why that song?" he asked Bran as they walked back to the hotel.

"Because she knows you speak Cornish?" his brother suggested.

Jowan shook his head. "She could have chosen any number of Cornish songs, but she picked that one. Is she the maid stolen away by the Bucca Dhu? Is she telling me she is lost forever, Bran?"

Bran shrugged. "Maybe she is asking for rescue? But why didn't she stay? We need more information, Jowan."

He didn't say that Jowan should have questioned Drew, or Snowden and his friends, but he didn't need to. Jowan knew it, but somehow, he felt too raw. "Lady Snowden has invited us to dinner tomorrow evening—or this evening, I suppose, given the time. Business and pleasure, I gather. In the morning, when we wake up, let's see the inquiry fellow that Snowden mentioned, and set him on the trail of Father's solicitor. Then we can call on Coombe again in the afternoon."

"Perhaps this Wakefield can tell us about Coombe, too," Bran suggested.

Chapter Seven

THE INQUIRY AGENT had his office in a terraced house on the outskirts of Mayfair. Five steps led up from the street to two green doors, one of which had a brass plate that read "Wakefield and Wakefield".

Bran plied the knocker. The man who opened the door said, "Good morning. Sir Jowan Trethewey and Mr. Hughes? Come on in. I'm Wakefield."

They followed him into an entrance hall and then through to an office that might at one time have been a parlor. Wakefield waved them in the direction of a couple of chairs and took a seat behind one of two desks in the room. "Your note said that you had been referred by Lord Snowden and that you are hunting for your father's solicitor. Can you tell me what has happened, in your own words, and what you want me to do for you?"

Jowan and Bran had discussed how best to describe the situation they found themselves in, and why they had allowed four years to pass before pursuing the matter. They had agreed that they should start at the beginning, and so Jowan did.

"My father…" He glanced at Bran and corrected his words. "Our father died when I was still seven months shy of my twentieth birthday, and my brother here had just turned nineteen."

He waited for Wakefield to comment or show any reaction to the disclosure that he and Bran were brothers. Wakefield did not turn a hair but merely nodded.

"Father had never permitted either of us to be involved in his business dealings, and we had, in any case, been away for two years at university. The executor of his will sent for us to return for the reading of the will. It was simple enough. Father left everything to me." His indignation at the man's self-centered arrogance colored his voice. There had been nothing for Bran, whom he had recognized as his son. Nothing for the housekeeper, Mrs. Roskilly, who had managed his house for fifteen years and warmed his bed for at least a decade. Nothing for any of the other servants.

Correcting those oversights had been one of Jowan's first tasks once he turned twenty-one. Or, at least, he tried, though Bran refused to take his fair share. And Mrs. Roskilly was then in her last illness and already living as his pensioner in one of his cottages. He settled it on her and gave her an income for life. He didn't like the woman, and he was certain she had been complicit in taking Tamsyn from him, but the way Sir Carlyon had treated her was unjust. As it was, she died three months later.

"I take it someone was appointed to manage the estates during your minority?" Wakefield asked.

"The local earl was appointed my trustee. He thought to leave the day-to-day management to those my father had employed—the mines to the mine manager, the land to the land steward, and other matters to the local solicitor. As for me, he told me I was an adult and could do as I pleased."

"The path of least resistance," Wakefield commented.

The shrewd comment summed up Lord Trentwood very well. "Exactly. His lordship is a pleasant fellow, much given to the joys of the table and disinclined to trouble himself. When I told him I wanted to find out how matters stood with my inheritance, he roused sufficiently to write letters to each of my stewards telling them I had his authority."

He sighed, remembering his own reaction to what they had discovered. "What Bran and I found was a mess. The land had been neglected—the steward said that my father refused to invest or to change to more modern practices. Some of the tenancies had fallen vacant because the cottages were unlivable. The same with the two tin mines—wages that could not compete with our neighbors, housing that was tumbling down, and old equipment that was increasingly dangerous. Our fishing villages were not much better."

The grim look on Bran's face was undoubtedly mirrored on his own, as he and his brother both remembered the shocking revelations from the manager and the steward. "Our income from tenancies, mines, and fishing catches had dropped and was barely enough to keep things going as they were, let alone to make the investments needed," Jowan explained. "Yet our father had continued to spend lavishly on clothing, wine, horseflesh, house parties, and his mistresses." His anger at the old man rose again to choke him and he paused to take a calming breath or two.

"He had other sources of income," Wakefield surmised.

"So we assumed," Bran volunteered. "And so the local solicitor confirmed. It took some persuasion to find out exactly what he had invested in, but we are Cornish boys, Mr. Wakefield, born and bred. My mother was a fisherman's daughter and I lived in her father's house until my grandmother died. Jowan ran with miners' sons from the time he could toddle. Both of us know what kind of enterprise is available to a man who cares about making high profits but who has no morals to speak of."

Wakefield nodded. "Smuggling, I take it?"

"Ess," Bran nodded, dropping into Cornish.

"Smuggling," Jowan confirmed. "While we were at war, mark you. He had other investments, too. Shares in manufacturing a mine pump, a row of houses in Truro, and a few other things. Enough so we could drop the smuggling and still raise enough to begin the improvements on the land and in the mines.

And one more investment we could find little about. We discovered income payments over the past four years, and two years before that a couple of large payments from the Trethewey accounts. The local solicitor confirmed that Father had another investment or investments but knew only that someone in London was handling it. Any papers to do with that investment, Father had kept himself. He was his own secretary, and if he had a system, we have yet to figure it out."

"It took us months to even find the name of the man in London," Bran said. "Jowan wrote to him and had no reply."

"I wrote several times," Jowan confirmed. "No reply."

He handed Wakefield the papers they had found regarding the solicitor and the investments—precious little, but enough to hint that there might be some money somewhere. He'd also included their notes about their actions to date.

"You did not come to London once you had this name," Wakefield noted, a statement rather than a question.

"We have had much to do in Cornwall," Bran explained. "Fortunately, Lord Trentwood was only too willing to let us—or Jowan, rather—make the decisions and take the actions needed to put our affairs to rights, but it has taken years of hard work to make the land, the mines, and the fishing catch as productive as they should be."

Jowan cautioned, "We're not there yet, but we are at least far enough along to make this trip to London. We called at the address we had for the solicitor who was handling Father's investment, whatever it was, and he has been gone from there for at least four years."

"We realize that it may be too late to do anything about the money that has gone missing," Bran acknowledged, "but we would like to at least try to find the culprit."

"I will see what I can do," Wakefield answered. He waved the stack of papers. "This gives me a good start."

"There is another matter," Bran said, with a nod of encouragement to Jowan.

Wakefield raised an eyebrow.

Jowan wasn't sure where to start. "The singer, Tammie Lind. I need to know… That is, could you find out…" What? If she was a prisoner? It sounded ridiculous to his own ears, and he could only imagine what Wakefield would think of it.

"The lady is actually Tamsyn Roskilly, the daughter of our father's housekeeper," Bran explained. "She left Cornwall when she was sixteen, promising to keep in touch. She failed to write, even to her mother. When her mother died, shortly after our father, we informed her through the Earl of Coombe, her patron."

Wakefield, who had been toying with his pen looked up at that, his focus sharpening.

"We received no reply even to that," Bran continued. "When we called on the Earl of Coombe five years ago, and again on this trip, we were denied entry. It is possible that the lady has brushed the dust of her homeland from her feet and wants nothing to do with anything from her past. However, my brother fears that letters from home might have been kept from her, or that she is being suborned in some way, or both."

"Bran puts it very well," Jowan agreed. "We will leave her alone if that is her choice. But we owe her a rescue if she needs one."

"The Earl of Coombe has a dark reputation," Wakefield told them. "I can tell you that without any investigation at all. How much it is still deserved, I do not yet know. When he was last in England, he was infamous for his parties and his liaisons and known in certain circles for dissolute behavior beyond that normally expected of even a young British aristocrat. I have not followed his activities on the continent, but I know who might have done so. I can ask. Also, I have another client who has asked me to investigate his current activities. I can report on what I find to you if you wish."

"If you would," Jowan said.

"As to Miss Roskilly, or Miss Lind, as she is now known, I

should be able to find out what you want to know. You might not like any answers I find for you, however. Coombe was well known for his ability to corrupt innocence, and I cannot imagine that any young woman in his power would escape his attentions."

Jowan shut his eyes against the roaring in his ears. His sweet Tamsyn in the hands of a villain! He didn't want to imagine it but was besieged by a kaleidoscope of scenes of her calling for help while a malign presence assailed her.

"Jowan?" Bran's voice anchored him back in the present and allowed him to catch his breath. He used it to give the investigator his answer.

"Find out, Wakefield. It is better to know the worst rather than be haunted by speculation."

LADY SNOWDEN SET a good table, and her guests were an entertaining lot. Jowan found himself taking a Mrs. Ashby into dinner. She was accompanied this evening by her husband, a Mr. Elijah Ashby, and when Jowan asked if he was the famous travel writer, she smiled and blew a kiss at a gentleman halfway down the other side of the table. "He is, Sir Jowan," she told him.

She was an early reader of the popular books, she told him, and they discussed some of their favorite anecdotes from the volumes for the rest of the remove.

After the servants cleared the plates and brought in the next collection of dishes, he turned to the lady on the other side, a Lady Stancroft. They had been briefly introduced at the *musicale*. Once again, she was wearing an ornate mask that covered one side of her face. Given the minor scars on the visible side and the somewhat more unsightly scars on her neck, he guessed the mask covered damage she did not care to show in public.

"My husband tells me he is considering investment in your mine, Sir Jowan," she said after he had greeted her. "What is your position on employing children?"

Once again, Jowan found himself defending his stance of allowing those over the age of twelve to take up jobs in the mines. Lady Stancroft saw his point but insisted that families would never be able to drag themselves out of poverty if their children were not given the opportunity for education.

They had the opportunity, he explained, since he and Bran had funded a dame school. But, he told her, neither they nor their families could afford, in most instances, to take full advantage of it. Still, Jowan hoped that insisting on the little ones staying in school might change things over time. Surely a mother and father who had at least basic reading and numbering skills might see a benefit in encouraging a budding scholar if one of their brood showed talent.

He tried to express some of that to Lady Stancroft. Again, she was surprisingly sympathetic. "I see your point. It may take a generation or two, you think, to change minds and attitudes."

"Not always," Bran spoke across the table. "Two of our boys started apprenticeships in Plymouth this year, and one of the girls is being kept on at the school to train as a teacher. Jowan paid for the articles for both boys and is paying a weekly stipend for the girl."

"It is good business," Jowan protested. "The village lost its blacksmith several years ago. In time we'll be able to provide a living for one of the boys, and the wheelwright is growing older and has no sons to inherit his shop. If the village is to continue to thrive, we need to provide options for our young people. And a thriving village is good for me, as a landowner and a mine owner."

"Well said," commented a man from farther down the table. "I wish more landowners and industrialists took that view. So many see education as a threat to their positions, rather than as a way of bringing wealth to their area."

"Prosperity and happiness," commented one of the women, and the conversation became general, some supporting Jowan's standpoint, some wanting even more radical changes, and some espousing a more conservative, cautious approach.

It was far from the evening Jowan had expected in such high reaches of Society, and so he said to his host.

Snowden laughed. "You cannot judge all of Society by my friends, Trethewey, any more than you can judge them by the friends of, say, the Duke of Norfolk, or Viscount Sidmouth. The upper classes are not a single group in London any more than they are in any other part of the country, and though we meet one another at large events such as balls, we tend otherwise to gather with those of like mind. Indeed, even clubs and coffee shops attract Whigs or Tories or those with other interests such as fashion or horses."

"Birds of a feather flock together?" Jowan asked. "Does that make you and your friends Whigs?"

Snowden pressed his lips together and narrowed his eyes in thought. "Not exactly."

"I suspect we are too radical for the Whigs and too conservative for the radicals," Lady Stancroft interjected. "Not that we all agree, as you have seen, Sir Jowan. I should like to see better education for children, particularly girls, a reform of the voting system, and regulation of child labor. Most people in this room would say the same, but the details of what each of those means and of how to achieve those ends might have us arguing from now until the end of time."

"Legislation lags behind the dreams of reformists, whatever their views on the detail," said Mrs. Ashby. "Thank goodness for practical people like you, Sir Jowan, and others here. People who simply make the changes that kindness and justice demand without waiting for politicians." She nodded at Snowden. "Snowy's wife Margaret offers her services as an herbalist to a free clinic that provides medical services to those who cannot afford to pay for a doctor."

A second nod was for Lady Stancroft. "Arial and her husband Peter have established dame schools in their villages, to name just one of their innovations. I think I'm correct in saying that all the ladies here support the Duchess of Winshire's efforts to provide opportunities for women, and also the Dowager Lady Sutton's to provide a refuge for women in intolerable circumstances."

"And would you say you are typical of London's ladies?" Bran asked.

"Sadly, no," Lady Stancroft replied. "No more than our husbands are typical of London's gentlemen. Far from it, in fact."

In that case, Jowan thought, he and Bran had been fortunate to find themselves in a community of like minds.

Chapter Eight

AFTER THE CONCERT for Her Grace of Winshire, Guy was besieged by requests for Tammie to sing at a variety of entertainments for a range of different hostesses, from top-lofty duchesses and marchionesses to the wives of the wealthy middle-sort.

He picked and chose between them, but even so, Tammie sang for four or five evenings a week and several times a week at afternoon entertainments. She enjoyed it. Not only was she happy when singing, but Guy had to keep her well and content, which meant frequent doses of the drugs she craved, carefully measured to keep her floating but not totally detached from reality. And no sexual favors for Guy or men that Guy wanted to influence.

Matters could change, and almost certainly would. Tammie was seldom so deeply in her dream world that she forgot Guy might change his mind at any time, especially if she behaved in any way that the toffee-nosed upper classes regarded as scandalous. Little did they know how scandalous Guy was! Or perhaps they did not care. He was, after all, an earl and a man!

And an elf king. That realization was lodged in Tammie's brain, and though the rational part of her mind wanted to argue that elves were imaginary, the rest of her knew Guy behaved exactly like the faery folk of the songs and the stories—and got away with it, furthermore. Anyone else, even an earl, would have been caught and punished long since. What was that, if not faery magic?

As if to confirm her suspicions, or perhaps to mock her, the dark fire of his aura had coalesced into a crown. He was an elf king.

Her perfect behavior was rewarded early in the second week of such engagements. Guy had a request for Tammie that he really wanted to fulfill, but it was at a time when he needed to be elsewhere. The boy he had given Tammie to a couple of weeks earlier was showing signs of cold feet, and Guy planned a drunken afternoon with trimmings that would take the poor boy's freedom of choice away forever.

Tammie didn't want to know the details, but she hoped Guy failed. The boy was a naive fool, but not naturally vicious. The consequence of his preoccupation, however, was that Guy planned to send her to an afternoon concert with only her maid, two footmen, and one of Guy's muscle-men as escort.

Perhaps Jowan would be there.

"At least that Cornish fool won't be there to bother you," said Guy, seeming to read her mind. Typical faery magic, she thought. "He has somehow managed to gain entree to the Marquess of Deerhaven's crowd, and Lady Bevan has nothing to do with any of those."

Tammie spread her hand and studied the back of it. As always, she was only one step away from the dreams in which she preferred to live. She had never noticed before, but the blue veins formed letters. A "B" and an "L". Or perhaps the second letter was a "V". How interesting. Be Valiant. Is that what her hand was telling her?

She kept her eyes lowered for fear Guy would read the rebellion she planned. She had been searching the ballads for clues to an escape and had found some stories where the person stolen by the faery managed to escape, so it was possible.

She did not think she would be able to persuade Guy to sleep on her lap or come swimming with her, as the maidens in two ballads did, one killing the elf knight with the dagger he intended to use on her and the other also visiting the fate the elf knight intended on her, and drowning him. But there was still hope in the ballads, for some escaped, with help.

Not all rescues were successful, and none of the rescued were ever quite the same. Still, better to be free and damaged, or to die trying, than to remain enslaved to Guy.

Jowan would help if only she could reach him and convince him. She did not know how she would manage it, but somehow, she planned to see Jowan. Lady Bevan's would be a good opportunity if he was there. She had looked for him at every entertainment, but Guy's explanation of how he chose where to send her explained Jowan's absence.

No matter. If not this time, then another.

"Go, then," Guy said. "I will see you at dinner this evening."

Lady Bevan was one of those who thought herself too important to bother with politeness to a performer. Tammie's carriage was directed to the back door and met by a butler who echoed his mistress's superior attitude.

He led them to a little room lined with cupboards. It had three uncomfortable chairs and no other furniture. "You will stay in this room until you are called, as will these others," he instructed. "You will sing four songs while the guests are eating luncheon. When you have finished singing, you will return to this room, and your carriage will be called. You will not mingle with your betters."

"Miss Lind," Tammie said, in her most aristocratic accent.

The butler reared back in offense. "I beg your pardon?"

"Not granted," Tammie snapped back. "I find your tone offensive. If you are relaying your mistress's instructions, then I find Lady Bevan offensive. Henry, will you send for my carriage, immediately please."

Henry bowed. "Yes, Miss Lind." He turned towards the door,

but the butler moved to intercept him.

"See here," said the butler. "Lady Bevan is expecting you to entertain her guests. She has told them you are coming."

"You may inform Lady Bevan that I am an artist, and I do not sing for those who do not give my art the respect it deserves. Singing while people are eating, indeed! You might also tell her that an insult to me is an insult to the Earl of Coombe."

The butler backed away. "Wait here," he said.

"No," said Tammie, and she led the other four from the room, turning along the passage in the direction away from the door they'd entered by. The butler grabbed her arm, but Guy's brute put his massive hand over the butler's thin one and the butler fell back, wincing.

"You cannot go out there," said the butler, as Henry the footman opened the green baize door.

Tammie ignored him. Lady Bevan was in the entrance hall, directing footmen who were moving vases of flowers according to the lady's direction.

"Henry," Tammie said, "my carriage."

"Yes, Miss Lind," said Henry again, and negotiated a path across the room through the chaos of flower movers. Tammie seated herself in a comfortable chair and the rest of her minders gathered nearby.

"You!" Lady Bevan shrieked, pointing a finger at Tammie. "You cannot wait there. The butler will show you where you can wait."

Tammie smiled serenely. "No, thank you. I am comfortable here. But do not be concerned, Lady Bevan. My carriage will arrive shortly, and I shall be gone before your guests arrive."

Lady Bevan gaped at her, then, frowning, said, "Gone? But you came here to sing. I paid the Earl of Coombe." She flapped her hands as if shooing hens. "Go with my butler. He will show you where you are meant to be."

"Lady Bevan, I have performed before the crowned heads of Europe, before princes, dukes, and others who trace their blue blood back to the time of Charlemagne. Never have I been expected to prepare in a china pantry and to sing while people masticate their food. I will not remain to be so insulted."

Bewilderment and temper fought for supremacy in Lady Bevan's face and temper won. "The Earl of Coombe shall be hearing about this," she threatened.

"Yes," said Tammie, "for I shall tell him. An insult to my music is an insult to Lord Coombe." The one true thing about Guy was his love for music. In every other respect, he would do whatever advantaged him, even if that meant tramping all over his dependents and anyone else in his way.

"But… I have told my guests you will be singing," Lady Bevan complained.

That statement did not need a comment. Tammie ignored it.

"You have to sing," Lady Bevan declared.

Tammie glanced at her and went back to contemplating the footmen. That one near the door was going to drop his vase if he did not put it down soon. He was turning all sorts of interesting colors, his jaw was set, and his knuckles were white.

"Miss Lind! I am speaking to you!" Lady Bevan shrieked.

Tammie turned her attention to the lady. "Lady Bevan, I suggest you take any complaints to Lord Coombe. I will leave as soon as my carriage is ready."

The lady deflated. Tammie could almost see the bombast spurting out of her in red puffs. "What can I do to convince you to stay?" she demanded, pouting.

"All I need, my lady," Tammie replied—humbly, for she had won and did not need to crow about it—"is a parlor to wait in and a time to sing. Before or after the luncheon, whichever suits you. But not during, while your guests are busy with something else. Other than that, I need to speak with your musicians to ensure that they have the music to accompany me. That is all. If your ladyship can see your way to providing me with what I need to do justice to your good reputation and my own, then I would be happy to stay."

"Hmmph!" said Lady Bevan. She barked at the butler. "Bishop! See to it that Miss Lind has what she needs." She turned her back on Tammie just as the struggling footman gave up and the vase slipped from his grasp with a loud crash.

Bishop, the butler, looked at the chaos of the broken vase, flowers, water, and his mistress taking out her anger on the hapless footman, and crooked a finger at another footman who was not currently burdened. "See Miss Lind to the green parlor, and ask the leader of the musical quartet to visit her there."

"Bishop," Tammie said, "When you have a moment, please let Henry know to send the carriage back to the mews and to join me in the green parlor. Thank you."

She followed the footman away as Bishop began to try to restore order in the entrance hall. Poor man. He might be a pompous idiot with a stick where the sun did not shine, but he had her sympathies.

The green parlor was acceptable. Tammie asked the footman for a large jug of fruit juice or lemonade or some other cordial, and sufficient glasses for them all. Once he left on that errand, she invited her entourage to sit. "Good job with the lady, Miss Lind," said Guy's muscle.

Tammie smiled, vaguely. The muscle had a flask with her next dose of laudanum, which made it all the more important to have his approval.

The footman must have found the quartet before he fetched the lemonade, for the violinist who was their leader turned up just before Henry reappeared with a tray containing the requested jug and glasses. Nothing to eat, Tammie noted.

She discussed music with the violinist, and it was as well she did, for he was not familiar with one of the pieces she had chosen. It gave her the opportunity to ask if he knew "The Ballad of Tam Lin".

"No, Miss Lind. I haven't heard of that one."

"It is from Scotland's borderlands, I believe," she said.

"My cellist might know it," said the violinist. "Mac is from

Dumfries."

"Never mind," Tammie said. "I shall sing 'Sweet Nightingale', without accompaniment. We shall make it the last song, and you and your colleagues can take a five-minute break. I fear Lady Bevan might expect you to play straight through, otherwise."

They had settled the program just in time, for a footman came running to say that the guests had started to arrive, and Lady Bevan wanted to know why she only had a trio and not a quartet. The violinist scurried away.

After that, there was nothing to do but drink her dose of laudanum, wash it down with lemonade, and wait. Guy's muscle played cards with one of the footmen and Tammie's maid took out some sewing. Tammie sat idly watching the sunbeams that infiltrated the windows, splintered by the imperfections in the glass, and further distorted by the surfaces they struck: a mat, the legs of a table, the parquet floor.

When she was called for her performance, she drifted towards the door. Henry tugged on her arm. "Miss Lind, I shall order the carriage for forty-five minutes from now, so you do not need to wait after the performance." In an undertone, he added, "Sir Jowan Trethewey is in the audience."

That name penetrated the daze. She blinked a couple of times while she tried to remember what she wanted to say to Jowan. "The ballad." That was it. "Tell Jowan *The Ballad of Tam Lin*. Tam Lin. Remember that."

"Miss Lind?" The muscle had turned back in the doorway and was looking at her with suspicion.

"One moment," she commanded, putting on her imperious persona. "Henry, yes. Your suggestion is excellent. Henry is going to order the carriage now so it will be ready in forty-five minutes."

The muscle's face cleared. "Yes, Miss Lind," he said. "Run along, Henry. This way, Miss Lind."

There was something else. Tammie could not remember it. *Oh yes.* "Your message will be welcome, Henry," she told the footman. "Mac knows."

But for the life of her, she could not remember who Mac was. She could only hope that Jowan knew.

FOR ONCE, JOWAN and Bran had gone in different directions. They had bribed a street boy to keep up with the movements of the coach Tammie used, and the urchin had arrived with news of her arrival at the house of a Lady Bevan just as the brothers were about to join David Wakefield, whose agents had been watching the Earl of Coombe on behalf of Wakefield's other client.

Apparently, the uncles and former trustees of a viscount new to his majority were concerned about the company their nephew was keeping. Bran had gone to join Wakefield, and Jowan had searched through the invitations that had accumulated in their little sitting room since the Duchess of Winshire had noticed them to find the one that gave him entry to this, one of the most boring garden parties he had every attended.

Not that he was an aficionado of garden parties. He could count on one hand those he'd been to, and that included three in Cornwall over the past four years. Still, if he had been to two a week for four years, he could not imagine any of them would have been more stultifying.

This one had a string quartet providing background music, and a lot of people he would normally not be interested in meeting chatting loud enough to drown out the music. He didn't know anyone else at the party. The hostess introduced him to one gentleman and then abandoned him to the victim's increasingly desperate attempts to discover whether Jowan knew anyone who, as the man put it, mattered.

Once the man was satisfied that Jowan was hopelessly provincial and disastrously ill-connected, he wandered away to better company, leaving Jowan to sip at the wine he had been given, and to wander from group to group, listening in on what other people were saying.

Fashion, horses, scandal. Nothing momentous. Nothing interesting. Only overheard mentions that confirmed Miss Lind would be singing this afternoon kept Jowan from leaving.

At last, his patience was rewarded. Tamsyn appeared from the house, flanked by a couple of hulking footmen and with a maid scurrying behind. Lady Bevan stood on the platform of the little open summerhouse being used as a bandstand and tapped a teaspoon on a glass to attract attention.

"Ladies and gentlemen," she nearly shouted. "For your pleasure, I have brought the Devon Songbird to sing for you."

Tamsyn stepped up into the bandstand, curtseyed to Lady Bevan, and curtseyed again to the guests. A man standing near Jowan commented, "She can pleasure me, anytime." Which brought a chuckle to those with him and had Jowan forming fists of his hands and picturing the blood spurting from the idiot's nose all over the snowy lace of his cravat.

If you make a scene, you will be ejected, he reminded himself urgently, but nonetheless, he was breathing heavily when someone tapped on his shoulder, and he whirled ready to defend himself. It was the footman from Coombe's house, the one who had given Jowan Tamsyn's note. He gestured with his eyes and headed to the shelter of a nearby shrub.

Jowan followed him, realizing that the shrub masked him from the view of the singer and from those nearest to her, including her maid and her minders.

"Sir Jowan, isn't it sir?" checked the footman.

"I am," he agreed. "And you are Coombe's footman." He couldn't keep his disdain for the man from his voice.

The young man blushed. "Miss Lind's footman, sir. I have a message for you, from Miss Lind, sir."

"I hope to speak to her myself," Jowan told him.

The footman shook his head. "We have been instructed to keep Miss Lind from meeting with you, sir. I am sorry. It is as much as my job is worth not to obey. The other men will obey Coombe, anyway. And Miss Lind will suffer if she manages to speak with you. Please don't get her into trouble, sir."

"Is that your message?" Jowan asked, his anger at the thought of Coombe hurting Tamsyn making it hard for him to keep his voice to a low mutter.

"No, sir. The message is..." the footman frowned as if bewildered, "the ballad of Tam Lin."

Now Jowan shared the sensation. "The ballad of Tam Lin? What the hell does that mean?"

"I don't know, sir. I hoped you would. 'Tell Jowan the ballad of Tam Lin.' Oh, she also said, 'Mac knows,' sir." He shook his head as if that might dislodge some more information.

"I must fetch the carriage, sir. That is the whole message."

"Thank you," Jowan said, accepting that the young man knew nothing more. "Please let Miss Lind know I stand as her friend."

"I will, sir."

The footman faded into the crowd and Jowan moved far enough out from the shrub to be able to see Tamsyn. The ballad of Tam Lin? What on earth could that mean?

Tamsyn held the audience in the palm of her hand. Even the men in Coombe livery could not take their eyes off her as her rich voice soared over the garden. Jowan, too, truth be told, but he retained enough sense to keep close enough to cover that he could step sideways to be out of sight of Coombe's servants.

Quite apart from her magical voice, her appearance captured the crowd, and the way her eyes passed over them, pausing on face after face, then moving on. Jowan waited for her to see him, and at last, halfway through her second piece, her eyes met his, widened, and moved on.

Had she recognized him or not? Yes, she had, for a moment later, when the operatic aria she was singing called for a smile, she focused on his face for the full stanza. So much so, that one of the men in Coombe livery, a great brute of a fellow, turned to see what she was looking at. But not before Jowan ducked his head so all the man would be able to see over the crowd was Jowan's hair.

She didn't let her eyes pause through the next piece. It was a rollicking popular song, "The Barmaid's Catechism", where a cheeky barmaid sings about getting orders mixed up or serving meat that was questionable. Tamsyn managed to persuade even this jaded fashionable crowd to join in with the chorus, where the barmaid explains how she dashes away at the first sign of a complaint:

"And, if told of the error, though ever so small,

Break off with—Dear me, did not somebody call?

Lord bless me, where are all my people humdrumming?

I must e'en go myself—coming, sir, coming!"

Jowan compared this polished performance to the Tamsyn he knew, the shy musician who could only perform if she pretended she was alone. What else had changed?

"One more time, and louder!" she called out as they sang the last chorus, and the musicians obediently played the tune again. The crowd bellowed the words this time and were laughing along with Tamsyn as they roared out the final line.

"I must e'en go myself—coming, sir, coming!"

By the time the applause for that song had died down, the musicians had crept away, and Tamsyn was alone. With no accompaniment, she sang an old traditional Cornish song, one Jowan knew well. It was another courting song, "Sweet Nightin-gale", where the maiden feared to go home through the shadows but was reluctant to accept the boyo's escort. As the couple marry, Tamsyn met his gaze again, singing, "She was no more afraid, to go in the shade," before letting her eyes drift away.

Another message? He had no idea. He joined the applause and made no attempt to get closer to her as she thanked Lady Bevan for her hospitality, curtseyed to the crowd, and was escorted away by Coombe's servants.

After that, he saw no point in staying. He headed back to the hotel to wait for Bran, but it was still early, and he had another thought. Perhaps a bookshop might have the words of the ballad to which Tamsyn directed him. A friendly passerby sent him to Finsbury Square, where he discovered the biggest book shop he had ever seen.

The Temple of All the Muses said the sign above the door to an enormous foyer. Jowan asked at the counter for the ballad and was directed to the music section, up several flights of stairs.

A sales assistant then took over the search, finding the shelves that held traditional ballads, and soon unearthed a copy of *Scots Musical Museum*, which held a poem by Robert Burns actually called "Tam Lin", and the second volume of *Minstrelrey of the Southern Border*, by Sir Walter Scott, which had the words of a song called "Young Tamlane".

The assistant showed him to a table and chair and left him to read. The songs were related—the same story told with a few unimportant changes. A girl had an encounter with either an elf knight or her childhood sweetheart who had been stolen by the queen of the fairies. When the girl found she was with child, she was determined to rescue and wed the child's father.

She discovered she could break the spell holding her swain on one night of the year, and that by pulling him from his horse and holding him as the queen turned him into one monster after another. At last, the queen had to give up, and the couple had their happy ending.

Scott, in his introduction to the tale, explained there were a number of versions, but with the same basic tale. Was Tamsyn seeing herself as the elf knight, the stolen sweetheart? If so, Jowan was Janet, the girl who outwitted and outlasted the fairy queen. He would, as Burns put it, hold her fast. At least, he would if he could once get his hands on her.

Jowan went looking for the assistant and asked for a pen, ink, and paper. He had to pay for them, but it was, after all, a shop. He settled back at the table with the books and wrote out the words of each song.

Was he fooling himself? He'd show the lyrics to Bran and see if his brother came to the same conclusion about Tamsyn's purpose in sending him to find the songs. The question remained, how could he get at Tamsyn when Coombe kept her so close? Also, who was Mac? And what did he know?

Chapter Nine

JOWAN'S DETOUR AND the time he'd spent copying out the verses had taken longer than he'd expected. Bran was already at the hotel and waiting eagerly to tell him about their disappointment.

They had, as planned, hidden themselves to watch Coombe take his young victim into a brothel that catered to those attracted to young boys. After that, nothing went to plan.

It transpired that the youthful peer was not nearly as drunk or drugged as Coombe believed. He very quickly realized the main business of the house and lost his temper. The Wakefield agent who was inside the house said the more Coombe tried to charm his mark into a better mood, the louder the man became.

Hearing the shouting, the viscount's uncle, who had insisted on coming along but had promised not to interfere, forgot his promises and raced into the building to rescue his nephew. That led to more shouting, as the uncle explained his presence by telling the young man, at full volume, everything Wakefield had found out about Coombe's habit of inveigling young men into his orbit and then keeping them there with drugs, alcohol, sex, and blackmail.

Wakefield sent in the constables he'd alerted to the practices happening in the house, but the proprietor and her stock had taken alarm at the noise and left by a secret exit in the cellar. With nothing to show what happened in the building, the constables could do nothing. Coombe declared that he and his friend had accidentally arrived at the wrong house, and no one could prove otherwise.

"Wakefield says they have nothing that will stand up in court," Bran explained. "On the good side, the viscount didn't believe Coombe any more than we did. He went home with his uncle."

He took a sip of the brandy Jowan had poured for him. "I hope you did better."

"I don't know," Jowan said. "I saw Tamsyn but didn't speak to her. On the other hand, she sent me a message. *The Ballad of Tam Lin.*"

"*The Ballad of Tam Lin?*" Bran frowned. "That's it? That's the message?"

"Not the whole of it. Apparently, Mac knows."

Bran's frown deepened. "Who is Mac? And what does he know?"

Jowan sighed. "I have no idea. But I did find the lyrics of the ballad. Two ballads, actually. The biggest bookshop I've ever seen had books with them inside, and they sold me writing materials to make copies." He picked up the sheets and passed them to Bran.

"She wants to be rescued," Bran commented. "It's the same story, only with Coombe as the elf king and her as his prisoner."

"And me as the fair Janet," Jowan agreed, with a grimace. He didn't much like the casting. "That's what I figured, but I wondered if I was reading my own desires into it."

"I don't think so." Bran grimaced. "Jowan, Wakefield says that Coombe is known to use drugs to keep his victims compliant. Opium, ether, alcohol, magic mushroom. Other stuff, too, that he brought back with him from his travels. Hashish and more. Once people are slaves to the drugs, they will do anything, he says, for a dose. Your Tamsyn might be past saving."

"I can't accept that," Jowan said. "I have to try. The question is how to get close enough. She is always guarded."

"I can think of a few more questions. How will you take her, yes. Also, where will you take her? Coombe will claim she is under contract, or she is his ward, or some other relationship exists that means you are breaking the law."

Jowan nodded. "You make good points."

"I have more. What will you do once you have her? If she needs the drugs to survive, will you provide them? And where will you get them?"

"I need more information," Jowan decided.

"We can take Drew into our confidence," Bran suggested. "Possibly Wakefield, too. Probably Wakefield. He really, *really* does not like Coombe."

"You will help me, then?" Jowan asked. Bran hadn't sounded at all enthusiastic.

"Of course," Bran told him. "You need to do this. At the moment, you are stuck. If it turns out to be a disaster, at least, you will know."

→≫≪←

GUY RETURNED FROM his afternoon excursion in an evil temper. By the time he sent for Tammie, the whole house knew he had been crossed in some way, and would be dangerously unpredictable until he had calmed down.

"Sing for me," he demanded when she entered the room; it stank of brandy. A quick scan showed a decanter that had been hurled into the—fortunately empty—fireplace with sufficient force to shatter it. The broken remnants of a vase showed it must also have offended Guy in some way.

He had a footman on his knees, the man's arm twisted up behind his back. Who knew what the poor man's sin was? Guy always required perfection and was impossibly particular when angry.

"Sing!" Guy bellowed, making Tammie jump.

She opened her mouth and began belting out the first song she thought of—the silly ditty about the barmaid she'd amused an audience with earlier this afternoon, but she knew before she got to the chorus that it was the wrong choice. Guy didn't want to hear about excuses for poor service.

The music at the front of her mind was the ballad with her hope of escape, and that would never do. She had to think fast, and the laudanum she'd taken when she arrived home was casting a fog over her mind. Fortunately, one occurred to her before Guy could take out his impatience on her.

Ah! That would do. A remarkably filthy song about a sailor Guy had enjoyed teaching her when she was still a shy virgin. When she was still Tamsyn, who hadn't understood most of the references or a lot of the words.

She began to belt it out, surprising Guy into a smirk when he realized what she was singing. The tension went out of him as she sang verse after verse, interspersed with the highly suggestive chorus. The risk was that she'd arouse him, but he had a new pet, a little violinist he was personally coaching, so he'd probably call for her, and sure enough, after ten or more verses, he was fondling his crotch and calling for a footman to fetch Miss Tempest.

Hadn't he been more charming and less offensive when Tamsyn first met him? Or had the naive girl just been too stupid to see what he was like? Perhaps he no longer made an effort when Tammie was his main audience.

Certainly, he stopped rubbing himself as Miss Tempest hurried into the room, her face eager. "Guy? You sent for me?"

"Deidre, darling," he cooed. "I am upset. Won't you play for me? That's enough, Miss Lind. Miss Tempest will soothe me now. Everyone else, get out."

Tamsyn was only too glad to obey.

The following day, Guy had talked himself—or more probably screwed himself—into a more cheerful mood. He decreed his entourage would once again make a display at Hyde Park during the fashionable hour. Miss Tempest would ride alongside him, while Miss Lind rode near the back.

Miss Tempest, foolish girl, stuck her tongue out at Tammie when Guy turned his back. Tammie swept her a full-court curtsey in response, which had Miss Tempest furrowing her brow as she tried to work out whether or not she had been insulted.

Was it worth trying to talk to the girl, to tell her what Guy was truly like? Tammie felt that she ought to, even if she was punished for it. On the other hand, Miss Tempest was unlikely to listen any more than Tamsyn would have in the beginning, when Guy was exerting his full charm to ensorcel her.

The two cases were different. Tamsyn had taken two years to allow Guy to bed her, whereas Miss Tempest had been in Guy's bed from the day he'd brought her home. That, though, made it more likely the girl would not hear anything against him.

But, from what Tammie had heard, Deidre Tempest was a much tougher female than Tamsyn had been. The shy country girl sent away against her wishes had few defenses against Guy's persuasion and manipulations.

Only her love for Jowan had kept her from submitting to Guy for the two years it took to accept that Jowan was not going to even reply to her letters, let alone come looking for her. Later, of course, she realized Guy had kept their correspondence from reaching one another.

La Tempest was a city child, born to a stage dancer, raised in London theaters, and orphaned since she was thirteen. She'd made her way doing odd jobs until she'd gained enough skill with the violin to join the theatre's orchestra.

Unlike Tamsyn, who had been sold by her mother, Deidre had sold herself, placing herself in front of Guy, demanding an audition, and impressing Guy enough that he had signed a contract with her then and there, and brought her home. Who seduced whom was an open question.

Did Deidre mean to take Tammie's place as Guy's princess?

She was welcome to it, but Tammie still felt she should warn the girl about the likely costs.

The company was turning in through the gates to Hyde Park, riding four abreast. They split into two columns to pass an open carriage, and Tammie nodded and smiled at the ladies and the gentleman in the carriage. One of the ladies waved, but the others looked as if they had swallowed something sour.

The procession was having the intended effect. People looked, even if they refused to acknowledge the riders. Gentlemen on their own hailed Guy and well-born members of his entourage, as did some ladies. A few gentlemen even waved at some of Guy's musicians and singers.

But even those who pretended Guy and his people did not exist altered their course around the group of riders. And those of the lower sort had no hesitation in enjoying the display, waving and calling out. Several boys ran along beside the horses.

Tammie imagined Guy's pleasure at the response, though he was too far ahead for her to see his face. Nonetheless, she felt her tension ease. Nobody in his household or his wider orbit could relax when Guy was out of sorts.

They did a complete circuit around the park's main ride. Tammie wished they would hurry. The craving had started, reminding her it was time for another dose of laudanum—Guy continued to allow her enough to prevent the worst of the suffering of going without, and not enough to fully immerse herself in the dreams.

She shifted uncomfortably, glad they were once again approaching the gate on the way home. The craving had, as always, started as an itch at the back of her mind, but was now beginning to crawl over her body.

She looked around again, hoping for a distraction. A man stepped out from the shelter of several trees and removed his hat. Jowan! He was looking directly at Tammie, and she could not prevent her smile. A quick look around suggested that no one had noticed.

She turned her eyes back to Jowan. He was still watching. He nodded, his face still and his gaze intent. Had he received her message? Did he know she was a prisoner of the elf king? She returned the nod, then tore her attention away before someone in the company remarked on her interest.

She tried to tell herself that Jowan would rescue her, but hope was too precious, too pure for the likes of her. He had only to ask in theatrical circles and he would soon know that Tamsyn was lost beyond redemption, and Tammie was too corrupted, too broken to save.

Chapter Ten

W AKEFIELD HAD A report for them the next morning on the missing solicitor. "The short version is that he died four years ago. His files were boxed up and sent to his only surviving cousin, a widow who lives in Devon, in Plymouth. It isn't necessarily bad news. If you can find the paperwork that links your father to the investments he made on your father's behalf, you will be able to claim the proceeds."

He handed over the name and last known address of the widow.

He also had news about Thatcher, the man who had fled a couple of weeks ago before he could be apprehended. He had not outpaced his crimes, however. He had been arrested in Oxford after another cheated client recognized him. Since Jowan and Bran had left statements with the magistrate here in London, they would not be needed for any court case, and they'd found their own investors to put the new mine project back on track.

"So, we've succeeded in two of the tasks for which we came to London," Jowan mused. "And I have a plan for the last."

"You've been able to speak with Miss Lind?" Wakefield asked.

"Not precisely," Jowan admitted. "She sent me a message."

Wakefield shifted, a rare sign of unease in a man who was usually highly controlled. "I have not yet finished writing up my report on Miss Lind, or Miss Roskilly, as she was when you knew her. The information is... disturbing. She may well hope for rescue from Coombe—she has made previous attempts to escape. However, it is unlikely she will want to return to Cornwall. She certainly is not the girl you remember."

Jowan fought down the urge to loudly refute Wakefield's point. The man spoke the truth as he saw it, even if the medicine he administered was bitter. "Once she is out of Coombe's hands, we can ask her what she wants."

"She may not know, or she may change her mind," Wakefield warned. "She is an opium user, Sir Jowan. Other things, too. Ether. Alcohol. An eastern drug called hashish. If you know anything about opium eaters, you will know it is a disease with them. It seizes the mind, until, deprived of the drug, the eater will do anything at all for a dose, whether it is immoral or not, illegal, dangerous, or improper. I have heard of rare cases where long-term users break free of the yearning for the drug, but through a long hard path that few can follow."

Jowan swallowed. "She was my father's responsibility," he replied. "He brought Coombe to St Tetha and brokered what I can only call a sale between Coombe and Mrs. Roskilly. I owe Miss Lind a rescue, Wakefield, and whatever help she needs to regain her health, if she chooses to take that path."

If she chose to leave Jowan again, then so be it. What he had just said to Wakefield was the truth, and his own hopes and dreams were none of Wakefield's business nor any of Tamsyn's responsibility.

"You have a plan, you say?" asked Wakefield.

"The beginnings of one," Jowan admitted. "I think our best chance to take her is when Coombe and his acolytes and pet musicians ride in Hyde Park, which they do at least once every week. Miss Lind rides near the rear of the procession, and Coombe near the front. I propose to swoop in on a fast horse, scoop Miss Lind up, and ride away."

He'd only thought as far as the escape. "We will have some

kind of a shell game, swapping to another horse, or having several similar horses with riders and pillion passengers, but the real horse will be led out of sight once Miss Lind is in an anonymous carriage. After that—obviously, I will need a place to take her and a plan to prevent Coombe from finding her."

Wakefield nodded. "That could work. And Miss Lind is in favor?"

"Miss Lind suggested it," Jowan insisted, and then honesty forced him to admit, "sort of."

That needed explaining, and Wakefield was highly skeptical. "You are proposing to turn Miss Lind's life upside down based on your interpretation of a ballad," he said. "A ballad about fairies."

"She went to the trouble of sending Jowan the message," Bran pointed out. "Jowan's interpretation makes sense. And we cannot ask her, for Coombe has put guards on her to prevent Jowan from speaking to her."

"In fact, he is keeping her from all of her admirers," Wakefield disclosed. "She is escorted to her performances, kept apart in a guarded room, escorted to the stage, and then taken home immediately after she sings her last song. However, I might have a way." He walked to the door of his study and said a few words to someone in the hall, then resumed his chair.

"I have sent for my wife. If I can be certain that Miss Lind wants this abduction, then I have some ideas about how we might help. You might also ask your friend Lord Andrew Winderfield to help you source the horses. His family has the connections."

A tap on the door was followed by the entry of a pretty woman, neatly dressed as befitted the wife of a successful businessman. The three gentlemen rose, and Wakefield presented Jowan and Bran to Mrs. Wakefield.

Once she was seated, he explained Miss Lind's guards, Jowan's plan, and Wakefield's reservations.

"You are thinking of a maid, David," Mrs. Wakefield said. "It would be best if it was at a home where we have friends. Can you discover Miss Lind's program of engagements?"

"I have a footman who keeps me informed," Jowan said. He listed the commitments for the next three days.

"Lady Hamner," Mrs. Wakefield decided. "She is a family connection. That gives us two days to prepare. I will send her a note and ask for a few minutes to explain what we need."

Bran had an objection. "Miss Lind travels with her own maid."

That was true. If Mrs. Wakefield planned to use the private moments between a lady and her maid, the other maid would be a hindrance.

"So, we need to manufacture an errand for the maid. I shall think of something, Sir Jowan. Leave it to me. David, I take it you want at least an initial indication of whether Miss Lind objects to going back to Cornwall since that would certainly put a spoke in any attempt by Coombe to retrieve her."

Jowan brightened, but Wakefield grimaced. "It might not serve. Coombe's family seat is in Devon. East Devon, but ask, by all means. Meanwhile, Sir Jowan, Mr. Hughes, read the reports. I will send you the one on Miss Lind by tomorrow morning."

"And we shall speak with Drew," Bran said.

ANOTHER EVENING, ANOTHER concert. They merged into one another, distinguished only by the color of the parlor Tammie was given for her dressing room, and the quality of the supper supplied to her, and sometimes to her minders.

Tonight had another feature—the accident on the way in, when a clumsy maid spilled a huge vat of punch all over poor Daisy. Full of apologies, the housekeeper sent Daisy off with three maids to have a bath and change.

Tammie assured the housekeeper that she could manage without her maid, but the housekeeper insisted, so here Tammie was, waiting for the substitute maid to bring her something to drink.

At least, if the household truly was sorry about the accident, Tammie and her entourage might receive decent refreshments.

A tap on the door proved to be the substitute maid and a footman, both with trays. And yes, the supper looked sumptuous. The maid's tray held a teapot, a cup, a glass, and a plate of mixed savories and sweet tarts and cakes. The footman carried two jugs, three glasses, and plates piled high with more savories and cake.

"Ale and cider," he said, cheerfully, as he put the tray on a table on the other side of the room, near Tammie's minders. "Let Prue know if you need anything else." He nodded to the maid and left.

The maid had put her tray on a side table next to Tammie. "Will you have your tea now, Miss Lind?" she asked in a low voice, "or would you prefer lemonade first?"

"Tea, please," Tammie told her. "Prue, is it?"

Prue nodded and bent to the teapot. "Milk, Miss? Or cream?" she asked, as her eyes slid towards Tammie's minders, who were fully focused on their tray. Without changing her tone or volume, she added, "Sir Jowan plans to abduct you when you are riding in the park with Lord Coombe and his entourage. Do you take sugar, Miss Lind?"

Tammie blinked as she attempted to keep her expression from changing. If this was a hallucination, it was the strangest she had ever had. "Did you just say…?"

"That Sir Jowan plans to abduct you? Yes. He has asked his friends for help. They wish to check that you are willing."

That was surprisingly logical for a hallucination. "Willing and eager," Tammie assured the maid.

The maid was adding cream and sugar to the tea. Tammie realized she had pointed to them without thinking about it. "May I make you up a plate, Miss?" asked the maid. "He will take you somewhere safe. London? Or Cornwall? Or somewhere else?"

Does he not want me in Cornwall? "I long for Cornwall," Tammie insisted. The maid's hands moved swiftly to put a selection of edibles on a pretty china plate with the same pattern as the cup and saucer.

Tammie took a sip of the tea as the maid said, "I shall pass those messages on, Miss Lind."

At that moment, Guy's muscle called out, "What are you about, Prue or whatever your name is? No gossiping with Miss Lind. She is preparing to sing."

"Is there anything else I can help you with, Miss Lind?" Prue said, ignoring the man as if he had said nothing.

"Thank you, no. I shall sip my tea and rest. Perhaps, if Daisy is not back in time to do my hair, I might need you. Tell Jowan's friends that I am anxious to escape, and I want to go home to Cornwall."

"I shall, Miss Lind."

The maid moved to a chair a few yards away and the muscle relaxed. But when the footmen started to play cards, Tammie beckoned the maid. "Put up the dressing screen and begin on my hair, please, Prue."

The muscle looked up and then returned to watching the card game. As soon as Prue was near enough, she told Tammie, "Wear a cape that is easily given to a decoy."

Tammie had something she needed to say, too. "Tell Jowan not to listen to me. When I beg for the drugs, he must not listen. He must refuse."

The door opened, and in came Daisy. Prue had time to say, "I will tell him," and then Daisy sent her away and took over. Tammie let her grumble about the accident and praise the treatment she received afterward. "I would have been back earlier, Miss, but her ladyship herself came to tell me how sorry she was, and she kept me talking. I hope you didn't mind, Miss. It was so nice of her, and I did not wish to offend."

This had been a very efficient operation, Tammie realized. She wondered if Guy knew that Jowan had such useful and clever friends. *Well.* He wouldn't learn it from her.

✦

Chapter Eleven

"I F THIS FAILS, we will try something else," Bran said, as they waited on a ride that Coombe and his entourage would pass as they returned through the park to the gate nearest to Coombe's townhouse.

Bran was trying to soothe Jowan's anxiety, but it wasn't working. Jowan had several other plans, or at least the first inklings. Abducting Tamsyn from a public place with her consent was the only one that didn't cross the line from probably legal to definitely criminal.

Kidnapping her from Coombe's carriage was arguably highway robbery. Taking her from a concert or other engagement would mean fighting those Coombe had assigned to keep her caged. Perhaps Coombe himself, and Jowan's heart leapt at the possibility.

But they would risk injury, arrest for assault, and worse, failure.

There was always an invasion of Coombe's house. Jowan had even thought of a way to make that somewhat legal. If someone provided the appropriate magistrate with enough evidence of crimes to justify a warrant to search and seize, they could get in and bring Tamsyn out with them.

But that would mean waiting until they had collected definitive evidence, for raiding the house of an earl was not undertaken lightly.

He had better make a success of this abduction in the park. And he would. He and his accomplices had spent hours thinking of everything that could possibly go wrong and deciding on countermeasures.

"They're coming back, guv!" said the boy who was a few paces ahead, keeping an eye out for Coombe and the riders.

It was time, then. Jowan mounted his horse. "Wish me luck, Bran."

"Always," Bran replied from the back of his own steed, extending his hand. Jowan shook it and then Bran rode off, away from the main ride.

After a nod for the boy on lookout, Jowan nudged his horse into a swift walk. So far, so good. Coombe kept coming. Jowan tucked in his chin so that the hat would shade his face. The conspirators had calculated that Coombe would not give Jowan a second look, given he was on a branch ride and not likely, at his current pace, to reach the main ride before all of Coombe's retinue had passed.

Good. Coombe was beyond the intersection of the two rides. Jowan gave the horse the signal for a trot, then a canter. *One... Two... Three...* By the time he counted to fifteen (and he was counting quickly), he was pulling the horse up alongside Tamsyn's, clasping her around the waist, and lifting her to sit on his pommel. The clever lady had already kicked her feet free of her stirrups, and so the transfer took a count of two, but that was enough time for one of Coombe's men to react, forcing his horse forward to block Jowan's escape.

The horse Drew had provided for the rescue shouldered the other horse out of the way and bounded away, reaching a gallop within a second. Ten strides and they were through the gate. They slowed and turned left, continuing to reduce speed. Drew had assured Jowan that the horse would be able to stop within ten yards of the gate, and so two of Jowan's accomplices waited at that point.

The horse was still moving, if slowly, when Jowan let Tamsyn down into Drew's arms. By the time he had dismounted himself, Tamsyn had abandoned her riding cape to Prue Wakefield and was donning the hat Prue gave her—a stylish flat hat that tied on with a scarf and hid part of Tamsyn's face.

Jowan tossed Tamsyn up into the saddle of one of the two horses a boy was holding, then the lad mounted the other. Meanwhile, Prue had put on Tamsyn's cape. Drew tossed her up on the horse Jowan had abandoned and mounted behind her.

"Thank you both," Jowan called to them, and they rode off along Park Lane. Jowan led Tamsyn in the opposite direction. They had organized several more decoys. Drew would fire off one of them as soon as he reached the corner of Cullross and Park. Drew's horse would go one way along Park, and the near-identical horse that was standing at wait would go the other.

They'd repeat the ploy at three more corners, until sixteen bay geldings spread out across London, all around sixteen hands high and all bearing a rider in a black coat and top hat, with a passenger sitting on the front of his saddle. All those decoys had to do was stay out of reach of Coombe and his men, but even if they were caught, they all had good reason to be out on the roads on such a day.

Meanwhile, Jowan must trust them to know their work, for his part of the plan was to turn off into a street away from the shell game of the multiplying horses, where a hackney waited that would take them west to Bran and the traveling carriage.

"We will go to Ealing tonight," he told the woman in his arms. He didn't want to celebrate yet, but he couldn't stop the feeling of joy that spread through him. Tamsyn! His Tamsyn. She was in his arms, and he was holding her close, just as he'd dreamed about for so long. "It's about an hour away, so we will not need to change the horses."

"They are lovely horses," Tamsyn said, her voice distant as if she was thinking of something else.

"We will send these beauties home to their owner," he told her. "We turn here, and there, up ahead, is our transport for the next step. It's not the final step, though. The hack will take us to the last vehicle of the day."

Tamsyn giggled. "It is like the children's game. Stop the music, and if there is not a horse to plop down on, you lose."

She willingly allowed him to help her down from her horse and see her into the hack.

So far, so good.

⇒⇒⇒⇐⇐⇐

BY THE TIME they left London, Tammie's mind was clear enough to be certain that this was reality and not another dream. She was impressed. The rescue had come off without a hitch. A friend of Jowan's called Drew had supplied the horses—no fewer than eighteen had been needed in total—another friend the hackney coach, and a third the travel carriage they would use to go to Cornwall.

But not immediately. Jowan said they would spend a few days in Ealing at a house belonging to one of Drew's friends. Just an hour from London, it was apparently used largely as a rural retreat.

"Drew tells me the house has a caretaker in the village," Jowan explained, "but no permanent staff, since the owners usually bring their personal servants and a cook, and otherwise prefer to hire casual help from the village, as needed. Mrs. Wakefield—she played the maid who talked to you—has chosen servants who can be depended on to keep our secrets, and they will be waiting for us."

"How long will we stay there?" Tammie asked. "Can we go straight to Cornwall? Or do you have business keeping you near London?"

"You are our business," grumbled Bran. "By the way, who is

Mac?"

She shook her head. She didn't know anyone called Mac.

"Your footman told me that Mac knows," Jowan said. *"The Ballad of Tam Lin. Mac knows.* That was the message."

No matter how she wracked her brain, Tammie couldn't figure out who Mac was or what he might know. "But you worked out the important part," she pointed out to Jowan.

Bran groaned. "Jowan and I will spend our lives wondering who Mac is," he complained.

Tammie didn't know what to make of Bran. She had seen him with Jowan several times—in Hyde Park and when she was singing for ladies of the ton. It was a surprise to discover he was Jowan's brother. There was a story there, and Tammie meant to find out what it was.

Bran was polite, but it was clear to Tammie that he was no happier about being part of a threesome than Tammie was. It was illogical of her to be upset. Of course, she hadn't expected that she and Jowan would fall back into the same close friendship they had enjoyed before she was sent away. Nor had she expected them to be alone. She'd had a vague idea that he would provide a maid for propriety.

"We will go on to Cornwall once you are well again," Jowan explained. "You told Mrs. Wakefield that you wanted to stop taking opium and the other substances?"

"I do," Tammie declared, all the more strongly because she was not convinced she would succeed.

Jowan's pleased nod made her even more determined to try. "You will be sick, they tell me, though they cannot be sure how sick. We will stay at Sunnynook—that is the house we are borrowing—until you feel ready to travel again."

Tammie had to accept that. She had tried to stop before and had given up when the pain and the yearnings became too much for her. "Don't let me have anything, Jowan. You must promise. Do not give me opium or alcohol or anything else. Promise me."

Jowan searched her eyes. "I promise," he replied solemnly.

Tammie was not satisfied. "No matter what I say, no matter how much I beg, hold fast," she insisted, and Jowan nodded.

"You, too, Mr. Hughes," Tammie said, fixing Bran with her best stare. "Promise you won't let me have any drugs. I know it is going to hurt. I know I will feel as if I am dying, and Jowan will probably think the same. It is worth it. People hardly ever do die, or so I have been told. But if I do, at least I will have chosen. At least I will no longer be a slave to my own cravings."

Some warmth came into Bran's eyes for the first time. "I promise," he said.

"You will have a nurse," Jowan told her. "Someone who has been through this with other people. I don't know how many or whom—Mrs. Wakefield mentioned men who had been put on laudanum after suffering injuries during the war and women who had taken laudanum for their nerves and then taken more and more. She knows what she is doing, Mrs. Wakefield says."

"We'll also have a cook and a general-purpose maid," added Bran. "Just as well, for I don't think you would want to eat my cooking."

Tammie appreciated the man's effort to lighten the moment but she had another concern. "Isn't it dangerous to stay so close to London? What if Guy finds us? The Earl of Coombe, I mean."

Jowan shook his head. "The only people in London who know where we are going are the Wakefields and Drew, and no one in Ealing will know who we are or why we are there. That's why we are hiring our own servants."

"We will be using false names," Bran added. He pointed to his brother. "John Riddick." An inclination of the head to Tammie. "Thomasina Riddick, his wife." He put his hand on his own chest. "Barney Riddick, brother to John."

"Clever," Tammie acknowledged. "Enough like our own names that we are unlikely to be caught out."

Conversation lapsed after that, and Tammie allowed the movement of the carriage to rock her into an uneasy sleep.

They arrived just at dusk. Tammie woke as they were pulling

up to the house—little more than a large cottage set in an acre of gardens. The travelers stepped out of the carriage to be welcomed by candlelight in the windows and the smell of newly baked bread.

The driver helped Bran carry their bags while Jowan escorted Tammie inside. The driver, carriage, and horses would stay at an inn in Ealing until they were sent for. If anyone asked, the driver would say his master was visiting someone in the neighborhood.

It suddenly occurred to Tammie that she had no baggage, but Bran gave one of the bags he was carrying to the maid who opened the door to their knock. Perhaps the ineffable Mrs. Wakefield had packed for Tammie as well!

"If you come this way, Miss, I shall show you up to your room," said the maid.

"The house looks immaculate," Tammie commented.

"The owners always have it cleaned top to bottom when they wish to use it, Miss. Or so I was told. I'm glad, for it will be much less trouble to keep it that way than to clean it all from the beginning. This is your room, Miss."

She opened the third door on the right from the top of the stairs and stepped back for Tammie to enter.

It was a pleasant room. Not nearly as sumptuous as some of those Tammie had slept in while on tour—Coombe tended to stay in palaces, mansions, and castles with the blue-blooded and the rich. Much more comfortable than most of them, though.

The paneling was painted a peaceful shade of mint green, and the same color dominated the wallpaper—a print with leaves and here and there a little bird. A woman waited for her there.

The maid undertook the introductions. "Miss Riddick, this is Mrs. Evangeline Parkerdale, who will look after you while you are here."

"Mrs. Parkerdale," Tammie said. "I am pleased to make your acquaintance." The maid-nurse was younger than Tammie expected—a tall, sturdy woman of around Tammie's age with a pleasant if somewhat nondescript face and a brisk, competent manner.

The woman curtseyed. "Miss Riddick. Call me Evangeline, please. Richards, could you fetch hot water for Miss Riddick's wash?" Richards bobbed a curtsey and left. "Miss Riddick, may I help you to change? Or do you wish to lie down for a while? Traveling can be tiring."

An hour's carriage ride? Tammie had traveled all over Europe and the Middle East and was not at all bothered by an hour's drive on good roads. "A change would be good," she said. "Let us take a look at this bag and see what might be suitable."

"There is more, Miss," said the woman. "Mrs. Wakefield sent a trunk with me. If you will step behind the dressing screen?"

Sure enough, once the bag was also unpacked, Tammie owned four night rails, six chemises and six pairs of daytime stockings, with garters to hold them up, two sets of stays, four day dresses, two evening gowns, a redingote, a soft warm shawl, and two pair of slippers. She also had handkerchiefs, a pocket, a hairbrush and pins, tooth powder, and a toothbrush.

By the time she had ascertained the state of her wardrobe, the maid Richards had returned with a bucket of hot water. "Dinner shall be in thirty minutes, Miss, if it please you," she said.

Tammie removed her clothing behind the dressing screen so that she could retrieve Jowan's ring from her hidden pocket. For the first time in half a decade, she put it on her finger, though she had lost so much weight that it had to go on the middle finger of her right hand, not on the ring finger.

Once she had washed, she allowed Evangeline to help her into one of the evening gowns. "The slippers are a good fit," she commented after she'd put them on her feet.

"Mrs. Wakefield hoped they would be suitable," Evangeline replied. "She thought you were perhaps a fraction larger than she, so she purchased slippers that she found loose."

"She did very well," Tammie acknowledged.

Evangeline also did a good job of putting up Tammie's hair. "You are good at that," Tammie commented. "I understand that your primary task will be to nurse me when I am suffering from the illness that comes on those who give up opium. I did not expect you to also make an excellent maid."

"It is how I started," the woman explained. "I was maid to a lady who took laudanum and looked after her when her son emptied all the bottles and refused to allow more in the house. After the first time, she went back to the laudanum as soon as he thought she was safe to leave to herself, so I nursed her through the relinquishing pains twice."

"The poor lady. Did she manage to stay away from the horrid drug the second time?" Tammie was already desperate for her dream world. Was it really possible to get past the desperate yearning?

"Yes, Miss. She did. And she became anxious about one of her friends who used laudanum, so she loaned me to the friend, who had a friend with a son… Suffice it to say you are my eleventh patient, Miss Riddick, and I am determined to help you all I can."

Tammie took both of Evangeline's hands in her own. "I am grateful. I have asked the two Mr. Riddicks for a promise, and I would have the same promise from you, Evangeline. Do not give in to me. I would rather die than go back to taking the drug, but when the pain and the craving are bad, I fear I will beg for it. Do not give it to me. Keep me from it. Will you promise?"

"I will, Miss. I can tell you this if it helps, none of my patients have died. We will fight this together, Miss."

"Excellent. Thank you."

With those reassurances, Tammie went down to dinner.

Chapter Twelve

I N THE MIDDLE of the night, Tammie's own restlessness woke her. She could not get comfortable. Her legs first and soon her arms had to keep shifting, trying to find a more comfortable position only to discover after a moment or two that the new position was as impossible as the one before.

Tammie recognized the beginnings of what would soon be hell. Next would come a fever and the aches throughout her body, turning into bone-wrenching pain as her own stomach and bowels turned against her. Even worse was what followed, but she had never gone very far into that. Always, she had stepped back from the brink, or Guy had found her and forced her to drink laudanum—by then, she had not resisted him, for she had believed her quest for a normal life was doomed.

Thank Jowan and Mrs. Wakefield for Evangeline! Evangeline swore it was possible to leave the drugs behind. If she wanted it enough. Evangeline had seen it with eight of her eleven patients, though two of them had tried twice and one four times before he succeeded.

"I will stay with you until you no longer need me, Miss Riddick," she had assured Tammie.

That was acceptable. Tammie had tried at least five times, so she was due a win this time.

She was clearly not going to sleep. She had noticed books in one of the downstairs rooms. Perhaps one of them would suffice to take her mind off her growing discomfort. Her new wardrobe did not include a house coat to put on over her night rail, but she wrapped herself in one of the shawls and put on a pair of slippers. It would suffice.

With a candle to light her way, she found the room with the books. It was something of a general-purpose room, with comfortable chairs and sofas, a games table in a corner, a desk in another corner, and a wall of bookshelves.

Tammie headed for the bookshelves but tripped partway on something she didn't see in the dim candlelight. She went down with a crash, and the candle guttered and disappeared into the sudden darkness.

Her shin hurt! Tammie sat on the floor, hugging it and swearing under her breath. She had recovered enough to feel around her for the candle when a voice from the doorway said, "Show yourself." Jowan, sounding grim.

"Did I wake you?" Tammie asked. "I tripped over something. I am sorry for the noise."

He sounded relieved when he said, "Tammie. Bran, can you light a candle or something?"

A moment later, candlelight revealed the brothers standing just inside the door, each barefoot and wearing no more than pantaloons and loose shirts. Tammie could also see a footstool lying on its side a yard away. "That must be what I tripped over," she said. She looked around. There was the candlestick, within reach of where she fell. The candle had fallen out and rolled a few feet away. "Thank goodness it went out when I fell."

Jowan took a few steps and offered Tammie his hand to help her up, and Bran passed her to fetch the candle. The brothers worked smoothly together. In the seven years since Jowan and Tamsyn had been so wrapped up with one another, Jowan had found a similar partnership with his half-brother. One without the complication of the physical attraction that had led his father and her mother to exile Tamsyn.

Tammie was jealous and ashamed of herself for the feeling. She should be glad for Jowan. She was!

"Having trouble sleeping?" Jowan asked.

Tammie nodded. "It is the beginning," she explained. "An ache in the muscles that can only be relieved by movement, but it doesn't go away when you do move. So, you move again, and again. But all the time it gets worse and affects more of you."

"You sound as if you have done this before," Bran commented.

They might as well hear the worst of her. They would see it soon enough. "Five times," she said. "Twice, I only got this far, and Guy saw how restless I was and made me take a dose. Twice, I was really ill before he found me. Once, I managed to get far enough away from him that I made it all the way into hell." She swallowed hard and admitted. "When he found me, I was glad to take the dose. I hope this time, with support to continue through the worst of it, I might make it out to the other side."

The two men exchanged glances, and then Bran spoke, his voice gentle. "How bad will it get, Miss Lind?"

"Call me Tammie," she said. "You are about to know me far better than you want to. That is if you plan to stay while I go through this."

"We all plan to stay," Jowan said. "Ruth, the doctor I mentioned? She says you need someone to be with you. Evangeline, yes, to nurse you. But just someone to keep you company when you cannot sleep, to listen when you need to talk, to read to you when you need to be distracted. Bran and I will take turns, if that is acceptable, Tamsyn. Tammie."

"Tamsyn is dead," Tammie explained. "I had to kill her, Jowan, or I would not have been able to endure. Perhaps, when I am no longer a slave to the drugs and the alcohol, she will be able to return, but for now, I am Tammie." That was a hope she had never articulated before, even to herself. That Tamsyn might live again. Might write music again. Might once again enjoy a sunrise over the moors, a rainbow in the mist, the wild sea crashing on the sea cliffs with the gulls wheeling above.

Jowan swallowed hard but nodded. "Tammie, then."

Bran had asked something, but it had skittered away from her jumpy mind. "What did you ask me, Bran?"

"How bad will it get?" Bran repeated.

"Very bad. First comes the restlessness and the itching. Next, the aching gets worse, until every muscle and bone in my body feels sore, my head hurts, and my nose runs, as if I have a bad ague. Then, and I do not know a polite way to say this, my body rejects food. I vomit. I have watery stools. By that time, I will be feeling hot, then cold, then hot again. I will sweat even though I am shivering with cold, and my body is covered in goosebumps. Then, in a blink, I will feel as if I am burning."

"Is there anything we can do to help you feel better?" Jowan asked.

"Not that I know. Evangeline might know of something," Tammie said.

Evangeline spoke from the doorway. The nurse was also in a night rail and wrapped in a shawl. "I treat the symptoms," she said. "Cold cloths for fever. Warm ones to remove sweat. Blankets for cold. Drinks help, too. I have made several gallons of lemonade, so you have something to be sick with. It is worse, those of us who nurse such patients find if the patient does not have enough to drink."

"Did I wake you?" Tammie asked. "I am sorry. I came down to find a book to read because I could not sleep, and I fell over a footstool."

Evangeline dismissed the apology with a wave of her hand. "No matter. It is useful to hear how you have responded before. It will help."

"Then you get better?" Jowan asked.

Tammie wished that was so! "Then it gets worse," she explained. "It turns to hell. That is when I need you to hold fast. I shall beg for any release from the pain. Drugs. Alcohol. Death.

Any release. You must keep me from them. I might see or hear things that are not there. I might fight you, believing you have turned into some kind of monster. And all the time, right through it, I will be longing for opium, for a drink. Craving them beyond anything you can imagine. As if they would grant me a day in paradise, though I know full well their promise is a lie."

She took a deep breath. "When the craving is on me, I will do anything and say anything to make it stop. To make the pain stop. I have failed five times. I have never yet managed to get through to the other side."

"But there is another side, and you *can* reach it," Evangeline said, reassuringly. "I have seen it repeatedly. Just when you think the hell will go on forever, you will find yourself coming out of it. You will sleep for the first time in days, and when you wake, the worst of the symptoms will be gone. Then, each day after that, you will feel more well. You will be able to see the beauty around you again. Life will be worth living once more."

That was what Tammie wanted. That was what she hoped she could hold on to when the pains and the cravings were at their worst. "If I can reach the end, it will all have been worthwhile," she said. "But it is not the only possible outcome, Evangeline, and you know it. If I die in the coming days, you must all three remember I prefer death to living in thrall to the poppy and the booze. Do not blame yourselves. Do you hear me? If death is my way to freedom, then so be it."

IT WAS AS bad as Tamsyn had described. No, worse, because the beginning was so benign. Jowan sat up with her for the rest of the night, and they shared memories of the childhood they had shared when he was the only son of the baronet, she the only daughter of the housekeeper, and both were neglected by their parents.

A "do you remember" would set off a torrent of stories to take out of storage and bring into the light. Some things, they remembered differently, and when that happened, they argued amiably, even as they had back then, when in all the world there was only Jowan for Tamsyn and Tamsyn for Jowan.

By dawn, her nose had begun to run, and her eyes were red and itchy. The aching had increased, too. She did not complain, but she shifted again and again, never still for more than a moment, and, while she kept her trained voice light and easy, the strain on her face spoke of pain.

It was downhill from then. Jowan went to bed after breakfast. Tamsyn ate little but seemed cheerful enough when he left her playing *vingt et un* with Bran. By the time he woke, the next stage had begun. She was calling for a chamber pot every half hour and complaining of the cold while sweating profusely.

As day turned to night and back to day again, they pushed her to drink lemonade, mint tea, broth—anything she could tolerate. Evangeline was calmly determined. "You must drink, Tammie."

To Tamsyn's complaint, "I will only bring it back up again," she said. "Enough of it will stay to do some good." Sure enough, it inevitably came up again. The maid was kept busy bringing clean chamber pots upstairs as Evangeline removed the one that was recently filled.

Evangeline took most of the burden of care, cleaning up after Tamsyn, sponging her face with cooling water, helping her to change—which she did every couple of hours since she sweated so much.

Jowan and Bran sat with her when Evangeline slipped away for a couple of hours of sleep and also took turns to keep her company throughout the day. Tamsyn said little as she walked up and down or shifted, tossed, and turned in her bed. She was absorbed in her fight against the pain and the fever, which the willow-bark tea Evangeline made did not seem to touch.

On the fourth day, Tamsyn began begging. For opium, for alcohol, for anything that would relieve the pain. "It is crushing my bones. I cannot bear it."

Each of them had their own way of coping with her increasingly desperate pleas. Evangeline reminded her of the goal—a life no longer in thrall to the drugs and the people who gave them to her. Bran scolded that she had made him promise to say no, and he intended to keep his promise.

The first time she pleaded with Jowan, he thought his heart would break. "You don't want it, Tammie. Not really. Not deep down. Take my hand. If you need to, squeeze it. Hold me fast, dearest, and we shall get through this together."

When he relinquished her to Evangeline or Bran, his hand was bruised from her squeezing, but he always offered it again, and again.

By now, she was not just shivering, but shaking, and her fever was so high they were constantly changing the water they used to sponge her down. Even so, she was losing touch with reality, casting each of her carers as a person from her past—a dresser she once knew, her mother, a rival singer, a lover. In those hours, Jowan learned more about her past than he wanted to know.

Around the middle of the day, she sat up straight, her eyes wide with horror. "Snakes!"

Jowan followed her eyes. Nothing.

"Coming out of the wall," Tamsyn insisted, her voice shrill. "Help me! They are coming for me. Won't somebody help me?"

Jowan put his arms around her, and though she struggled, saying the snakes were coming, he would not let her go, but held her and murmured to her that she was safe, that he would let nothing hurt her.

A short time later, she fell into convulsions, her shakes turning to full-body shudders, her eyes wide open and staring at nothing, her legs and arms stiff, her teeth clenched. Evangeline was perturbed, though she remained calm.

"Talk to her, Jowan," she recommended. "Anything you like. A human voice might help, and she knows yours."

Jowan obeyed, telling an oblivious Tamsyn about the nefarious agent Thatcher, and how Drew had helped him and Bran find replacement investors.

He didn't get far. According to Bran, the fit only lasted a couple of minutes, though it had seemed much longer. Afterward, Tamsyn slept briefly, only to wake convinced that Jowan and Bran were bears, coming to eat her.

It was the beginning of days of fits and delusions. *The shaking frenzy*, Evangeline called it. "I should have realized Tammie was drinking heavily, as well as taking drugs... Ah, well. We are started now, and must stay the course," she said.

"Can you do nothing for her?" Jowan asked.

"If it was just the alcohol, I would give her laudanum to calm the symptoms," Evangeline explained.

"Ah."

Evangeline nodded. "Ah, indeed."

Jowan slept in snatches. Tamsyn barely slept at all. She was incoherent much of the time and confused even when she was mostly conscious. She was locked in a world of pain, peopled by spiders, snakes, bears, lions, and other threatening entities. As far as he could tell, Tamsyn held the worst of them to be the elf king.

It was the elf king who directed all the other delusions. Jowan couldn't tell whether his goal was Tamsyn's death or her capture. Perhaps Tamsyn herself was not sure. What she did believe, Jowan came to realize, was that the Earl of Coombe—Guy, she called him—was the elf king.

"He is coming for my music," she told Jowan once, during one of her semi-conscious states. "He wants to consume it. Then he shall be full of music, and I shall be empty. Forever empty."

Hour followed hour, and day followed day. The excellent cook sent up meals at measured intervals. The maid came and went, nurturing the fire, bringing trays, and then fetching them again when the food and drink had been consumed. Tammie continued to suffer.

The three caring for her fell into a routine. If her fever spiked, Evangeline would wash her. If she convulsed, whoever was with her would make sure she had something soft under her head and was lying on her side. If she was frightened by the figments of her imagination, Jowan or Bran would hold her until the delusion went away.

Then one day, her temperature fell almost to normal, and she did not convulse. Not even once. She fought imaginary creatures only twice in the entire day, and several times roused enough from her confused state to know their names and remember the escape from London.

And when she went to sleep that evening and slept right through the night, Evangeline said, with a relieved smile, "She is on the mend."

$$\smile$$

Chapter Thirteen

TAMMIE WOKE. HER body ached as if she had walked too far or ridden a horse for the first time in months, but the pain was gone, a vanishing memory. She had a dull headache and a dry throat, but the uncomfortable feeling in her gut felt more like hunger than sickness, and her mind was clear in a way it had not been for a long time.

She opened her eyes. Sunlight stretched across the floor from the window, gilding Jowan's silhouette as he sat by the window, studying some papers. His orange and green aura was barely perceptible, perhaps because she was sober. As she watched, he turned a page and shot her a glance, putting the papers down and standing when he saw that she was awake.

"How do you feel?" he asked.

"Hungry. Thirsty. As if I have been in a fight."

He grinned. "Thirsty I can deal with immediately." He crossed to a jug on a chest of drawers and poured some of the contents into a glass. "Here. Shall I help you?"

She took the glass, shaking her head. "I can manage. Thank you." She had fractured memories of him holding a glass to her lips. Him, and also his brother and the nurse, Evangeline. Bran's aura was predominately blue and yellow, while Evangeline's was pink.

"I will order a tray," he said and left the room. He was back in less than a minute. "As to the fight, Tamsyn—Tammie, I mean— it was one hell of a fight, and from the looks of you this morning, you won."

Suitable food for an invalid was delivered within thirty minutes. Scrambled eggs on toasted bread, and a glass of milk. It looked wonderful and tasted good, too. By that time, Evangeline had ordered Jowan from the room so Tammie could attend to personal needs and have a quick wash.

"My ring," she said, when she got as far as washing her hands. "What happened to my ring?"

"You said that the elf king was turning it to fire, and asked me to look after it for you," Evangeline explained. "It is here, on your dressing table." Tammie tried to put it on, but it hung loosely on her middle finger, and it would not go over the knuckle of her thumb. Evangeline tied a piece of ribbon to it and knotted the ends so that Tammie could slip it over her head.

Jowan returned to watch her eating, and Bran put his head in to express his delight at her improvement. Jowan looked exhausted. In fact, all of them bore the signs of sleepless nights. "How long has it been?" Tammie asked. "Since we left London, I mean?"

To Tammie's amazement, Jowan replied, "We have been here for ten nights." *Ten nights!* Tammie remembered the first clearly and perhaps three more. Long tortuous nights, with equally long miserable days in between. After that, nothing that could possibly be real.

"Ten nights! No wonder you all look as if you have been run over by a carriage."

Jowan gave a huff of a laugh. "I could do with a decent night's sleep," he admitted. "I guess we all could."

They had suffered those ten days and nights with her, these three. Tammie felt a surge of love and gratitude. "You held on," she said. "All of you. I cannot thank you enough. I know it must have been difficult."

"I've known easier days," Bran admitted. "But it was worth it, Tammie. Or it will be if you stay off the poppy and the booze." The last few words were stern.

"Of course, she will," Jowan told his brother. "You've done it, Tammie. I don't mind telling you I was worried a time or two." He shuddered.

"You will need to rest and recover," Evangeline decreed. "Eat well. Sleep a lot. The rest of us, too, must sleep and recover. But Jowan is correct. You have won. You should be proud of yourself.

"I had help," Tammie said.

EVANGELINE DECREED A week of convalescence. On the first day, Jowan wrote to David Wakefield to see what his surveillance of Coombe had disclosed. Jowan couldn't believe that the man had let Tammie go without some reaction.

On the second day, Evangeline allowed Tamsyn out of bed to sit up in the cottage's sunroom, provided someone carried her down the stairs. Jowan volunteered and was shocked to find how light she was. She had already been thin to the point of gaunt, but she now seemed to be little more than skin and bone.

She had little appetite, too. She approached her meals with gusto but lost interest before consuming even half of the small portions she had been served. Evangeline said her capacity for food had shrunk but would expand again quite quickly. "She will need to eat as much as she comfortably can, and do it often," Evangeline said and had a word with the cook.

In the afternoon, Tamsyn begged to go for a walk in the garden. Evangeline agreed, provided Jowan or Bran was on hand to help her if she became unbalanced or overtired. "Afterward, you may feel like a rest," she added. Tamsyn pointed out that she had already had a morning nap.

Jowan offered his elbow and let her set the direction. As they made their slow way around the garden, Bran and Evangeline followed, chatting quietly. Apart from noticing that Evangeline was laughing, Jowan ignored them, all his attention on Tamsyn, who was examining everything they came across as if it was new to her.

"It feels… real, Jowan," she said. "The colors, the shapes, the smells." She stopped and put her head back, her eyes shut. "The wind." She looked up at Jowan. "I did not even know I missed this. The poppy blurs the pain, but it also blurs the edges of everything else." With a soft smile, she stroked a leaf and then the bark of a tree. "Can we sit down? I *am* a little tired."

He conducted her to the bench they'd almost reached and handed her onto the seat, then sat beside her. Evangeline and Bran nodded as they passed and continued down the path, still talking. Jowan sat with Tamsyn, content to be silent if that was what she wished.

He was weary to the bone. If she had another nap, he would take one himself, but he was somehow afraid to sleep when she was awake as if she would be snatched back by the fairies if he did not keep a close lookout. Which was a silly thought, and just proved how tired he was.

Had Janet, the heroine of the ballad, looked at the knight she had stolen from the faery queen and wondered if she could live up to the expectations of someone who had been in faery land? Or if she even wanted to?

Was she haunted by the shapes her knight had taken in her arms and the secrets he had disclosed in his torment? What simple maiden could hope to have the bedroom skills to satisfy one who had been with the Queen of the Fae—and who knew how many of her ladies?

What simple boyo from Cornwall could hope to measure up to the sophisticated lovers his Tamsyn had had, starting with Guy, and including how many others? The names she mentioned in her delirium echoed in his brain, but he had no desire to count them. Jowan, who had twice been with a bargirl in Oxford, and had visited a cheerful widow in Launceston once a week for a six-month, had otherwise sought satisfaction on his own. He knew nothing by comparison to those sophisticates.

She had turned to him for help but as a friend, not as a lover. Their youthful promises were seven years in the past, separated from the here and now by a mountainous terrain of broken promises and different experiences.

He would not press her. Perhaps, in time, this Tamsyn, the one shaped by the past seven years, would come to love this Jowan. In the meanwhile, all he could do was offer her his support. The devil of it was that he had not changed. Not in the essentials, not in his love for Tamsyn.

In the past ten days, he had come to know her again, at least a little. And surely the Tamsyn he saw in her agony was a true picture of the woman—still determined, still passionate, still brave and intelligent.

He'd learned more than he wanted to know about what her life had been like, but it didn't change his love. She had been debauched. He blamed Coombe for it. She had been actively involved in orgies. Coombe's fault again. She had helped Coombe to capture others and addict them so Coombe could force them to his will. She hated herself for it, but Jowan absolved her and blamed Coombe.

Coombe needed to be destroyed, but Jowan had no idea how a country baronet from a remote corner of England could manage to take down a popular earl with contacts throughout the English aristocracy and beyond into Europe.

He was roused from his thoughts by Tamsyn's voice. "I do not think I can walk inside, Jowan," she told him. "Not up the steps, at least. Will you carry me?"

"I will carry you to bed," he said, "and then I will find my own. An hour's sleep would be a good idea."

By the third day, she was eating more and staying awake for longer between naps. And Evangeline and Bran both looked better for a couple of good nights of sleep. Jowan, too, when he examined his face reflected in a shaving mirror, was less pale and the bags under his eyes less pronounced.

That was the day that David Wakefield and his wife Prue arrived from London. He had sent two reports over the past few days. In one, he had mentioned that Thatcher had been let out on bail and had disappeared. The other had been about Coombe's efforts to find his missing Devon Songbird.

"We thought we would see how you were, and let you know what we have discovered," David explained after the initial greetings were over. "It is, after all, only an hour's drive and Coombe has no watchers on us since he has not discovered our involvement in the rescue."

"Not for lack of trying," Prue added, dryly. "He or those working for him have been questioning everyone they found that came in touch with either of you gentlemen. Including David, of course."

David chuckled. "A couple of locals, which was useful, for they knew enough about me not to be stupid. I told them that I never discuss my clients' business. They attempted a bribe but didn't bother with any threats. Coombe came himself but got no further."

Prue was indignant. "The man tried to bully you, David. He must be an utter fool."

"He has an elevated opinion of his importance, Prue," David told her.

Tamsyn was clearly concerned. She leaned forward in her eagerness to convince the Wakefields. They did not know Coombe the way she did. "You must take him seriously," she said. "He is friends with the king, and has other highly-placed friends, too. And if seeking to have you harassed by the magistrates and planting rumors to destroy your reputation does not satisfy him, he is not above hiring low criminals to attack you directly."

"We appreciate your warning, Miss Lind," Prue said, "but you must not worry. A relative of David's has already had a word with the king, and we have far too many allies in Society for any rumors to take root. In fact, any attempt to destroy our reputation is likely to backfire and undermine Coombe's, which is no more than he deserves."

"David is a half-brother of the Duke of Haverford and a protégé of the Duchess of Winshire, and he and Prue have worked for at least half of the ton," Jowan explained.

Tamsyn opened her mouth, but Prue spoke first. "As to your other concern, our house is well guarded and we and our children travel with armed guards, some in plain view and some not. We rather hope there is an attack, for we shall catch the attackers and perhaps follow the trail back to Coombe, which would be the best possible outcome."

Jowan could see by Tamsyn's face that she was still worried about Coombe. She said nothing further, but he had a concern of his own. "They would not have followed you, would they?"

Prue's look was reminiscent of a governess attempting not to laugh at a silly question, but David said, "We were not followed. We did not leave our house by carriage or as ourselves, and we had people checking for trackers." He chuckled. "We will have the carriage drop us off directly at our house though. Let the watchers explain that to Coombe."

He sobered. "I have a full report which I will leave with you, Jowan, but the short form is that Coombe has been overreaching himself, inveigling the sons of the aristocracy into his web. At least a dozen peers have sons or nephews who fell into or just avoided Coombe's toils on the Continent, and he has made two failed attempts and begun grooming another two young men since he returned to England."

He handed what must be the report to Jowan. "We haven't definitive evidence of anything illegal, though many of his tactics skirt the edges and are at least immoral. But if we cannot get him on breaking the law, we probably have a large enough group of annoyed parents to force him offshore again."

Jowan wasn't satisfied with the idea of letting the man go.

"He must have broken the law. He is too immoral and too arrogant not to."

"Look at singers or musicians who died unexpectedly, or who disappeared," Tamsyn suggested. "I can give you names and approximate dates."

Everyone in the room turned to stare at Tamsyn, Jowan with dawning horror as he realized how frightened Tamsyn must have been over the years. With no one else to turn to, and the knowledge that people who displeased Coombe ended up dead, what could she do except disappear into the false dreams of the poppy and other substances?

How strong she must be to have survived.

WHEN TAMMIE HAD answered all his questions, Wakefield was bluntly honest. "I'll do my best, Miss Lind. But I am not hopeful. It will be next to impossible to prove Coombe guilty of any of the disappearances that happened in Europe or even farther abroad, and the flutist who died shortly before he took you overseas was six years ago. I'll check the coroner's report and follow up with witnesses. Perhaps we will be lucky."

But more likely they would not. That was what he was really saying. Tammie was not surprised. Guy seemed to live a charmed life.

"One point worth considering is whether Coombe thought the evidence might point to him," said Mrs. Wakefield. "After all, you say this was shortly before you left for overseas. Odd to go on a concert tour in the middle of a war. Was it a trip he had planned for some time, do you know?"

"No," Tammie replied. "No, it was not. One day he was talking about funding an opera at the Royal, and the next, my maid was told to pack my bag, for we were leaving."

"Interesting," Wakefield commented. "We might find something after all."

I trust you have finished with my patient," Evangeline interjected. "She is almost asleep on her feet."

It was true. She was tired. How lovely to be tired when she knew she would be able to sleep and would wake refreshed!

Wakefield and his wife apologized. "We should have remembered that you are convalescing, Miss Lind," Mrs. Wakefield said. "I hope we have not caused a setback."

"Not at all," Tammie assured them. "I am ready for sleep, but I am better every day. Am I not, Evangeline?"

"Ask me again in three more days," Evangeline replied dryly.

THE JUICE OF the poppy kept one from having to face unpalatable facts. Or liquor would do, at a pinch. Tammie was not going to admit to the wonderful people who had seen her through the torment of the past fortnight that she still yearned for peace, the freedom from care. It was a false freedom, and she was determined not to succumb again.

However, being faced with a future in which no one else made her choices for her had its negative sides, too. Apparently, Prue Wakefield had asked if she wanted to return to Cornwall, and she had said yes. Since the day she woke without a fever, everyone must have assumed that was the plan. Until this morning, six days later.

It came up for discussion at breakfast. "Are we going to be able to leave tomorrow, as planned?" Bran asked Evangeline.

"I see no reason why not," the nurse replied. "As long as we travel at an easy pace. Tammie's health is much improved."

"Six days on the road," Jowan suggested. "Six to seven hours a day with a long stop in the middle of the day. Will that do, Evangeline? And a longer stop if Tammie needs it. You do still want to go to Cornwall, Tammie, do you not?"

More than anything. "Yes, I do," Tammie said. It was only then she realized that what she wanted was to go back to the Cornwall of seven years ago, and the Tamsyn who existed then. Cornwall would have moved on, just as Jowan had.

In the last six days, she had been watching him. He was not the boy she remembered. It was not just that he was a grown man. The seven years had changed him. For a start, he had the same easy friendship with his half-brother that he had had, in her memory at least, with her. He was also the baronet, and that meant he had work to do.

Important work on which other people's livelihoods depended. The work didn't stop because he was in hiding. He had given his stewards and managers Wakefield's address, and messengers from Wakefield arrived every other day, bringing him letters and reports and documents to review, and taking away his answers to the previous dispatches.

Bran was fully in his confidence, and acted as his secretary, his sounding board, and, at times, his adversary, forcing him to fully articulate the reasons he was leaning towards a particular decision. Robust discussions would leave the room they had adopted as their office and carry on through meals and into the evening, so Evangeline and Tammie were spectators to their debates. Sometimes, Bran would change Jowan's mind. Sometimes, Jowan would change Bran's.

Tammie's envy of Bran's relationship with Jowan grew by the day, and embarrassed her mightily, for she had no right to feel Jowan was her property.

It would be worse in Cornwall, because Jowan had a place there, and so did Bran. Tammie did not have a place anywhere. On the stage, perhaps. But she could not risk returning to London. Guy would have her back under his control again before her bag was unpacked.

"What will I do in Cornwall?" she wondered.

"Rest and recover," Jowan ordained.

"At your expense?" she asked, the weight of all he had done

for her suddenly presenting itself. "I have no money," she realized. "No way to support myself. Not in Cornwall. I cannot even begin to pay for what you have done already." Not that he would demand payment. Jowan was not like that. But, if she understood some of the conversations she had overheard, the baronetcy had been left in a parlous state. Jowan had mended things, but he was not wealthy.

His response was to be expected. "You owe me nothing, Tammie. I was glad to help an old friend."

"What of your earnings from your concerts?" Bran asked, his eyes narrowing in suspicion. "Has it all been spent?"

"Bran!" Jowan warned. "It is not our business."

"It is a fair question," Tammie said. "But I do not know the answer, Bran. Guy handled my bookings, my contracts, any expenses, and any payments made. I was never asked to pay for anything, and I was never given money. Oh, but I have jewelry. I forgot! I sewed some pieces into the hem of the skirt of my riding habit. How could I have forgotten? We can sell it, and I can at least pay whatever you are charging, Evangeline. And perhaps have enough that I will not be a charge on you, Jowan."

"Your skirt may be hanging in your room," Evangeline suggested. "You were wearing it when you arrived here, so we will be able to find it."

She stood as if to look straightaway, and Tammie rose, too. "You will let me pay my way, Jowan, will you not?"

"You have your inheritance from your mother, too," Jowan told her. "You have her cottage and her savings. I instructed the lawyer to invest the savings for you and to rent the cottage until we could ask you what to do with them, so I expect you have a tidy bit there."

That news stopped Tammie in her tracks. "I have a cottage?" She and Mother had lived at Inneford House when she was last in Cornwall. Mother kept the house and warmed Sir Carlyon's bed.

Jowan merely nodded. "Go and check for your jewels. But you need have no worries about supporting yourself, Tammie.

You are a woman of property, if not substance."

But not a woman with a future, Tammie mused, as she followed Evangeline upstairs. *Or, at least, not a future I can work towards. I need a goal. I need some reason to keep breathing and to keep away from my personal demons.*

Chapter Fourteen

THEIR GOAL ON the fifth day from Ealing was Exeter or perhaps a little beyond. When they stopped for their midday break, Jowan figured they were making good time, so they could linger for a while here, or get a bit closer to home later in the day.

Bran had something other than their progress on his mind. He and Jowan went for a walk to stretch their legs and were heading back to the inn where Tamsyn was resting and Evangeline was watching over her.

"She has been another man's mistress, Jowan. Hell, from what I heard while she was ill, she has been little better than whore to Coombe's pimp," he said.

He put up his hands and stepped back at Jowan's expression. "I wouldn't repeat it to anyone else, but I've always told you the truth, and I'm not about to change now."

Jowan had always believed that when he met Tamsyn again, the spark would be there, or it wouldn't. They would either pick up where they left off, or they would see nothing was left to pick up and go on with their lives. In fact, after seven years of silence, he was fully expecting to find that Tamsyn was not the girl he remembered.

He had been right. She was not, and part of the reason was the experiences she had been through. But the spark was still there, fanned to flames as he got to know her again over the week of her convalescence and the days of travel on their way to Cornwall. Bran didn't understand.

"Then tell me this," Jowan said. "In her situation, as a sixteen-year-old girl in the hands of a man with no conscience, would you have done better? Remember, she knew her mother had sold her, and that my father would simply return her to Coombe if she turned up on our doorstep. She had no money and no friends. Even I, as far as she knew, had abandoned her. What would you have done?"

Bran opened his mouth to argue, then closed it again. After a moment, he said, "Fair point. But I don't see why you still want her, for all of that. I accept it wasn't her fault, but she is used goods, Jowan." He frowned. "It wouldn't be fair to take her as a mistress, at least not yet. She is too vulnerable. But you cannot be thinking of marriage."

Jowan was thinking about punching his brother. "First, never call Tamsyn 'used goods'. Not ever again, or I'll punch you through to next week. Don't even think it. That's a horrible thing to think about a human being. Used goods, as if she is yesterday's tea leaves. She's not someone's property that they're tired of, any more than your mother was."

That was a low blow. Bran's mother had died when he was a baby, but those who raised him, apart from his beloved grand-mother who died a week before Bran turned up on the doorstep at Inneford House, never tired of reminding him about her disgrace. He reddened at the comparison but said nothing.

"Second, I'm not thinking of marriage. Or, at least, not yet. I'm not thinking of anything. As you say, she is vulnerable. She needs to live a little, get used to how life is without the poppy or the brew. Find out what she wants from life. I mean to help her if I can and stay out of her way otherwise. Do I have hopes for the future? I won't lie to you, Bran. I can't help but wonder if we might mean more to one another in time than we do or can now. If that happens, I would hope my brother would be happy for me." In its way, that was a lie, for he glimpsed what their love could be. He yearned for a future with Tamsyn as his wife and would do whatever he could to make it happen. Whatever he could without spooking her.

Bran didn't respond as Jowan hoped. "Evangeline says, the chances are she will go back on the opium or at least start drinking heavily again. She was clearly a lush, and we know how hard it is for them to stay sober."

"We shall see," Jowan said. "I think she means what she says. I think she has the courage and the determination to keep sober. If she doesn't..." he shrugged. "We'll deal with that if it happens. Bran, don't tear her down. That's all I'm asking."

"My uncle drank," Bran told him. "My grandfather, too. Neither of them ever managed to give it up. I don't trust her, Jowan. But I won't tell her or anyone else. As for being happy for you, I guess we will have to deal with that when it happens, too."

Jowan understood Bran was concerned for him. There was no point in resenting the man for it. The truth was that Jowan, too, thought he might be riding for a fall. Not because he expected Tamsyn to turn back to the drugs and booze. He knew how determined she had been as a child, and believed she would surprise her detractors.

His problem was he couldn't believe that a sophisticated woman of her beauty and experience, who had thrilled audiences in all the great cities of Europe and beyond, would choose him and St Tetha. Who was he, after all, to win such a prize? Only Jowan Trethewey, a man of little fortune, not very much experience, and no particular talent, who had lived most of his life in a tiny village in Cornwall and was committed to staying there.

The inn was within sight, now. A cluster of people were gathered in the courtyard, and as Jowan's eyes focused on what was happening, he broke into a run, Bran speeding up to run with him. A stranger had Tamsyn by both wrists and was dragging her towards a carriage while several other men held off Evangeline and their driver and groom, and the inn's keeper and servants watched without interfering.

Bran fell away. Without asking, Jowan knew he would be loading the pocket pistol he carried. Jowan didn't wait, but hurled himself straight at the man holding Tamsyn and fetched him a mighty clout to the head that had him letting go of Tamsyn and falling to the side.

➤➤➤◀◀◀

THE MEN HAD burst into the private parlor where Tammie and Evangeline were talking over a cup of tea. "That's her," said one, whom Tammie recognized as Paul Willard, one of Guy's most fervent acolytes. The other men also had muddied auras in Coombe's signature colors. "Get the treacherous bitch," Willard said. Another two men grabbed Tammie by her arms and dragged her to the door, though she dug her heels in and fought to be freed.

As she tossed her head about, she could see a fourth man holding Evangeline at bay.

Those hauling Tammie ignored the protesting innkeeper, but Tammie could hear Willard telling the man that Tammie was his master's runaway wife, whom they had been sent to retrieve.

"Lies!" Tammie yelled as they forced her out into the inn yard. "He lies!"

Jowan's coachman and guard emerged from the public room, calling for Tammie to be released. Other guests in the inn made themselves scarce and the innkeeper and his servants stood and watched as Willard grabbed Tammie's hands and the other men formed a barrier between the pair of them and Tammie's would-be defenders.

Willard was dragging her towards the open door of a carriage when Jowan appeared, seemingly out of nowhere, and knocked him flying.

Tammie fell back into the mud of the courtyard. Jowan offered her a hand up. "Get behind me, Tammie. Who are they? Coombe's men?"

"Yes. The one you hit is Paul Willard. I do not know the others."

Willard was groaning. The other three men were holding the line but casting anxious glances behind them.

Jowan said, "Tammie, go to our carriage without getting too close to those villains, and bring me the flat wooden case under the rear-facing seat."

His carriage pistols. Of course. Tammie edged sideways, keeping an eye on the men, and then made a dash for the carriage. A gunshot made her look back. One of the men was a few paces closer to her but had flinched backward, his eyes on Bran, who was standing in the shadow of Willard's carriage, a smoking pistol in one hand and another pistol in the other.

Tammie hastened to fetch Jowan's pistol case, her heart leaping into her mouth when the carriage rocked while she was in it. Then a voice spoke from above her. "I have them covered, Sir Jowan. Scurvy knaves."

The guard! He must have taken his chance and gone for his blunderbuss. Tammie scrambled from the carriage and carried the case to Jowan. While Willard lay in the mud and the other three stood glowering at Bran and the guard, Jowan loaded both pistols and the coachman returned to Jowan's carriage and produced his own pistol. Evangeline showed an unexpected talent, taking Bran's spent pistol and reloading it.

The innkeeper decided to take a hand. "That one on the ground said the lady was his master's wife," he said.

"That one on the ground lied," Jowan replied. "Is there a magistrate nearby, innkeeper?"

"No, sir. That is, Lord Brant is our magistrate, but he is away over in Kent visiting his daughter. The nearest magistrate is twenty miles away."

"Then call the constable and have these four locked up," Jowan ordered. "My party and I shall make sworn statements before we leave. We cannot wait for the magistrate, but these four can."

"The woman belongs to the Earl of Coombe," insisted one of the other men. "Mr. Willard recognized her. And she recognized him, too."

"That's right," said another. "She is Miss Lind, the singer, and the Earl of Coombe is her patron. She ran away from him, and he has a right to get her back."

The innkeeper looked to Jowan for his response. "See?" Jowan said, "Already, they contradict themselves. That man lied when he said my sister here was Coombe's wife, and now they claim that Coombe owns the famous singer, Miss Lind. Slavery is illegal in England in case you have not heard. If you keep the leader separately from his henchmen, your magistrate will have the chance to question them before they can conspire on an answer."

"Miss Lind?" said one of the inn's grooms. "I've heard of her. The Devon Songbird, they call her. I don't rightly like foreigners coming into our village trying to steal away the Devon Songbird."

"That's not her, you fool," said another groom. "You heard the gentleman. They tried to steal the wrong lady. This is the gentleman's sister."

They continued to argue the matter as they efficiently tied up the Londoners, including Willard, who had recovered conscious-ness only to start yelling threats. His father the viscount was going to eviscerate them all, apparently. Tammie, now they'd decided the attempted abduction was a case of mistaken identity, didn't want to upset the harmony by explaining that Willard's father had disowned him for being a drunken degenerate.

She went inside with the rest of her party and wrote a state-ment saying she recognized none of the men except the Honorable Paul Willard whom she had met while in London. She said she was not, nor had she ever been, married to the Earl of Coombe, who was, as far as she knew, a bachelor. She was traveling home to St Tetha with Sir Jowan Trethewey, Mr.

Branoc Hughes, his brother, and Mrs. Evangeline Parkerdale, a friend, and could be contacted through Sir Jowan.

She signed as Tamsyn Roskilly, though the name felt like a suit of clothes she no longer fitted. On the other hand, Tammie Lind did not fit, either. Who would she be now?

"I signed as Tamsyn Roskilly," she told Jowan. "Which I suppose will spoil your claim that I am your sister."

"Not really," Jowan said, with the cheeky grin she remembered from their joint childhood. "I told him Bran is my brother by a mistress, and you are the daughter of my father's long-time housekeeper. He can draw his own conclusions."

The innkeeper conducted them to their carriage, apologizing all the way for not defending Tammie from the invaders. "I did not know what to do," he kept saying. "I did not know who was in the right."

"I don't have much confidence that they will hold out for long against Willard's threats," Bran commented, as the carriage rolled out of the stable yard.

"All we can hope," said Jowan, "is they won't let those villains go before we have a chance to get home and marshal our defenses."

"We should have questioned Willard himself," Bran said, "to find out whether they knew where we were, or whether they found us by chance. There may be other parties out."

Jowan pressed his lips together and frowned, then shook his head. "A fair point, but I doubt we'll get much sense out of him, and I don't want to waste any time getting home. We could be there tonight if Tammie is well enough for a long run this afternoon."

Evangeline looked concerned, but Tammie nodded. "Better a long afternoon and evening's carriage ride with the three of you than as a prisoner of one of the Earl of Coombe's men," she said. "I doubt they would have been as considerate."

But what if his people are waiting for me in St Tetha? "Jowan, they might be in St Tetha ahead of us," she warned.

He nodded. "Bran and I have discussed that," he said. "We'll stop at Wheal Trethewey, at the mine manager's house. He'll be able to accommodate you ladies for the night while Bran and I drop by some of the cottages and ask about strangers in town."

"If they are there, they will be facing the whole village, Tammie. If need be, we'll call in the militia," said Bran.

"I do not want anyone to be in danger because of me," Tammie insisted.

"We have no intention of allowing Coombe to take you back and make a slave of you again," Jowan replied. "You cannot ask that of us, Tammie."

Tammie turned to the nurse, who had become a friend in recent weeks. "Evangeline, this is not your fight."

"It *is* my fight," Evangeline answered. "I have been fighting to save those in thrall to the poppy. How much more important is it to fight those who deliberately subject people to overuse of that and other things?" She was pink with indignation and distress. Bran put his hand on hers, and she turned her hand over to form a clasp.

Bran and Evangeline! That was an interesting development. Evangeline continued. "To enslave people, as Jowan rightly says. Indeed, I hope I will have the opportunity to give witness to the condition you were in, Tammie, thanks to that monster. The very idea!"

Tammie blinked back tears. How long had it been since she had had people who would take her part? She felt a surge of affection for them all. Had she been asked a few weeks ago, she would have said that opium and other substances opened her eyes and her mind to another world, a fantastic world of colors and sounds that did not exist in the mundane world.

That was what Guy had always claimed, and Tammie had believed him. In the past few days, however, she had discovered she had been seeing the real world through a wall. A crystal wall, perhaps, like a thick window of multi-colored glass that dulled and distorted what she saw, heard, and scented. And beyond that, what she felt.

She might not be able to see the indescribable colors from her poppy dreams, but the colors she could see were brighter and crisper. The same for all the other senses. As for emotions, she felt everything more intensely. Fear. Gratitude. The only thing dulled was her ability to perceive people's auras. Only careful concentration let her see them now, a shadowy remnant of the colors and shapes that used to be so obvious to her.

Her friends were smiling at her. "I am more grateful than I can say," she told them.

Jowan had clearly given orders for speed. The coachman kept the horses to a trot or even a canter whenever the road allowed, and they stopped twice as often as before to change teams, losing ten minutes in the change but gaining that time back doubled with the faster pace.

They went through Exeter in the mid-afternoon and kept going. By nightfall, they were in Bridestow, where they stopped to change their team once more and set out extra carriage lamps.

"The moon is full, Sir Jowan," Tammie heard the coachman report. "It will rise in about thirty minutes or so, I think. I suggest we take the time to get something to eat and otherwise look to the comfort of the ladies."

It was a good suggestion. After nearly a fortnight of Evangeline's coddling, Tammie's appetite was improving to the extent that she had moved Jowan's ring from the ribbon to her middle finger. Mention of dinner had her longing for it.

"Will it be safe to continue by moonlight?" she asked. Jowan was escorting her and Evangeline into the inn to order their meal while Bran helped the coachman inspect the available horses to decide which would be best to carry them further on their way.

"Yes, with tonight's clear skies it should be easy," Jowan replied. "We will have to go more slowly, though. Nothing above a trot or a fast walk. I should think we'll be home by midnight."

They set off again at moonrise. Jowan and Bran had so far traveled with their backs to the horses, but this time they suggested Jowan sit beside Tammie and Bran beside Evangeline. "Being larger," Jowan explained, "we're better anchored. If you ladies wish to sleep, you can use our shoulders as pillows."

Tammie yawned, which made the others laugh.

They took the seating Jowan suggested, but for the next stage of the journey they talked, and it wasn't until they pulled out of Okehampton that Tammie finally succumbed to her weariness. She must have slept through the change at Lifton and the moment when they crossed the Tamar into Cornwall, for she woke to Bran speaking through the hatch to the coachman. "Take the next right and look for a house on the left around 500 yards down that road."

She was sprawled on a man's chest. She didn't have to look to know it was Jowan's. Even after the day on the road, he still smelled of whatever lotion he used after he shaved and of something that was undefinably Essence-of-Jowan. He had propped himself in the corner, so he was sitting semi-sideways on the bench seat, and he had an arm around her to anchor her in place.

He gave way immediately when she pressed back against that arm.

"You're awake," he commented. "We're nearly there, Tammie. No sign of any trouble."

The mine manager said the same when they woke him, apologizing for the imposition. It was Thomas Penrose, whom she remembered from the years she had lived at Inneford House, though he was several years older than her and Jowan. Back then, he had been assistant to his father, the previous manager of this mine.

He recognized her, too. "Tamsyn Roskilly," he commented. "You've brought her home, Sir Jowan."

"I have, Thomas. But I had to extract her from the hands of an evil man who was trying to keep her against her will. We encountered his men on the way here and had to foil a kidnap attempt. That's why we haven't gone straight to Inneford—in case they are here ahead of us."

"No strangers in the village that I have heard about," Penrose said, "but why don't you stay here for the night, and we'll check out the area in the morning? You'll be safe here, Miss Roskilly. There isn't a man, woman, or child who isn't proud of our own Cornish Lark, even if you did call yourself some outlandish thing while you were away."

"Not my doing," Tammie assured him. "The Earl of Coombe decided that Cornwall was as good as a foreign country to most of England and would not listen to what I wanted."

"I remember him," Penrose commented. "Obnoxious Englishman. Looked down his nose at all of us. Laughed at Sir Carlyon behind his back, and the rest of us to our faces. Is it him you're running from?"

"It is," she confirmed.

"Let him come, I say," said Penrose. "Come on inside. Sir Jowan, you know the way to the drawing room. Fix your party something to drink against the cold, and I'll sort out beds for you all, and stabling for the horses."

"Perhaps the ladies would prefer a cup of something hot," said a woman's voice. A young woman of about Tammie's age was on the stairs, dressed, but in a way that hinted the gown had been thrown on over her night rail, with the back left unlaced and a shawl worn to cover the gaps.

"My dear," said Penrose. "We have guests for the night. Sir Jowan Trethewey you know, and Mr. Bran Hughes. Miss Roskilly and Mrs. Parkerdale, my wife. Virginia, Miss Roskilly is the Cornish Lark. You will have heard the folks around here speak of her. Mrs. Parkerdale is her companion. If you can manage a bedroom for the ladies, I'll see to the carriage and then organize somewhere for the gentlemen to sleep."

"I'll see about your tea first," Mrs. Penrose said. It wasn't long, though, before all was sorted, and Tammie and Evangeline were tucking themselves into a large, low bed in what was clearly a child's bedroom. Tammie fell asleep wondering who they had displaced.

Chapter Fifteen

J OWAN AND BRAN went out with Penrose at first light, leaving Tamsyn and Evangeline with Mrs. Penrose and her children. The coachman and guard stayed behind to act as guards, and Penrose also warned his servants to keep watch.

They stopped by Wheal Trethewey first. The miners and smelterers were just gathering for work, so Jowan spoke to them before they went underground, telling them about Miss Roskilly's desire to come home to Cornwall, Coombe's efforts to stop her from leaving or even seeing Jowan, the rescue, and the attack at the inn.

He was heartened by the shouts of approval for his actions, and the grumbles against foreigners.

"She's one of ours, men, and she has come home. I mean for her to be safe here in St Tetha. Are there strangers hereabouts? They might have been sent by Coombe."

"There's that mine fellow," shouted one of the men.

"Aye, Thatcher," said another. "He be tromping about telling us you don't have the money for the new mine. Is that true, Sir Jowan?"

Thatcher! So, this was where that villain went. "It's a damn lie," Jowan told the questioner. "Bran and I went to see him in London and found he was trying to steal from us. Getting people to put money into the mine just so he and his partner could run off with it. He and his partner were arrested, but they let him out of prison while he was waiting for his trial, and he ran away. Bran and I found our own investors and we can start whenever we like."

"If you know where he is staying, tell me," Bran added. "I have a few words to say to him before I hand him over to the magistrate."

A couple of the men chuckled. "He's staying with the magistrate, Mr. Hughes, so that'll be right easy." The local earl, Lord Trentwood, was also the magistrate. The job was normally a sinecure, but today the man might have a bit of work to do.

"He's the only one," one of the others commented. "The only stranger, that is. That I know of." He looked around at the other miners, eliciting a buzz of agreement.

"You'll let me know if that changes?" Jowan asked.

"Aye. That we will, sir," the miners agreed, and several commented they would be happy to do whatever they could for Miss Roskilly.

The word was the same in the village. The only stranger was Thatcher, who had been there for several days, doing his best to stir trouble. "We played dumb," one of the shopkeepers told him. "Didn't know what he was at, but we weren't going to believe a foreigner over you, Sir Jowan. You've dealt fairly with us since the day you took over from your Pa."

"Bran, you call by Inneford and see there's no sign of Coombe or his men, and I'll visit the earl," Jowan suggested.

"Perhaps I should send for the earl to meet me at the inn," Penrose suggested. "If this Thatcher fellow gets wind of you being here, he will take off again."

That was a good plan, so Bran headed for Inneford House, and Penrose and Jowan walked back to the inn, which had been one of their first stopping points.

It was still early, but that was all to the good. Thatcher, who had pretensions as a gentleman, might still be asleep. Penrose wrote his note and sent an inn servant to the earl's house, then Jowan and Penrose settled down in the snug with a glass of ale. They instructed the innkeeper to send Lord Trentwood in when he arrived, but to keep Thatcher out of the snug if he turned up.

They waited over an hour. Jowan filled in the time by asking Penrose for a report on the mine for the past few weeks. Bran arrived to join them, reporting that the Inneford servants had seen no sign of strangers and that bedchambers had been prepared for the two lady visitors after Jowan's message from Ealing. Bran, too, had an ale.

Eventually, the earl arrived and was shown through to the snug. He stopped in the doorway. "Trethewey. I didn't know you were back. Hughes, too. I've a guest who is stirring trouble for you. Thought I'd keep him here till I could find out what was going on. Sent a letter to you in London a week ago, but I thought you'd write, not come back."

"I left London nearly three weeks ago. I was in London when Thatcher was arrested for stealing from me and others. I got a letter where I was staying out of London to tell me he had been let out on bail and had disappeared. I'm not surprised to hear he's in St Tetha causing trouble."

As Bran told Tamsyn and Evangeline when they rejoined them, that was that for Thatcher. "Lord Trentwood took our sworn testimony and went home to turn his guest into his prisoner. I don't suppose we'll be able to recover any of the money he stole, but at least most of the investors had not made good on their commitments before we put a stop to his tricks. Lord Trentwood thinks he will refer the man back to London for trial since most of his crimes were committed there and his accomplice is there."

Since they'd made sure no other strangers were around, there was no reason not to take Tamsyn and Evangeline home, and so they did.

IT FELT STRANGE to be back in Cornwall—back in Inneford House, especially. Good, but strange. Things were familiar but different. Everything around Tammie was what she had grown up with, but as she'd expected, it was not the same.

The people had grown older. Some had retired, or even died, and others—often their children—had taken over. Even those who seemed much the same had memories from the seven years Tammie had been gone that she didn't share. They would refer to "the year Sir Jowan caught the smugglers" or "that winter when vicar be snowed in on the downs for two days with t'earl's daughter", and she would want to hear the rest of the story, which everyone else clearly knew and took for granted.

The people who owned the village shop when she was a girl were gone, retired to live with a daughter in Truro, and the family who owned it now were newcomers, though Cornish born and bred, and related to the family who owned the inn.

Houses had been repainted or bits had been built on or taken down. The church roof, which the parish had been saving through Tammie's entire childhood, had now been replaced. A whole line of trees was missing behind the village green—blown down, apparently, in a dreadful storm that was another of the events referenced when people wanted to date something. "The year the elms be blown clear down over by green."

Up on the moors, the ground had been cleared and building begun for the new mine about which she had heard so much. They were going to build a new and better smelter there, too, which would process the ore from all three mines.

In Inneford House itself, Jowan's hand marked every room. The old, dull, dark interior had been brightened with paint and furnishings. And Sir Carlyon's study was one place that had changed beyond recognition. It had been a place of fear where Sir Carlyon sat in state behind the desk while miscreants, or those he regarded as miscreants, were called to be berated and punished.

Now Jowan had made of it a library and business room combined, with bookshelves lining the walls, two desks in well-lit positions by the windows, and comfortable chairs near the fire.

The upstairs bedrooms, too, had all been refreshed with paint, even to the servants' rooms in the attic. The housekeeper's little domain belowstairs—the two rooms that Tammie remembered most clearly—had changed almost beyond recognition, with new paint, new furniture and curtains, and completely different paintings on the walls.

And a new coal range in the kitchen made meal preparation much easier for the cook who had taken over from the tyrant who used to rule there—a grumpy woman who lived in a state of perpetual feud with Tammie's mother.

It was disorienting. Close enough to Tammie's memories that the dissimilarities always caused a moment of shock. "Even with all the changes," she told Jowan a few days after their arrival, "I keep expecting to turn a corner and see Mama bustling by with the keys clinking at her waist."

Jowan and Bran had been busy since their return. Out around the estate, or at Wheal Trethewey, Trethewey Two, or the new mine site, or visiting the local gentlemen to catch up on all that had been happening in their absence. They had twice ridden over to the coast, where Jowan had shares in a couple of boats and owned a fish cellar, where the pilchard catch was processed.

They had been home for dinner every evening but had then retreated to the library to work for another hour or two. "We'll soon be over the hump of the work and coasting down the other side," Bran assured Evangeline, "and then I will show you the countryside."

He and Jowan had asked both ladies to stay in the house and garden unless one of them was available as an escort. Just until they knew that Guy had been, as Jowan put it, *defanged*. Tammie wanted to show Evangeline the places of her childhood, but she settled for those at Inneford House, for she certainly did not want to fall into Guy's hands again.

Bran was continuing his courtship of Evangeline with small presents and posies, frequent touches, and occasional ardent embraces when they thought themselves unobserved. Jowan had settled into a cheerful but slightly distant friendliness, though occasionally Tamsyn caught an expression in his eyes or a color in his aura that hinted at more passionate thoughts and that eased the empty ache she felt in her heart for the man she'd once loved and probably never had stopped loving.

One lovely discovery in the house was a new pianoforte in the music room. The old harpsichord on which Tammie had first composed music had also been restored, and both instruments were in tune.

How long had it been since she last wrote her own music? Or even heard fragments of melody or a beat that she would weave into the fabric of a piece?

In the early days with Guy, he had discouraged her from, as he put it, "wasting your time fiddling around with little tunes. No one wants to hear music written by a woman. You should be developing your voice, Tammie. Your great gift."

She had continued in private, unable to avoid documenting what she felt and experienced through the medium of music. At some point, under the dulling influence of the poppy and the oppression of the purely evil elf king, the music had died. But as they drove away from the abduction attempt at the inn east of Exeter, the hoof beats and wheel noise, the fear and the relief had begun to resonate in her mind, gelling into fragments of sound that, over the next few days, began to form a coherent piece.

Not a full symphony. Not yet. But one movement of a symphony. She sat at the piano and experimented with the motif and its variations. She was not too rusty. Fortunately, some people had been willing to pay for the Devon Songbird to sing while accompanying herself on the piano or another instrument, so Guy had been willing to allow her to spend time practicing.

She lost herself following where her fingers led her, not even distracted from the growing orchestration with the need to score what she was playing, what she was hearing. She only surfaced from the music when she heard herself vaguely thanking someone for placing a candelabra on the little side table she had been using to hold her paper, pen, and ink.

She blinked a couple of times and looked up. Jowan was smiling at her, and dusk filled the room.

"Good gracious, Jowan. It cannot be nightfall already!"

He did not bother to comment on something so obviously false, but nodded towards her stack of musical notations, now much easier to read thanks to the candles. She had not even realized she had been squinting in the poor light.

"You have been busy," Jowan said. "I know how you get when you are composing. I did not mean to disturb you, though I would have had to soon, for Evangeline says we cannot permit you to miss dinner."

Evangeline's professional opinion was reinforced by a loud and embarrassing gurgle from Tammie's middle. "It was time to disturb me. I have caught the spirit of it, I think. Now I need to shape it into something worthwhile."

"What I heard sounded wonderful," Jowan told her. He had always said that, but the opinion warmed her, anyway, as did what Evangeline said when Tammie saw her as they both went upstairs to dress for dinner.

"I heard what you were playing and thought it was beautiful. I told Jowan I didn't recognize it and he told me you were a composer. That was one of yours?"

"One I am writing," Tammie admitted. "It still needs a lot of work."

Evangeline stopped on the landing and touched Tammie's arm as if to check she was flesh and blood. "I am amazed," she said. "I suppose I always knew real people write the music I loved, but I never thought I would meet one."

"It is inspired by our escape from Coombe's men," Tammie explained. "At least, that is where it started." She could share her excitement with her friend, she realized. And then, it occurred to her that it had been so long since she had had a friend that she had forgotten the joy of celebrating her own achievements with them, and theirs in their turn.

"Evangeline, I haven't been able to write music in years. Coombe did not like my music and tried to prevent me, and somehow, I stopped hearing it. I feel as if I had lost both of my arms and today I discovered they were growing back and beginning to work again." On impulse, she hugged the other woman, and tears rose to her eyes when Evangeline hugged her back.

"I am so happy for you, and I wish I could kick that horrible man. To ignore such a talent! I thought he was supposed to be such an expert in music, but clearly, both of his ears must have been painted on if he did not like what you do."

Her indignation made Tammie laugh, even as the tears overflowed. "He said no one wanted to hear music written by women," she explained.

"Stupid, as well as horrid," said Evangeline, firmly. "Are those happy tears, Tammie? I hope so, for they should be. You have your music back."

"And I have a friend," Tammie noted. "If you are willing, that is."

"I am your friend," Evangeline assured her. "And will continue to be so, I hope."

⭆⭅

THAT NIGHT AT dinner, Evangeline and Bran raised the topic of their wedding. "I see no point in waiting," Bran commented. "We are both mature adults, and we have made up our minds."

Given the nighttime traffic Jowan had heard passing his bedchamber door, he was not surprised an early wedding was in the cards, but he was not as certain it was a good idea. Evangeline had a different concern.

She addressed it with Tamsyn. "I came to be a companion to Tammie. I do not wish to leave you in the lurch, Tammie. If you move to your mother's cottage, you will need another lady living with you to safeguard your reputation, and if you stay here, even more so, with a single gentleman in the house."

No way. Jowan shook his head. "I do not like the idea of Tammie alone in Apple Cottage, or even with servants and a lady companion. Not while Coombe is still at large. But if you two marry, you will be living here, will you not? A married woman in the house is all the protection Tammie needs."

"We talked about doing up the steward's cottage when I married," said Bran. "However, I don't see any reason why we cannot live here after our wedding until Coombe is dealt with or until Jowan is satisfied that Tammie is safe." At least Bran was making some kind of sense.

"I do not want you delaying the wedding on my account, Evangeline," Tammie insisted. "Nor do I wish to stand in the way of you and Bran having your own home. Jowan, I am sure there must be another lady who could be found to live with me. Perhaps we could advertise in the Plymouth papers if none of the local ladies is interested. As to Coombe, surely I will be safe in Apple Cottage? It is in the village, after all. And is there not a little stable with accommodation for a groom? If we looked for a strong and able man, he could also provide further security."

Jowan was trying to find the words to explain those plans could not work when Bran spoke.

"Both cottages need work," he commented. "We need to get the roof repaired or replaced, some plastering done, and a few other things fixed before either of them is livable."

Good man. Delay. That was the thing.

Jowan didn't want to be left alone at Inneford House. Bran and Evangeline could stay here permanently, as far as he was concerned. There was plenty of room. As for Tamsyn, he hoped to persuade her to stay permanently, too. As his wife. Too early to talk about that, yet, he supposed.

Bran, though, had other ideas. "What do you say, Evie, darling? Shall we arrange for the banns to be called and live here till the cottages are ready? And Jowan, we can arrange extra security for Tammie for as long as she needs it."

Bran seemed to think that was the final word. Jowan couldn't think of anything to say apart from, "I do not see any reason for any of you to move out. Inneford House has room for the three of you and more." And there would be more, the way Bran and Evangeline were going.

Bran smiled. "None of us will be moving straightaway, Jowan. Tammie, I don't suppose Jowan has had time to show you Apple Cottage yet." *The traitor.*

"Not yet," Tamsyn answered.

"We could walk down tomorrow afternoon," Jowan offered, surrendering to the inevitable. At least he would be able to point out all the problems that needed to be fixed.

"We can all go," Bran suggested. "We can inspect both the steward's cottage and Tammie's." And so, it was settled as things fell into place.

Chapter Sixteen

J OWAN AND BRAN had a morning of paperwork but finished everything essential by noon. Tammie and Evangeline arranged for the cook to fill a basket with foods that could be easily eaten under a tree somewhere, and the two men took it in turns to carry the basket.

They went to the steward's cottage first. It was in the grounds of Inneford House and on the banks of the river that gave the house its name, and right beside the bridge that had taken the place of the ford that used to give access to the village on the other bank. The walk from the main house took five minutes, and its upper floors could be seen through the trees.

Built, like most of the local houses, from granite with a slate roof, it had been part of the estate for two hundred years but had been empty for the past twenty, since Sir Carlyon decided to be his own steward. When Bran picked up the steward's role, he had continued living in the main house, so the only work done on the cottage had been essential maintenance to stop it from crumbling.

Evangeline and Tammie could both envision it as it could be, going from room to room, full of ideas about changes that could be made and furnishings that would bring the place to life.

"I suppose it is our part, while they talk about curtains and carpets, to notice the patched roof that needs to be completely replaced, the window frames with a touch of dry rot, and the floor boards and stair boards that need to be nailed down," Bran commented, dryly, to Jowan.

Evangeline heard. "Yes, that is not my area of expertise, Bran. But I do have some opinions about improvements to the kitchen and scullery. Also, once we've seen the attics, can you show me where the cottage gets its water?"

Tammie had some of the same questions when it came to her cottage. It had been lived in more recently and needed fewer urgent repairs, but neither had any money been spent to update either utilities such as coal ranges or furniture and decoration.

It was furnished with a chaotic mix of hand-me-down furniture, old and not-so-old, finely wrought and rough, in different styles, woods, and colors. Some of it, Tammie remembered from the housekeeper's rooms at Inneford. The paintings now missing from those rooms hung here, not so much adorning the walls as haunting them.

The apple orchard that had given the cottage its name had not had any pruning or feeding in years, and the whole garden was overgrown, though Tammie could see a few roses and other summer flowers splashing color here and there against the tangle of weeds and brambles.

It would take work. Still, Tammie thought she could be happy here. She could imagine herself on a winter's evening, with a roaring fire in the grate of the parlor, which was a decent size, so a piano in the corner should be far enough away from the heat not to dry out too rapidly.

Could she afford a piano? She needed to talk to Jowan about going to Plymouth to sell her jewelry. Quite apart from the piano and some gowns suitable for winter, she should be responsible for the repairs and upgrades on the cottage that she owned.

She would not raise it now. Looking at the cottages was making Jowan unhappy. Perhaps he was worrying about Tammie again, or perhaps he was not looking forward to Bran leaving him.

They walked back to Inneford House, Bran, and Evangeline absorbed in a conversation about the changes they'd like to make to the steward's cottage, which left Tammie to walk with Jowan. He was silent, and she was reluctant to disturb his mood. No. She had learned caution with Guy, but this was Jowan, and she trusted him not to lose his temper, even if he did not want to talk about what was bothering him.

Whatever they might be to one another now and in the future, they were friends, and friends looked out for one another.

"What is troubling you, Jowan?" she asked.

"Do you think they are wise?" he asked, nodding at the couple ahead of him. "They have known one another...what? For three weeks? Four? And they plan to be wed within another three. What do we know of Evangeline, after all?"

"That I owe her my life?" Tammie pointed out. "It has been an intense four weeks. Are you afraid for your brother? I do not think you need to be, but who can really know what another person is like? They are adults, Jowan, and will make their own decisions."

She hesitated to raise their own relationship but reminded herself again that this was Jowan, her friend. "I would wish to go more slowly. I *do* wish to go slowly. You have been giving me time, I think. Is that true?" She peered up at him, trying to see his reaction.

Jowan met her gaze, the heat she had sometimes detected burning in his eyes. "My wishes have not changed, if that is what you are asking. I am willing to wait until you trust me, Tamsyn. I still want forever with you, once you are ready."

"It is not that I do not trust you," Tamsyn corrected, "but I do not trust myself. I find that I hardly know myself, Jowan. Can you understand that?"

"I think you are calling me a hypocrite, Tammie. Wanting to rush into the romance that you and I were denied all those years ago and crying caution to Bran and Evangeline."

Tammie's heart leaped at the confirmation that Jowan still

wanted her, but she kept her voice level. "I think we each know our own motivations and can only guess at those of others. Our friends will marry, I think, whatever we think or say. And so, I will support them, and hope for the best."

"It was going to happen sooner rather than later," Jowan acknowledged. "Better now than in a rush to beat the stork. I wish everyone didn't feel the need to leave Inneford House, though."

"If it helps," Tammie said, "you have an open invitation to take your dinner at Apple Cottage."

It helped her. Even if she could find a suitable companion, she foresaw some lonely evenings.

Time for a change of topic. "I will need to convert my jewelry into money. Is there a suitable jeweler in Plymouth?"

"I would think so," Jowan said. He called out to Bran. "Bran, Tammie wants to go into Plymouth to see a jeweler, and you and I need to make a push at finding Mrs. Mayhew." To Tammie and Evangeline, he added, "we are trying to track down some papers that our father's London solicitor had. He died at about the same time as our father, and we recently found out his effects were sent to a cousin in Plymouth. We know she is a widow named Mayhew. But we don't have a current address."

"She might have married again and have another name, or she might have moved away from Plymouth, but I suppose we need to try," Bran commented.

"I would not mind visiting a fabric merchant," said Evangeline. "Mrs. Penrose says that the dressmaker in the village is quite good, but I will need to buy fabrics and notions if I am to have a new gown made up. I thought of going to Launceston, but I imagine Plymouth will have a better range of choices."

"Perhaps you should do both," Tammie declared. "You need a new gown to be married in. You also need several new gowns, in brighter colors than you currently wear. As Mrs. Hughes, wife of the steward and sister-in-law to Trethewey himself, you will need to look prosperous."

Evangeline started to chuckle, then looked at Bran for reassurance. "She is joking," she said.

Bran shrugged. "Dress however you like, Evie. You always look lovely."

"Jowan?" Evangeline asked.

"Tammie is not wrong," Jowan offered, cautiously. "Men are judged by the appearance of their ladies. If you look like a lady of the prosperous gentry, that will reflect well on Bran. And on me, too."

"Mostly by the women," Tammie clarified. "They are the ones doing the judging, I mean."

"Right. A new dress, then. I will if you will, Tammie."

Tammie nodded. "I will need a few new things. I will have to see how much the jewelry fetches. I want to buy a piano for the cottage."

"You can continue using mine," Jowan assured her. "Nobody else is doing so. I can have it moved to the cottage if you wish. After all, I did buy it with you in mind." He lowered his voice and leaned closer. "And if we do end up together once you've had the time to fully recover, we won't need two pianos."

⇶⟨⟨⟨

THE FOLLOWING MORNING, Jowan received three pieces of mail. There was a report from Wakefield and Wakefield and a letter from Drew Winderfield. The third letter proved to be a note from the mail receiving office in Launceston reporting that a letter from Plymouth awaited him and would need to be paid for.

"Shall we take the carriage and the ladies into Launceston, pick up the mail, and do some shopping?" Bran suggested when Jowan read out the note.

Jowan hesitated, but the report from Wakefield and Wakefield set his mind at ease. "Coombe has left London," he said. "He is believed to be heading for France. Wakefield says he has annoyed several powerful people, including the king, who was upset when certain dukes mentioned that Coombe has been terrorizing Miss Lind and had attempted to corrupt the second son of a powerful duke. His Majesty gave Coombe the cut direct and Coombe must have decided discretion was called for."

He handed the report to Tammie to read and opened the letter from Drew.

"Drew has much the same news." This letter he passed to Bran, thinking the details of the type of corruption that young Lord David Versey had confessed to his father was not a topic for a breakfast table or for two ladies.

"Let's get ready for a day's outing. One of the inns in Launceston has a sort of tearoom. We could have lunch there if you wish."

"You realize that Tammie experienced the kinds of practices that had Coombe kicked out of England," Bran pointed out to him as they waited by the carriage for the ladies.

Jowan shuddered. "Not something I want to dwell on too hard," he responded. "The things she has been through horrify me!" He braced himself for another attempt by his brother to persuade him that Tammie was the wrong wife for him.

"She is a strong woman," Bran commented. "The better I get to know her, the more impressed I am."

Jowan waited for the "but". After a moment's silence, he said, "That's it? You are not going to try to tell me not to rush into anything?"

Bran shrugged. "First, Tammie is doing a good enough job of that herself. Second..." He pointed to Jowan and then to himself. "Pot. Kettle."

Fair. "She says she needs time to find out who she is, whatever that means."

"It means she has been out of her mind for the past five years, is what it means. This must all be very strange for her. When you think about it, she was a child, and then she was Coombe's... whatever. She is an adult woman who has never been allowed to be an adult."

Bran was right. When Jowan looked at it like that, Tammie's insistence on living in her own cottage made sense. "I'd find it easier to let her go if I knew she would come back to me in the end," he admitted.

"She will," was Bran's unexpected answer. "Trust the connection between you, Jowan. It is obvious to everyone else. Which is another good reason for her to move to her own cottage, if she is not going to marry you straightaway. People around here are inclined to be proud of her stage career, but there are a few ready to say like mother, like daughter."

"Who?" Jowan asked, his fists already clenched in preparation.

"I've only been told by people who claim not to believe the stories and who won't say who is passing them around. You know how gossip is. Best not to take any notice of it except to make sure that nothing you do gives it credence."

The ladies exited the house, then, and their moment of privacy was over. Jowan supposed he was going to have to give in on the cottage. Coombe had been his last argument with any chance of success and the man was gone. At least until the king forgave him.

Jowan smiled at Tammie as he handed her up into the carriage. He could wait until she was ready. He had waited seven years, and a few more months would not hurt him. Or, at least, not hurt him mortally.

THEY SPLIT UP in Launceston, Tammie, and Evangeline heading for the drapery and the men to collect the mail and to run a few errands that took them to, among other places, the saddlery, the wheelwright, and the blacksmith.

When Jowan and Bran met the ladies for lunch, they were

able to report they had several large packages to be collected but were finished with their shopping.

"We have, too," Jowan said. "We managed to get most of the items on our list. The letter was a surprise. It was addressed to my father and signed *Patricia Mayhew*."

"The solicitor's cousin," Tammie exclaimed. "The one you were going to hunt for in Plymouth."

Jowan nodded, looking delighted at this turn of events. "As it happens, she has not changed her name," he said, "so we probably would have been able to find her. It is good to be saved the hunt, though." The news got better.

"She asks if my father wants papers with his name and address that have been discovered in records kept by Timothy Trantor, Solicitor, of London."

Tammie exclaimed, "How fortunate. You do, of course. Oh, Jowan. I hope that those papers will help you recover your money!"

"I do, too," Jowan said, fervently. "She said she wrote twice when the records were first sent to her after her cousin died, but received no reply. That must have been while Bran and I were still away at Oxford and my father was making a muck of things."

Bran took up the tale. "Mrs. Mayhew is moving and cannot keep anything that remains of her cousin's files. So, she thought she would make one more attempt. Jowan is going to let her know we are visiting Plymouth in a week and will call on her in Plymouth to retrieve the papers."

Chapter Seventeen

T HEY ARRIVED IN Plymouth in the middle of the afternoon and checked into the inn. The rooms they had reserved by letter were spacious and comfortable and included a private parlor where they could take their meals.

After refreshing themselves with a cup of tea and a wash, they sallied forth to tick off the first item on their list—a visit to the jeweler who Jowan thought would be the best to appraise Tammie's jewelry. "You will come with me, will you not, Jowan?" Tammie asked. "I trust you to help me decide whether to accept the man's offer."

Bran and Evangeline declared their wish to join the expedition. "We are going to choose Evie's wedding ring," Bran explained.

The shop was larger inside than it appeared from the street and looked prosperous—all polished wood and plush furnishings, with the hushed air of a temple. The jeweler's appearance and demeanor were reassuring. He was a man in his middle years and of average height and build, but he had kind eyes and a warm smile.

Tammie's cynical side, the one fed by years of exposure to Guy and his cohorts, suggested that such an impression would be helpful in cheating his customers. When he heard what they wanted, he introduced Bran and Evangeline to his assistant, who took the couple to another counter.

He asked Tammie to show him the jewelry she wanted to sell, and she emptied the contents of her cloth bag onto the counter. He examined the items, one set at a time.

They were items that had been gifted to her by Guy, by other lovers, by theatre managers for particularly memorable successes in ticket sales, and even by theatre followers who hoped for a closer relationship. They were part of the history she would prefer to forget, or at least move past.

The jeweler was putting them into three piles, and once he finished, he explained why.

Of the first pile, he said. "These are not particularly valuable pieces. The workmanship is not outstanding, and the items themselves have little intrinsic value, being of inferior materials."

The second pile, he said, was, "aesthetically pleasing and well made, though unlikely to command the highest of prices because the jewels are paste." Both piles, he thought, could appeal to some buyers. He would take them on commission and sell them.

That left the third and smallest pile—a diamond and pearl necklace, a ruby and diamond parure, several lesser necklaces, bracelets, and rings, a tiara, and a handful of jeweled hair ornaments. The value he placed on each had Tammie's eyes popping. Over one hundred pounds for the diamond and pearl, nearly as much again for the parure, and five pounds apiece for the pins.

"That, you understand, are the values you would insure them for, Miss Roskilly. If you wish to sell them on commission, I shall set the price at that level, but take thirty percent of the sale price as my fee. If you wish to sell them immediately, I hope you shall give me the right of refusal. My price will be the stated value less twenty percent."

They left the shop with the jeweler's promissory note for three hundred pounds and another eighty pounds in bank notes—more than sufficient to cover the cost of fabric for new gowns and to make a start on the repairs and alterations at the cottage. And Bran and Evangeline had chosen and purchased a wedding ring.

Very pleased with the outcome of the errand, they walked together back to the inn, Evangeline on Bran's arm and Tammie and Jowan a few paces behind the other couple. Suddenly, Tammie felt sure that someone was watching her. She wanted to discount it as her feelings and emotions had been unpredictably divorced from reality in recent years. Rather, she thought, make that in the past seven years, ever since Guy pretended to befriend her and then took her away from everything and everyone she knew.

She looked around, and no one was there. Of course. But the feeling persisted. Wait, wasn't that Guy's valet Marco, just twenty paces away on the other side of the street? He appeared out of nowhere as if the thought of Guy had conjured him up. *No.* He must have stepped out of a building, for when he saw her watching him, he stepped backward and disappeared again.

Her heart began to pound, and she wanted to run away, as fast and far as she could. But she forced herself to remain calm, or at least appear so. "Marco is here. Guy's valet," she told Jowan.

Jowan stopped, his arm tensing under her hand. "Where?"

"Just up ahead. I saw him, but just for a moment, then he moved backward. Into a building, I think. No, look!" They had walked another dozen paces, and Tammie was now close enough to see a narrow alleyway opening into the street just where Marco had been standing.

"He must have used that alley to get away," she said.

Jowan and Bran exchanged glances. "You escort the ladies to the inn," Jowan told his brother. "I'll see where this goes."

But when he joined them at the inn fifteen minutes later, he'd seen no trace of Marco, Guy, or anyone associated with them.

THEY HAD BEEN planning to split up on the second day—Bran and Jowan to meet with Mrs. Mayhew and Tamsyn and Evangeline to shop for fabrics. Jowan decided they should keep together. "If there's a possibility that Coombe is about and knows Tammie is here, I do not want you two ladies to be facing him on your own."

Evangeline was inclined to scoff, but Tamsyn shuddered and agreed. "He is unpredictable, Evangeline, and no one has ever said 'no' to him and made it stick. He thinks he is above the law… or if not that, precisely, that the law is only relevant to other people."

Bran agreed they should stick together, and Evangeline declared herself outvoted, so they all arrived at the address Mrs. Mayhew had given them. The house showed clear signs of the proposed move—light shapes on the darker walls that indicated where paintings had recently been removed, an empty tea chest in the parlor to which the maid showed them, and a flour bag alongside filled with wood shavings ready to protect whatever fragile objects were to be stowed in the chest.

The lady, when she arrived, proved to be a vigorous little woman in her middle years. She was removing a voluminous apron as she entered the room. "Sir Jowan Trethewey?" she asked, addressing her question to the space between Jowan and Bran.

"I am Trethewey," Jowan told her. "And I assume you are Mrs. Mayhew. May I make known to you Miss Roskilly and Mrs. Parkerdale? Also, my brother and steward, Branoc Hughes. Bran and I escorted the ladies to Plymouth for shopping. I hope you do not mind us all descending on you like this. We have a number of errands today and thought it better to stay together."

Mrs. Mayhew nodded politely to the others. "You will be wanting the papers regarding the work my cousin handled for your father," she said to Jowan. "I have them here."

She indicated a stack tied with string, sitting on a table in the window embrasure. "If you do not mind, I would like you to check them to make sure that they are as you expect. My cousin's files were in disarray when they reached me. He had apparently been ill for some time, and his filing had suffered. Also, whoever packed up his files took no care regarding what went where. While I have done my best to sort everything in order, there may still be elements missing. I have two boxes of papers for which I have not been able to discover logical places."

Jowan thanked her, and he and Bran took a seat at the table and began looking through what was there. Jowan was not sure he'd be able to recognize whether something was missing, since he did not know what to expect, but all that he and Bran could do was their best.

As he and Bran went through the papers, he heard Mrs. Mayhew offer Tamsyn and Evangeline refreshments, and lead them from the room. A short while later, a maid brought a cup of tea and a slice of lardy cake, and put them by his elbow, and he glanced up to see that Bran had been given the same.

He gave the maid a smile and his thanks and turned back to what he was reading. It was soon clear that the relationship between Trantor and Sir Carlyon lasted for more than a decade before the two men died within a couple of months of one another.

Sir Carlyon had started with a few small investments in cargoes and had reinvested his earnings and principal. Jowan began sorting the pile by investment and date. Bran pulled out a notepad and a graphite pencil and began calculating the investments and returns.

"We have the information we need to assert ownership of each stock," Jowan concluded after a while. "I'd venture to suggest some correspondence might be filed elsewhere or might have gone missing altogether."

"If we can recover the sums owed, you'll be a rich man," Bran responded, turning the pad around to show Jowan the total he had underlined and then circled.

"Three thousand, five hundred, and twenty-one pounds,"

Jowan read, awed.

"Don't forget the three shillings and nine pence," Bran commented. "Mind you, I don't swear to any of those. If the money has been reinvested, or even just put in a bank on deposit, there could be more. And, of course, some or all of it might have disappeared since the baronet lost track of it."

It might have been true, but Wakefield had reported that Trantor had a reputation as a trustworthy solicitor, at least until he fell ill. So, there was at least a chance that some or all the money was waiting for them somewhere. Waiting for the Trethewey estate, which meant Jowan. But he would at least be able to give his steward an increase in salary.

"Three thousand, five hundred pounds," he repeated slowly. Trethewey 1 and 2 combined gave him one hundred and fifty pounds a year. Wheal St Tetha was expected to do better, but only after it ate money for the first year or two. All the tenancies on the estate together didn't gross more than three hundred pounds, and he had to take repairs out of that.

The first step would be to track down what had happened to the stocks and shares. "How do you and Evangeline feel about taking a honeymoon in London?" he asked Bran.

⇢⇢⇢✳⇠⇠⇠

THE LADIES HAD spent the hour helping Mrs. Mayhew. She was in a difficult situation. The house that she had shared with her husband had been left to her husband's son by an earlier marriage. The son was an officer with the East India Company and had been happy for his stepmother to remain in the property while he was in the Far East, but he had resigned his commission and was on his way home.

"It is natural for Nigel to want the house for his wife and children," Mrs. Mayhew explained. "It is certainly not large enough for an unwanted dependent. Not that Mr. Mayhew left me penniless. My widow's portion will afford me an adequate income, particularly if I can find an inexpensive cottage to rent. I have been saving, too, so all shall be well, I am certain."

The worry in her eyes told another story, and when Evangeline asked when she had to be out of the house, Mrs. Mayhew admitted that it could be as soon as two weeks, depending on when her stepson's ship docked. "If I have not found a place to stay, I will put my boxes into storage and rent a room somewhere."

An idea popped into Tammie's mind, but it would be rash to say anything. After all, she did not know the lady. Certainly not well enough to propose living together. On the other hand, Mrs. Mayhew seemed pleasant enough. She had a clean bright aura in which greens and pinks predominated, which meant she was probably nurturing and kind. She had shown herself to be honest in contacting Jowan about her cousin's files. She had nice manners and her servants appeared to treat her with respect and affection.

Tammie was going to need a respectable woman to live with her in her mother's cottage. A respectable lady, furthermore. A companion, not a servant. She had asked in the village. No one could think of someone suitable who wanted the work.

Perhaps asking Mrs. Mayhew was not so outrageous after all.

By the time Jowan and Bran were finished, the ladies had packed two tea chests with china, carefully wrapping each item in paper and nesting it in wood shavings. And Tammie had made up her mind to discuss her idea with her friends.

They may have good reasons why having Mrs. Mayhew as her companion would not be appropriate. Or they might agree with her own assessment. Either way, she now had friends she could trust, and talking to them would help her make up her own mind.

Accordingly, when they had said their farewells to the lady and were waiting for a hackney, she introduced the topic.

"I am considering making Mrs. Mayhew an offer," she said.

"She needs a place to live, and I need a respectable lady to live with me."

Evangeline thought it an excellent idea. Bran and Jowan were more cautious but acknowledged they had not spent much time with the lady. "Why not offer to have her on a trial basis for two months?" Evangeline suggested. "She can use that time to search elsewhere if she finds the situation not to her liking."

"How much will you tell her about you?" Bran wanted to know.

"Branoc Hughes, Tammie does not need to put all of her linen out on display," Evangeline scolded. "Mrs. Mayhew needs only to know that Tammie has inherited her mother's cottage and needs a companion so that she can live there after you and I are married and have moved into our own house."

Tammie was not so certain. For one thing, the village gossips would certainly fill Mrs. Mayhew's ears with their interpretation of Tammie's history. For another, it would be unfair not to let anyone who lived with Tammie know about the possible danger from Guy and his minions. And then there was the point that Tammie did not drink nor use laudanum, which was unusual enough to require an explanation.

"If she is to live with me, she needs to have a picture of my history in at least broad brush strokes," Tammie decided. "If, after that, she decides she does not want to take up my offer, then so be it. I certainly do not want to live in close quarters with a companion I must deceive to have her respect."

A hackney approached, and running alongside was the boy they had sent to fetch it. Bran assisted Tammie and Evangeline aboard while Jowan paid the boy for the errand and gave the address of their inn to the coachman.

It was a drive of only a few minutes. Tammie was soon walking into the inn with Bran and Evangeline arm-in-arm behind her while Jowan settled with the hackney driver. She came to a stop two paces into the entrance foyer.

The Earl of Coombe turned from his conversation with the

innkeeper and strode towards her. "Tammie. That fool denied you were here," he said. "I have come for you." Tammie stared at him. Had he changed drastically in the few weeks she had been gone, or was it just that distance—and sobriety—meant she was seeing him as he was? Surely those wrinkles were not new? Nor the jowls under his chin, and all the other signs of dissipation and age?

His aura was duller than ever. It was as if smog or mud obscured the light.

"Well, Tammie?" he demanded. "Send for your bags and come along."

It was the harsh tone that presaged punishment, and Tammie quailed. But Evangeline stepped up beside her and took her hand. On her other side, Bran stood so close his arm touched her shoulder.

Tammie took strength from their presence and from the knowledge that Jowan was only moments from joining them. "I am not coming with you, Guy."

"Now, now, Tammie. You have had your little rebellion. But you have caused me trouble enough. Get your things or leave without them. I do not care, but we will leave together."

"No," Tammie said, the habit of obedience so ingrained in her that the single word was all she could manage.

"The lady has refused you, Lord Coombe," said Jowan's voice, calm and strong. "She wishes nothing further to do with you."

"Impudent puppy," Guy scoffed. "Let her look me in the eyes and say that."

Tammie summoned all her determination and stood straight and firm. She met Guy's eyes with her own. His were bloodshot. "I wish to have nothing to do with you, Lord Coombe."

For a moment, indecision and surprise showed on his face, but he rallied, taking a step closer and putting out a hand. With his most charming smile on his face, he said, "If Daphne Tempest bothers you, she need not. She cannot replace you, Tammie. You will always be my princess."

The name he had given her, said in that wheedling tone of voice, suddenly disgusted her. "My name is not Tammie. Tammie Lind is no more. Leave me alone, Lord Coombe. Tammie Lind is gone. She is free of you and all your manipulations and deceits."

As she was speaking, Jowan changed places with Bran and took her hand to place it on his arm. Guy reddened, either at Jowan's action or what Tammie—no, Tamsyn—had said. "You don't belong in some lowly pigpen with this gape seed, this country bumpkin," Guy insisted. "You deserve to be courted, admired. To dazzle with your voice and your beauty. You know what I can give you, Tammie."

"Goodbye, Lord Coombe," Tamsyn replied. "Sir Jowan, I wish to retire to our suite."

Jowan nodded and began to lead her to the stairs, making a wide circuit around Guy.

"You don't want her, Trethewey," Guy jeered. "Or you will not, once you know what she is. A whore. *My* whore, who has spread her legs for anyone I chose." Jowan's stride hitched and his arm under Tamsyn's stiffened. "You speak of Tammie Lind, the celebrated singer. You subjected her to opium and worse. You abused her. And now you have lost her. I am not surprised you cannot show your face in London and have been repudiated by the king."

"Tammie, I can give you whatever drugs you want," Coombe pleaded.

Tamsyn refused to look at him. Jowan snarled, and—to Tamsyn's surprise—Coombe quailed.

"Sir Jowan?" said the innkeeper, stepping between them and the stairs. "I do not want any trouble." He waved a hand at Tamsyn. "If this—ah—person is—er..." He trailed off as he took in Jowan's expression.

Bran took a hand. "Innkeeper, the Earl of Coombe has been driven out of London in disgrace for attempting to debauch and disgrace young men. I would not take his word for directions to a privy. I suggest you move out of our way and let us return to our rooms. Or do you wish us to take our custom elsewhere?"

The innkeeper stepped aside, and Jowan and Tamsyn led the way upstairs.

Chapter Eighteen

JOWAN COULDN'T BELIEVE that Coombe had just given up, even after they discovered the inn he had been using and were told that he had paid his bill and left.

Jowan and Bran hired a cadre of off-duty sailors to escort them and the ladies whenever they went out, and perhaps that was enough to deter the villain. However, they saw no more of him in their remaining days in Plymouth.

When they left, it was with a cart to carry their purchases and Patricia Mayhew's possessions, for she had accepted the position of Tamsyn's companion.

They were back in St Tetha on a Friday, and on Sunday, they were all present in church for the second reading of banns for Bran and Evangeline. They lingered in the church yard after the service to accept congratulations and to introduce Patricia to their neighbors. Word of her arrival had, of course, already spread, and the forthcoming wedding had to vie for first place in conversations with what was being done to the cottages to prepare one for the newlyweds and the other for Tamsyn and Patricia.

Not that either would be ready in time for the wedding. The reroofing would start this week, as would some of the other major repairs and alterations, but neither place would be habitable for at least two months. Jowan was glad of it.

"I am in no hurry to see you go," he told his friends.

"We are not going far," Bran pointed out, which was true, but a separate house a few minutes' walk away was not the same as being under the same roof.

On the other hand, Jowan had to admit that living with Tamsyn, given the way he felt about her, was playing havoc with his emotions and his sleep. His brother had been right to warn him that the Tamsyn of today was very different, in many ways, to the Tamsyn of seven years ago. But this had only given Jowan the opportunity to fall in love with her all over again.

Her strength of character and of purpose, her courage, and her determination, all attracted him as much as the quiet sense of humor, the curiosity about the world at large, and the kindness that remained of the girl he once knew.

As for attraction, he had been almost ashamed of how drawn he was to her when she was little more than skin and bone. Now that her curves were returning, along with color in her complexion and a sparkle in her eye, he was uncomfortably aware of her whenever she was near—a discomfort that was only alleviated during dreams in which she was finally his.

He had promised to respect the time she needed to come to terms with the woman she now was, but it was a daily, and sometimes an hourly, challenge not to show her how much he wanted her. Even with Evangeline and Patricia living in the house with them, he was afraid that temptation would overcome him. The last thing Jowan wanted to do was to emulate Coombe by putting pressure on her. He had seen how much she hated and despised the fiend, even as she feared him. But every time he saw Bran tug Evangeline into a sheltered corner for a kiss and a cuddle, his frustration with his own situation threatened to overwhelm him.

It was just as well that the wedding was fast approaching, and that the newlyweds had agreed to his proposal to take their wedding trip to London, where Bran would attempt to track down the investments for which they now had documentation.

Four days before the wedding, a letter from Coombe's solicitor gave the couple another task in London.

THE LETTER WAS delivered just before breakfast. Addressed to Miss Tamsyn Roskilly, it was waiting for her when she came to the table. She opened it and gasped.

"What is it, Tamsyn?" Patricia asked.

"A letter from a solicitor. The Earl of Coombe is suing me for breach of contract." Her eyes continued to move to and fro across the paper. "He claims that I was under contract to sing where and when he instructed me and that I have lost him…" she turned to the next page and peered at the writing. "An absurd amount of money by running away." She turned to Jowan, indignation and alarm battling for dominance. "This cannot be legal."

"No," Jowan agreed. "Of course, it is not."

Bran stretched out his hand. "May I see?"

Tamsyn handed him the letter.

"Do you remember signing any such agreement?" Evangeline asked, but Tamsyn shook her head.

"Not ever. My mother might have done so. Or Sir Carlyon."

"Those would not count now," Bran said, his voice distant as he perused the pages. "You are now an adult, and any contract signed by your legal guardian on your behalf would have ceased to have effect when you turned twenty-one." He looked up. "You should look, though, to see if you can find something in your mother's belongings."

Tamsyn had been told the Inneford servants had packed Mrs. Roskilly's belongings into trunks when they cleaned up the cottage after she died. The trunks were currently in the Inneford attics.

"I'll do that," Tamsyn agreed. "He can't make me pay all of that, can he? I do not have anything except what my mother left me and the money from the sale of the jewelry."

Bran was cautious. "It depends on whether he can produce an actual contract that was signed by you after you came of legal age."

"But if you do not remember signing one…" Patricia said.

Evangeline shook her head and Tamsyn admitted, "I do not remember a great deal that happened in the past five years."

"What would be the benefits to Tamsyn of such a contract?" Jowan asked. "And where are they? If his contract with Tamsyn's mother gave Mrs. Roskilly a lump sum or a share of Tamsyn's earnings, what has happened to them? And the same with any more recent contract. How much did a performance earn you, Tamsyn? Roughly?"

Tamsyn frowned, bewildered by the question. "I have never been told," she said, amazed she had never considered the matter. "I have never seen any accounting… Guy…" *No. Not Guy.* He did not deserve that level of intimacy from her even if he never knew that she had taken to calling him by his title. "Coombe, I should say, told me my performances helped to pay for the costs of my keep. But that cannot be the entire truth, can it? Other star performers live off their earnings without the need for a patron. I have no idea what Guy charged for my performances, but I have been hired out to entertain audiences no fewer than four or five times a week for the past seven years, often more when I am also engaged for a theatre season. I should have savings, should I not?"

Her friends all nodded, and Jowan commented, "I wonder if Wakefield might have a way to investigate how much Coombe has stolen from you."

"You should counter-sue him for stealing your earnings," Patricia suggested.

Jowan's expression of fury slowly changed to a broad smile. "What an excellent response to his suit against you," he said.

"I'm not a lawyer," Bran said, "but I would warrant that his failure to give you any earnings due under a contract, if there is such a contract, is a full defense to any claim that you are in breach for leaving."

"You need a solicitor," Jowan declared. "Do you want to make an appointment with the man we've been using in Launceston? He will at least be able to advise us on what steps you should take next."

"This," Bran waved the letter, "was filed in a London courtroom. Our man will probably refer you to someone in London. You should go and see him today, Tamsyn."

"The wedding is in a few days, and we have a great deal to do," Tamsyn objected.

But Evangeline declared that sorting out Coombe was more important than folding table napkins, which was part of Tamsyn's list for the day. "In fact, Patricia and I will come upstairs with you now, if you like, and help you go through your mother's things. Then you can take it to show the solicitor. Jowan, send a groom to Launceston to make an appointment for this afternoon."

IT TOOK THEM less time than expected. Whoever had been in charge of the packing had written an inventory and placed it at the top of each chest, so once Bran had pried out the nails, they soon found the one with "Asst'd Papers" marked on it.

They carefully unpacked the chest to remove the top three layers and then divided the papers that filled the rest of the chest into three piles, each taking a pile to search through.

The listings on the inventories included linens, china, and other things that would be useful once Tamsyn moved into the cottage. She also noted several items that brought back childhood memories. "Blue and White Cow Mug." She had loved that mug when she was a little girl. "Silver T-Pot." It had been her mother's pride and joy, and Tamsyn had felt so proud when she was first trusted with polishing it.

She made a mental note to ask for the chests to be moved to

the cottage when the repairs were completed. No doubt everything would need to be cleaned, and some items would need to be mended, but she and Patricia had been given a fine start to their housekeeping.

Not that she wanted to leave Inneford House and Jowan, but it was necessary. She had seen how he looked at her when he did not think anyone was watching. His desire for her was great, but not, she was certain, as great as hers for him.

One night, when everyone was asleep, her longing for him would become too strong. She was certain Jowan would welcome her to his bed, just as she was equally sure he would regret it afterward, and blame himself for treating her with disrespect.

As if a person with her history deserved respect! And yet, Jowan had never made her feel he despised her for her dissipation and debauchery. Bran had, at first, though he had since become a friend. So had Evangeline, who had, after all, seen her at her worst. But never Jowan. She would have loved him for that alone.

"Here they are," said Patricia. She handed Tamsyn a sheaf of papers tied with string.

The outside label said, "Tamsyn's contracts."

It was easy enough to untie the string. The plural was appropriate. The package contained three contracts—the original, signed when Tamsyn was sixteen, a second when she was eighteen, and a third shortly after her twentieth birthday.

"This says that Coombe would keep fifty percent of my earnings for my keep, clothing, music lessons, and his services as my manager, and the other fifty percent would be sent to my mother," she said to her friends. "So, what happened to that money?"

Evangeline waved her hand to the rest of the papers. "Perhaps there is something else in these."

Tamsyn nodded. "I had better take everything down with me and go through them all, in case there is something else that helps."

"We'll just repack the chest," Patricia said and began picking up the wrapped items they had removed. With all three of them working, they soon had the floor cleared again. They each carried a stack of papers downstairs to the library. Tamsyn set herself up on the big library table, and the other two left her to it.

By the time Jowan came to call her to lunch and to tell her that they had an appointment in Launceston at three that afternoon, she had found a pass book for a Plymouth savings bank with quarterly payments that must be the earnings mentioned in the contracts and a staggering balance.

She also had two letters from Coombe's solicitors concerning the contracts they had already found, and half a dozen letters from Coombe to her mother reporting on Tamsyn's success and advising against making any contact with Tamsyn.

Those were all she had found concerning Coombe, but she wanted more time to consider other parts of her mother's life, as disclosed in the papers she had kept. For example, a handful of letters from her father to her mother, all dating to the early years of their marriage.

"My father was a sailor in the navy," Tamsyn told Jowan. "I never knew. Mother would not speak of him." The last letter had been written when Tamsyn was three and sent from somewhere called Bangalore. Tied in with the same bundle was a letter from Samuel Roskilly's captain, sending his condolences on Roskilly's untimely death of yellow fever.

Over lunch, she told Jowan and Bran about the contracts and the passbook.

"That bank has an agency in Launceston," Bran told her.

"Bring the passbook, Tamsyn. We'll have to show your mother's death certificate and evidence you are her sole heir, but I know where those papers are. They might have to send to Plymouth to find out what has become of the account, but we can at least set matters rolling."

At dinner that night, they were able to report on a successful day. "The solicitor is going to draw up a suit against Coombe for loss of earnings, using the sums in the passbook as a basis for the amount," Tamsyn reported. "He will write a response to Coombe's breach of contract claim, saying that I am not aware of any such contract, and asking for a copy."

"Hopefully, that will settle things with that horrible man," Evangeline said.

Tamsyn doubted that it would. Coombe was used to having his own way and would assume any court case was certain to go his way.

"What about the bank?" Bran asked. "Is the account still in existence?"

"It is," Tamsyn confirmed. "The surprise is that it is in my name! I just had to prove I was who I said I was, and since they knew Jowan and he vouched for me, there was no problem. They are sending the passbook to Plymouth to have it updated, but as far as they know, no withdrawals have ever been made from the account."

If that proved to be true, Tamsyn was surprisingly well off. She really did not want to dwell on how much money she might have in case it all proved to be a chimera.

"In any case, I have done what I can," she said, "and lost a day in doing so. Now I am available again to help with the wedding. Evangeline, what are the plans for tomorrow?"

✦

Chapter Nineteen

BRAN MADE A splendid groom. Jowan could not help but wish it was him, and that the bride was Tamsyn, but he kept his feelings to himself and devoted himself to making certain his brother was dressed appropriately and at the church ahead of time. Bran, usually the more level-headed of the two of them, was so busy imagining everything that might prevent the wedding from going ahead that he kept losing track of what he was meant to be doing.

They had spent the night in the village inn since all three women insisted it would be bad luck for Bran to see the bride on the day of the wedding, and Bran had been conjuring possible disasters since Jowan woke in the early hours of the morning to find his brother pacing the floor.

"No, Evangeline is not going to have second thoughts," Jowan said. He'd been saying that in one version or another most of the day. And that the weather had been fine for a week so the vicar who was coming to officiate at the wedding would not be prevented from fording any of the three waterways—more brooks than rivers—between the rectory and St Tetha. In the unlikely event that one or more of the bridges that had stood for a century or more chose today to fail.

Apparently, Bran was going to be marginally insane until he

had his ring on Evangeline's finger, for a runaway bride and flooded rivers were only the least unlikely of the disasters he had conjured.

Still, it would not be long now. From his post at the door between the vestry and the nave, Jowan was able to report that the church was filled almost to bursting with their friends and their neighbors, and more people were gathered outside—the estate's tenants, miners from the family's mines, and others, less closely connected to Bran and Jowan.

Patricia came down the aisle. The bride must be close behind. Patricia and Tamsyn were planning to stay with her until Lord Trentwood, who was going to give the bride away, arrived to escort Evangeline. Jowan nudged Bran and the pair of them left the vestry by the outside door to hurry to the lych gate leading into the churchyard.

They were in time for Bran to hand his bride down from the Trentwood carriage. The happy couple would walk up the aisle together, with Lord Trentwood proudly following them and the two official witnesses, Jowan and Tamsyn, walking behind him.

All of Bran's worries must have evaporated. He helped Evangeline from the carriage with his heart in his eyes and a broad grin on his face, and she looked as besotted as he did.

The bride and groom were leading the way into the church. Jowan offered Tamsyn his elbow, and they set off after Lord Trentwood. "Isn't Evangeline a picture?" Tamsyn whispered.

Jowan nodded, and it was true. Perhaps it was her happiness that took her from passably pretty to beautiful, or perhaps it was her gown or something the other ladies had done with her hair or her bonnet.

Despite Bran's fears, nothing happened to spoil the ceremony or, indeed, the day. From the bride's arrival at the church to waving the happy couple off from Inneford House after a delicious wedding breakfast, the day was perfect.

Once they were gone, the part of the day Jowan had dreaded most arrived. Tamsyn and Patricia had accepted an invitation from Lady Trentwood to stay until Evangeline and Bran returned or until their cottage was ready, whichever came first.

Jowan had argued that Patricia, as a widow of mature years, was chaperone enough for Tamsyn to stay, and Tamsyn might have been convinced, but Lady Trentwood overruled Jowan. "People will talk, Trethewey. People are already talking, but we shall at least stop their mouths over this matter. Also, I do not doubt that my support shall be of value in squelching the gossip. Miss Roskilly is accepted at the highest levels of London Society, or so I am informed. I am determined that those narrow-minded people in St Tetha who regard theatre people with such disdain shall be forced to think again when it comes to our Cornish Lark."

So, the day ended with Jowan alone in Inneford House. Alone, that is, apart from the servants, who were having a celebration of their own in the servant's hall and would not welcome their master putting a damper on their company by joining them. He sat in the library with a glass of brandy and did his best to brood, but scenes from the day kept interfering with his determination to be morose.

Bran and Evangeline when they first saw one another outside the church. Evangeline's face as she said her vows. The pride on Bran's face when the rector presented him and his wife to the congregation. The song Tamsyn sang so beautifully during the signing of the register, not skipping a beat when it was her turn to sign as witness. Evangeline's swollen lips, disarranged bonnet, and bright color when the newlyweds' carriage arrived at Inneford House.

So many special moments. Jowan wanted them for his own. His and Tamsyn's. He had promised to give her time to know herself, but he had not promised not to court her, had he? Would that be a breach of the agreement? He wasn't sure, but he intended to find out. Tonight, he would stop feeling sorry for himself and go to bed, and tomorrow, he would pick Tamsyn a posy of flowers and make a formal afternoon call when Lady

Trentwood was accepting visitors.

JOWAN WAS COURTING Tamsyn. He took her a posy of flowers the day after Bran's wedding. That first posy was followed by dozens of others—every morning, rain or shine, picking the day's flowers was his first task, and if his work commitments meant he was unable to pay a call to deliver them, he would send them with a groom and a note.

He begged leave to escort Tamsyn and Patricia to church on Sunday and it became a regular practice. He invited her to walk with him on the village green and to visit the inn's private parlor for tea and cake, meeting Patricia there for propriety's sake.

He bought her little gifts—a pair of gloves, a china dish for trinkets, a box of fudge in fancy wrappers. Tamsyn protested that he would set the gossips quacking, but he said they could quack away, for he had nothing that they could turn into anything but the truth—Sir Jowan Trethewey was courting the Roskilly girl. The one who had gone away to be a singer and had become famous.

And rich, at least by local standards. That had come as a shock. The bank in Plymouth had written asking her to present herself with evidence of her identity since someone else had recently claimed the account in her name.

Jowan went with her when she met the bank manager. "The Earl of Coombe claimed he was your guardian, Miss Roskilly," the man told her. "He was able to show us a contract with your mother, but he was not able to produce any evidence that he was executor or trustee of the account, and it was evident from the date on the contract that it was no longer valid. Without any authority from you to release the money to him, we refused."

"You were right to do so," Tamsyn told the man. "The Earl of Coombe was my manager but is no longer. He certainly has no right to my money, and if you had given it to him, you may be certain that I would not have seen a penny of it."

Jowan took her and Patricia out to lunch to celebrate the successful claiming of the account. "At least we know why Coombe was in Plymouth," he said. "He probably thought you were in Plymouth on the same errand and left before we had him arrested for attempted theft."

"Quite possibly," Tamsyn said. "It is certainly a large enough sum to tempt him. I cannot believe Mother never touched a penny. With the interest, the amount is… If I never work another day in my life, I will be able to live quite comfortably."

It was not what London people would call a fortune and thank goodness for that. When he asked her to marry him, Jowan didn't want her to think it was for her fortune. Nor, for that matter, did he want her to agree to marry him because of his.

The investments his father had made had multiplied in the years since he and his agent died. Most proceeds had been tucked into a bank account where they accrued a tidy amount of interest. One of the groups who had invested in a cargo, unable to find the missing solicitor and give him the profits owed to Jowan's father, had reinvested on the unknown investor's behalf, and they had been lucky. That particular investment had more than doubled in four years.

Jowan and Bran decided to leave it in the group, but from now on they would track the earnings.

⟫⟫⟫⟪⟪⟪

LADY TRENTWOOD AND Patricia smiled on Jowan's courtship, even if he was not yet certain Tamsyn did. They made excuses to leave the pair of them together—suggesting a walk in the garden or suddenly remembering an errand on the other side of the house that would require them both.

He and Tamsyn were not left alone for long, and never with a shut door between them and the household, but it was a sign of favor to his intentions. "They think you are courting me," Tamsyn said, a few days after their return from Plymouth. Lady Trentwood and Patricia had just declared an urgent need to visit the kitchens for a recipe supposedly promised to his cook.

What was Jowan supposed to say in answer to Tamsyn's comment? "I hope you think so, too," he offered. "I am not trying hard enough if you haven't noticed."

Tamsyn blushed. "I was not certain," she said. "I have never been courted before."

The artless comment had him flabbergasted. Certainly, what she'd said during her delirium had left him in no doubt that she had had many lovers.

"I have had stage-door followers, of course," she admitted. "But it is all pretend with them. For a start, they woo an illusion, not a real human being. Also, most of it is showing off for other men rather than aimed at the female they claim to wish to impress." Her blush deepened, and she looked away. He could barely hear what she said next, in a voice that would not have reached across the room. "You know I have had lovers. Or not-lovers. Seduction, I think, has little to do with love, and it is certainly not courtship."

If it had been left to Jowan, he could have lived the rest of his life, preferably with Tamsyn, without thinking about or mentioning her previous experience. But if she needed to talk about it, then he would have to find a way to do that, too. His mouth was dry, and his heart was pounding too fast, but he kept his voice calm and quiet.

"I have had lovers, too. And I agree that the word *lover* is misleading. Something was always missing, even when it was a coming together to meet mutual needs."

He had moved closer, and their bodies were almost touching when she looked up into his eyes, her own telegraphing a mixture of anxiety and hope. "You do not mind that I have been with other men?"

He minded fiercely, but that was the wrong answer. An incomplete answer, for what he minded was not that she had been with other men, but that she had been with men who did not respect her.

Something—perhaps it was divine inspiration—guided him to say, "I mind that you have been hurt, dearest Tamsyn." That was all the truth. The choices she had made in the past, the mistakes she had made, if any—those did not matter to him. But her pain mattered; would always matter.

She smiled, then, and the ease of it caused his chest to unclench and warmth to flow through him. "I am healing, Jowan. I shall always be grateful to you for that."

"You owe me no gratitude," he growled, offended at the very idea. "I did what was right for the friend of my childhood. And if I have fallen in love all over again with the woman you have become? The fault for that, if it is a fault, is all mine. You owe me nothing, Tamsyn. But I hope one day you will be willing to give me everything, not in repayment for a debt, but because you want to."

They were interrupted then, by the sound of loud talking as Patricia and Lady Trentwood made certain the courting couple knew they were about to have company. Jowan was satisfied enough. They had broken some new ground in their conversation, and he had declared his hand. The next move was over to Tamsyn.

BY THE TIME Apple Cottage was ready for her and Patricia to move in, Tamsyn had finished going through her mother's belongings. Many of them now graced the cottage, and she had had some of the old furniture refurbished. She had also spent some of her jewelry money on new furniture and furnishings and had taken money from her newly found bank account to pay for a square piano, which fitted more comfortably in the space than the massive piano Jowan insisted had been purchased for her.

Every day was still a challenge. Keeping busy with one project after another meant that the cravings did not dominate her days, but they were still present in the background.

She had a list of tasks to complete for Evangeline, to make certain the steward's cottage was ready for the newlyweds when they returned, but after that, she would need to make sure her mind was occupied.

What she needed was a purpose. Some work to do that gave her joy and kept her busy. She had her music, of course. She practiced every day. She continued to compose. Perhaps she could publish her work, in time, but Coombe had undoubtedly been right that it would be harder for a woman.

In any case, it would not consume her days and keep her mind from her cravings.

"Do you have any work I might be able to do?" she asked Jowan on one of their outings. They were at the site of the new mine, where work on the initial shaft was complete, the mine head was in place, and the smelting works were being constructed.

"Do you have time?" Jowan asked. "Whenever we talk, you've been busy."

"I need to keep busy," she told him. After a moment's hesitation, she explained. He claimed to be courting her, after all. If anything, talking to him about her lovers had made him more attentive rather than turning him away. But he had a right to know how damaged she was.

"I don't go a day without craving opium or alcohol or anything that will take me into the false promise of bliss. In truth, several times a day, I find myself thinking about how easy it would be to succumb, and how good it would feel, though I know the second part is a lie. The sensations I would have are transient and leave me worse than before. But I am constantly afraid I will forget that when the cravings are hard."

The color had drained from his face. "I had no idea," he said. "You seem to be managing so well."

"I can manage. I have been managing. But it is easier to forget the need if my brain and hands are busy." She frowned at the shock on his face. "It will get easier, Evangeline says, but it will never go away. That is how I live now."

"I..." He gulped back whatever he had been going to say, shoved his hand through his hair, and took a deep breath. "Yes. Evangeline warned us. I should have remembered. What can I do to help? Do you need something to do right away?"

Tamsyn could have flung herself at him and kissed him. Once again, she had shown him how broken she was, and once again, he had absorbed the blow and come to meet her. To give herself a moment to recover her poise, she outlined what she'd been doing and planned to do.

"I have finished going through my mother's papers. We will be moving into the cottage tomorrow, and it will not take more than a day or two to settle everything to our liking. And I've no more than half a dozen items to pick up for the steward's cottage, plus Patricia and I mean to see that the bed is made, that we've lit fires in the main rooms for several days ahead of their arrival to make sure the place is dry and warm, and that a meal is hot on the stove."

"So, after that?" Jowan asked. He had recovered his equanimity and had the look that meant he was coming up with a plan. "I was going to wait until Evangeline came back—I have been meaning to talk to all three of you ladies about an idea I had."

Tamsyn raised her eyebrows in question.

"You know Bran and I would like to offer more schooling for the older village children. Those who want to go further. I wondered if you three ladies might take on some of the children who are ready for more than our teacher can handle. The teacher is the wife of the innkeeper and is only able to give us four mornings a week. I thought maybe you ladies could teach the girls painting. Fine sewing. That kind of thing. Perhaps even music lessons."

She felt her eyebrows shoot higher. "Or classics and science if their talents lean that way. Patricia has a fine education, and mine is certainly up to teaching a twelve-year-old girl." *Painting and embroidery, indeed.* Sometimes, even Jowan could be a typical man. "We will need to talk to the others, and to the teacher. But I am eager."

He reduced the minuscule dent in her faith in him. "I imagine you will teach anything for which they have an interest or talent. Something their parents see a value in, but also things that will lighten their hearts and brighten their days—and those of their families in the future."

Still a very male point of view, to assume that the future of all those girls held marriage and children. But Tamsyn loved him. Not just the memory of the boy, but the wonderful man he had grown into. Her only doubt was whether her love was going to bring him joy or despair, in the end.

It was time to return to Lord Trentham's. Jowan helped Tamsyn into his curricle and set the horses trotting over the path out of the moors, and down into the valley. They were approaching the village when another vehicle thundered towards them—a carriage, pulled by four galloping horses.

The driver didn't shift from the center of the road—Jowan had to swerve his horses and curricle onto the grass at the side to miss being hit as the equipage hurtled by.

"Fool!" Jowan spat after the rapidly receding carriage.

Tamsyn was thinking of a few choicer words.

"Could you make out anything about the carriage or the driver?" Jowan asked. But the driver had been muffled in a scarf, with a hat pulled down over his eyes and a bulky coat concealing his form. The horses were two bays, a chestnut, and possibly a black, but the black was the rear offside, and neither of them had managed a good look as it raced past. And the carriage was plain and also black.

They were still discussing the incident when they entered the village and saw a knot of people gathered on the road outside of the inn. "What has happened?" Jowan wondered. Someone ran from the crowd to the inn stables.

"An accident of some kind?" Tamsyn speculated.

The scene was becoming clearer as they approached. Someone was lying in the road, but too many people were gathered around to see any details.

"It looks as if the victim has plenty of help," Jowan commented. "I'll just go straight through to the manor, shall I?"

Tamsyn was about to agree when she caught sight of the bonnet lying abandoned just beyond the cluster of people. She would know it anywhere. She had helped choose the colors for the ribbon and braid and had watched them being attached to the felted wool shape, stitch by stitch. Her heart rose to her throat, and she heard herself say, "No, stop. That is Patricia's bonnet," almost before she even thought to speak.

She leaped down from the curricle even as Jowan drew it to a halt, lifting her skirts so they would not trip her, and not waiting for Jowan's help. Because there was Patricia, lying in the road, her face white, her arm at an odd angle, and her gown torn, her green and blue aura torn by jags of dirty red.

One of the villagers recognized Tamsyn and made way for her to sink down beside her friend.

"She is alive," reported the innkeeper, who was holding a wadded-up neckcloth against Patricia's forehead, "but she has been kicked in the head."

"She didn't have time to get out of the way," someone else commented.

"He drove straight at her," said another. "Straight at her."

A horse erupted at a gallop from the inn stables, thundering off in the opposite direction. "Johnny has gone for the doctor," the innkeeper explained.

"Make way," said someone else. "Mother Wilson is coming."

Mother Wilson was the local midwife, and probably the best person after Evangeline to see to Patricia's injuries while they waited for the doctor, who lived ten miles away, and might not be at home even when the messenger reached him.

Mother Wilson knelt on the other side of Patricia, and Tamsyn took over from the innkeeper so the woman had more room. Behind her, she could hear Jowan organizing the villagers, sending some off to make a device to carry the patient, instructing two of them to take up positions on the road and divert traffic, and telling the rest to stand back and make room.

"I can't examine her properly without undressing her," Mother Wilson said, "which I cannot do on the road. However, I believe it is safe to move her. She reacts to pain, though she is unconscious, and she does not show any signs of pain when I touch her back or her abdomen. She might have one or more broken ribs, and she certainly has a broken arm, but with care, she can be shifted to somewhere close."

Tamsyn had retrieved Patricia's reticule and checked inside it. She must have been visiting the cottage, for her set of keys was inside. "Apple Cottage," Tamsyn said to Mother Wilson and Jowan. "We planned to move in tomorrow, but it is all ready, and it is just around the corner."

Some of the neighbors came back with poles and sheets, and within a few minutes, they had carefully slid the sheet under Patricia, made up the stretcher taking care not to jostle the patient, and were on their way.

Tamsyn hurried ahead to unlock the cottage and fold back the blankets and top sheet in Patricia's room. She then assisted Mother Wilson with her examination, and afterward let Jowan into the room to hear the experienced woman's assessment.

"The ribs are just bruised, I think, Sir Jowan and Miss Roskilly. In fact, most of the injuries are bruises or grazes. The horses would have tried to avoid her, of course. Even the kick to the head was a glancing blow, or she'd have a broken skull, and as far as I can tell, it is intact. And the wheels also missed her. Also, the arm seems to have a clean break, or two clean breaks, to be precise. It could have been much worse. She has been lucky."

Given that the doctor could be several hours, they decided Mother Wilson would clean and, where necessary, bandage the cuts and bruises. The leg she immobilized between two straight boards. "I'll not bandage it more than needed to keep it still, for the doctor will undoubtedly want to see it when he comes."

Tamsyn helped, and so was there when Patricia stirred and came to. "I hurt," were her first words.

"Just lie still, Patricia," Tamsyn told her. "You have been in an accident. Mother Wilson says it is mostly cuts and bruises, but you have broken your arm."

"Not an accident," Patricia insisted. "He swerved to hit me."

❧

Chapter Twenty

TAMSYN AND JOWAN explained it all to Lord Trentwood when Jowan took her to Trentwood Manor to fetch those items of hers and Patricia's that had not yet been moved to Apple Cottage. Trentwood sent for the constable, who was the head ostler at the inn and who had already, on his own initiative, questioned many of the witnesses.

"He came in on the Launceston Road, my lord," he told Lord Trentwood. "And drove off across Bodmin Moor. He was well muffled up, and no one could give me a description, but I've sent stable lads off to the likely inns where he might have changed horses with descriptions of the team and instructions to ask about the driver."

"Good man," Lord Trentwood approved. He was, as Jowan had told her, a remarkably slothful man, but he achieved the peace in which to be slothful by choosing good lieutenants and giving them their heads.

"We will find out what we can, my lord," the ostler said. "Miss Roskilly, will you let me know when Mrs. Mayhew is well enough to give me her statement?"

It would not be tonight, Tamsyn discovered, when she returned to Apple Cottage. The doctor was present and had approved the work Mother Wilson had done so far. After Tamsyn returned, he gave Patricia a dose of laudanum before he set the two bones and bandaged the arm firmly within its splints.

Patricia was unconscious by the time he was finished. He handed the bottle to Tamsyn. "She is to have no more than two tablespoons and not more frequently than every four hours, Miss Roskilly. Otherwise, give it to her as she needs it for the pain."

Tamsyn nodded while her mind whirled with confused longing and iron determination. She would not take the laudanum. She would not.

"The bruises and the wrenched knee will mend easily enough, and I do not expect complications. The main danger is infection in one of her scrapes or cuts. Even the arm could be a problem, but the breaks are clean, and the skin is not broken. Watch for fever. Send for me if you have any concerns. Can you watch her through the night? Don't be a fool about it. If you need someone else to share the duty with you, ask. Almost any woman in the village will be willing. They are all offended she was run down by a carriage on their Main Street."

"I can manage." Tamsyn produced the words with that part of her brain that was not totally focused on the mix of opium and alcohol sitting so temptingly within a few feet of her hand. She had to stay focused on her friend, whose aura was fading, and losing even more color as the energy leaked from it through several tears.

Jowan was waiting downstairs when she went down to see the doctor out. She sent the maid up to sit with Patricia, with firm instructions to call Tamsyn if there were any changes, and sat with Jowan to have a cup of the tea he had asked the maid to order from the kitchen and a slice of the cake the cook had sent up with it.

"Do you think it was Coombe, Jowan?" she asked.

"I cannot see why," Jowan answered. "What was to be gained? They cannot have thought she was you. She is six inches taller and far more buxom."

Tamsyn wasn't sure which was worse—to think Patricia was

run down on purpose because of some plot of Coombe's, or to believe it was a random attack from a stranger. For an attack it was. Patricia had been sure that the driver aimed his team and equipage directly at her.

One thing was certain. If it was Coombe, he hadn't finished. Tamsyn vowed to be very careful.

TAMSYN SAT THROUGH the night with Patricia. Twice, she fed her another dose of laudanum, struggling not to show how much the sweet perfume of the concoction affected her. For the rest, she sat with a book or a piece of needlework, fighting the siren call of the bottle. By morning, she felt as if she had climbed a mountain or run for miles—exhausted and aching in both body and soul. But she had not taken the laudanum.

After she and the maid helped a sleepy Patricia to attend to her bodily needs and wash, Tamsyn went to bed for a few hours' sleep. It was a blessing and a relief to leave the laudanum bottle behind and guarded. Her last thought as she dropped into oblivion was that she had faced temptation and won. This time, at least.

A WEEK AFTER the accident, Patricia was fretting about still being confined to bed, but the doctor forbade her to get out of it for at least another week. "After that, you can get up, but you are not to use the arm until the splints come off," he told her. She was still taking the laudanum at night. And Tamsyn was still fighting the urge to help herself to some of it. The desire dominated her days and kept her awake at night, but she was determined not to succumb.

The investigation into the carriage and its driver had stalled—

they had discovered the horses had been hired in Launceston, but the driver had been bundled against the cold and no one could describe him. The charge of horse theft had been added to the charge of assault by carriage since both vehicle and team had apparently disappeared. As far as the constable could discover, they had never emerged from Bodmin Moor.

Jowan had posted guards around the cottage for several nights, but nothing had happened. Then the local newspaper carried a snippet from the London papers about an embassy affair in Paris, where the Earl of Coombe was mentioned as one of the guests. After that, Tamsyn suggested that the men should be able to spend their nights asleep in their own homes, especially since it was raining day and night as if another flood was imminent.

Two nights later, the rain clouds cleared in the evening, and the sunset promised a fine day to come. Tamsyn went to bed wondering whether Bran and Evangeline would arrive home on the morrow. Their letter announcing that they were on their way had arrived days ago, but she was certain they must have been delayed by the weather.

She woke when someone clamped a hand over her mouth and hauled her upright by her arm. Before she was awake enough to struggle, whoever it was had her firmly grasped with an arm around her chest, her back to a hard body, both of her arms trapped inside the bedding that he'd hauled up with her.

Her heart was pounding, her stomach clenching so powerful-ly that she thought she would vomit, her mind screaming for Jowan, her heart plunging into a void of despair and loss.

"Light!" That was a voice she knew. *Coombe.* But the stench of his cologne had already warned her. Sure enough, someone set a spill to the embers of the fire and then to a candle from the mantelpiece, and she could see Paul Willard, holding the candle, and the dark outline of a man between her and the candle, whom she recognized by his shape and smell to be Coombe. Which meant the man holding her was probably Marco.

"You have put me through a lot of trouble, Tammie,"

Coombe said. "I am most displeased."

Anger came to rescue Tamsyn from the inertia that had kept her still. She would have spat had her mouth not been held closed, and even so, she struggled.

"I have come to collect you," he continued. "I advise you to come quietly. If you make a fuss, I shall have everyone in the house killed. You do not want to be responsible for their deaths, Tamsyn, do you? Your servants and your poor friend, who has had such a nasty accident." He finished with a giggle that told her exactly who was to blame for the accident. Where fear for herself had lost its power, fear for them held her still. For the moment.

"The drugs?" He held out a hand to Willard, who lifted the flap of a pouch he was wearing and handed Coombe an apothecary's bottle.

No! She couldn't! No drugs. Anything but that. Her heart gibbered even as the craving within her woke and yearned towards the bottle.

"I shall make it easy for you, Tammie," Coombe crooned. "Normally, you would have to earn poppy juice of this quality, but I know you must have been suffering supply shortages in this god-forsaken wilderness. No noise now! You can let her mouth go, Marco."

"No," Tamsyn said, shaking her head as soon as her mouth was free. "No drugs, Guy. I'll come quietly, but no drugs. I have had nothing since I left London. You'll kill me."

"Stupid bitch," Willard mocked. "A tart like you? No way."

"Rubbish," said Coombe. He narrowed his eyes. "What trick are you planning to pull? Take your dose, like a good girl." He tried to get the bottle between her teeth, but she shook her head and fought against the arms confining her, beyond rational thinking. Coombe swore when some of the liquid spilled. "Hold her head still," he ordered. Willard and Marco forced her head back and held her nose. Coombe forced the bottle between her lips and then held them closed on the liquid that managed to make it inside.

Now that it was too late to stop him dosing her, Tamsyn's panic subsided a little. Perhaps enough had escaped for her to survive such a huge helping of something Coombe described as *quality*. Or not. If Coombe was successful in taking her away, she would be better dead. *No.* She couldn't believe that. Jowan would come for her. Jowan would rescue her.

It was her last coherent thought, as a great cacophony of sound went up from close by. If that was angel bells, there was something wrong with them. They sounded appalling. Perhaps, after all, her recent repentance was insufficient, and this was the sound of hell.

WHEN EVANGELINE AND Bran called into Inneford House on their way home, Jowan was tempted to beg them to stay. This last week, in particular, with Tamsyn so busy nursing Patricia, he had felt very alone in the great house.

"How is Patricia?" Evangeline asked. "And Tamsyn! We almost rushed straight back after we heard about her accident. Are they still at the squire's?"

"They have moved into their new cottage," Jowan admitted. "Yours is ready too."

Tamsyn would be so pleased to see her friend back and to welcome her to the home that she'd put so much effort into preparing.

"I'll ride down with you. Let us go as far as Tamsyn's and check for lights. I know she'd want to welcome you home if she is awake."

They had just turned the corner to Apple Cottage when a great hullabaloo of sound began. The horses shied. Bran had to calm his horses, and the driver of the carriage that waited outside Apple Cottage was having a similar issue with his team.

Up on the second floor of the cottage, Patricia had her window wide open and was clanging a metal tankard against a chamber pot, while screaming for help. "Intruders! Help! Murder!"

"Evangeline, get down and run for help," Jowan commanded. The rest of the plan came to him as he spoke. "Bran, tie your reins up so the horses think they still have a driver and set your team to a trot, then jump off onto the carriage. We'll throw the driver off and then you can drive the carriage away while I wait for whomever comes out of that door."

By the time he'd got that far, Evangeline was gone, and Bran had the reins tied securely to the front rail of the cabriolet, with enough slack to let the horses keep moving. They were almost on the carriage. Jowan leaped from his horse to the driver's perch and kept going, taking the driver down the other side, trusting Bran to deal with the vehicle and team. And sure enough, both coach and cabriolet continued down the road, and his horse was following. Meanwhile, along both sides of the street, windows were opening and doors, too, as village men in nightshirts and hastily donned trousers tumbled out into the street. Many of them were carrying rifles—hunting weapons or souvenirs of the late war.

"Some of you go around the back to stop whoever comes out that way," Jowan ordered. "Patricia, what is happening?"

Patricia leaned out to call down, "Intruders. I heard a voice in Tamsyn's room. A man swearing, I think. Maybe more than one. Certainly, more than one person moving around. I shoved a chair under my door handle and came to the window to make a racket."

"You did well," Jowan told her.

A bang and a crash sounded from inside the house. Patricia looked away and leaned out again. "The chair held," she said, her voice shaky.

Silence then, for far longer than he had expected. What was happening? Were the servants safe? The two maids slept in the attics, and the cook in a room off the kitchen. If whoever it was thought to collect more hostages, the servants would be vulnerable. He should have thought to tell those covering the back door to get the cook out if they could.

Before he could send a message to that effect, the front door crashed back and three people burst out into the street, only to stand staring in shock at the absence of the carriage and the presence of a reception committee.

One he recognized as the moonlight fell on him. Coombe. *Not three. Four people.* Behind Coombe, another of the three was carrying a body. And not just any body—the slender form of Tamsyn, wrapped in a blanket, and limp. Jowan had a moment of screaming panic at the sight of her still form, but his rational self assured him she would be of no use to Coombe as a hostage if she was dead.

At the same moment, Coombe spoke. "We have Tammie Lind. Let us pass. Marco will slice a piece of flesh off the treacherous bitch each time anyone makes a single hostile move." The man at Coombe's side grinned and waved a knife that looked sharp enough to carry out Coombe's threat.

The other man swore and stepped back, shifting Tamsyn so her head, which had been hanging over his shoulder, was held away from his body. "Your whore just vomited again," he complained to Coombe.

They were his last words. A single shot rang out and he fell, Tamsyn with him. The neighbor on the other side of the road had been a sharpshooter in the Rifles, and he took his chance at a shot as soon as Tamsyn was no longer protecting the man's torso.

Several other men raised their weapons. Marco took a step towards Tamsyn, thought better of it, and took off at a run, and Coombe broke and ran a moment later. Several guns fired, but neither man stopped, so if any of the bullets had hit them, they had not done nearly enough damage.

Half the village took off in pursuit.

Jowan left them to it while he ran to Tamsyn. She was hurt. Unconscious. Vomiting, the villain who held her had said.

The villain lay sprawled back against the house at the top of the steps, his eyes staring, a small hole in his coat in the region of his heart explaining why. Jowan recognized him. *Willard*. The man who had led the previous kidnap attempt. Tamsyn had fallen mostly on top of him, but her head and shoulders dangled over the edge of the step.

At least she had not fallen headfirst onto the stone steps or the cobbles of the street. Jowan put his arms under her and lifted her just as Patricia opened the front door. Willard slumped into the house, and Patricia drew back. Jowan stepped over him and carried Tamsyn into the parlor. Her breath was broken and shallow, and when he set her down and checked her pulse, he could scarcely find it. He could smell the stink of vomit overlaying the sweet sickly stench of laudanum. Patricia was limping around the room, lighting candles from a spill as Evangeline entered, followed closely by Bran.

"How is she?" Evangeline asked, as she knelt beside Jowan.

"I don't know." Jowan grimaced. "He gave her laudanum. Didn't you say it might kill her if she had to give up again?"

Evangeline's eyes widened with alarm, but she spoke calmly. "She is still alive, and I shall do my best to keep her that way."

"She vomited," Patricia commented. "At least twice, by what that man said. That would have helped to get the poison out, would it not?"

"Yes, it would have," Evangeline agreed. "Patricia, are you not still recovering from your carriage accident? Get off your knee before you damage it further. On your way out, Jowan, send someone for the doctor."

Jowan cast a glance at the door, torn between his need to hunt down Coombe and his aversion to leaving Tamsyn.

"Tamsyn will get the best care I can give her," Evangeline assured him. "I trust you and Bran to capture that man and prevent him from hurting my friend ever again."

"I have horses," Bran said, "and you know the countryside as well as anyone in the village."

His mind made up, Jowan strode towards the door, where Tamsyn's maids and cook were standing, watching their mistress. They stepped out of his way, but he paused and turned back to Evangeline. She had not waited for him and Bran to quit the room but was unbuttoning Tamsyn's nightgown.

"She is my life," he said.

The nurse looked over her shoulder to meet his eyes. "I know. She is still alive, Jowan. Go and get that villain."

He nodded and left the room, Bran on his heels. As he stepped over Willard, who still blocked the doorway, he heard Evangeline say, presumably to the cook and the maids, "You, put some hot water on. I want warm water to bathe her. You two, fetch me towels and washcloths, and…"

Chapter Twenty-One

ONE OF THE village boys held the reins of two horses Jowan did not recognize.

"No time to go home or to chase after your horse," Bran said. "The innkeeper is providing horses for anyone who can ride."

Well enough. Jowan nodded, took the reins of the nearest horse, and mounted.

They followed the sound of the hunt—calls to alert the rest of the pursuers to sightings or redirections regarding places that hadn't been searched. From the sounds, Coombe and his valet had taken to Bodmin Moor.

Perhaps they thought it would be easier to lose the pursuit amongst the hills and valleys, the rocks and scattered buildings, not to mention the mists that would counter the assistance given to the hunters by the bright moonlight.

Or perhaps they thought the open moors would be less familiar to the villagers than their own fields, being ignorant city fools who did not know Jowan's people.

Certainly, they had reckoned without the blanket bogs and valley mires that every villager who lived on the edge of the moors knew how to recognize and negotiate. Whenever the two managed to evade the hunt, all Jowan and his allies had to do was cover the heights and wait for one or the other to get caught as the grasses over the peat gave way and the bog beneath captured a boot or even both legs in liquid mud that oozed away whenever its victim struggled.

Every time, the man who had been trapped yelled—for help, or just in fear and surprise. So far, the boggy snares gave up their captives before one of the hunters could reach them, but it was only a matter of time. And so far, the St Tetha side had followed Jowan's instructions not to use their guns. If Coombe still had any ammunition left—he had been shooting less regularly as the night wore on and had so far missed everyone he shot at—he would be most dangerous when cornered.

The full moon was at its zenith, but the mists had grown thicker. They could be at this all night unless something changed. But Coombe and the valet must be tiring faster than the St Tetha crowd. Quite apart from the energy sapped by the bogs, they were two city dwellers of sedentary habits.

The risk was that they'd make it to the edge of the moors at a time when none of the pursuers was close enough to prevent them from leaving, but so far, the hunt had driven them farther in.

Driving. That was a point. Up until now, they had not been herding Coombe and valet, but letting them set the direction. A destination popped into Jowan's mind. "Let's drive them towards Aermed's Hollow," he said to Bran.

Two other searchers who were close enough to hear turned to Jowan with a grin even as Bran chuckled. "Nice," he said.

Legend said that Aermed's Hollow had been created when a hero had fought a dragon there, to rescue the maiden Aermed. The hollow had been formed by the stroke of the hero's sword that split the dragon nearly into two, and the rocky walls on to north, west, and south were, so the story said, the bones of the dragon. Certainly, a rock near the entrance to the little valley looked, from a certain perspective, like the skull of a dragon.

If the mist cooperated, and Coombe and his man could be pushed in the right direction, they would find themselves trapped with near vertical walls on all sides but one, and no way out past those who waited on that side. And the walls confined one of the deepest mires on the moor—one that would, after the recent rain, be even deeper than usual.

The men who had heard his plan drifted away into the mist to set the word spreading. Perhaps it was Jowan's imagination, but a new sense of purpose hovered over the moor, and a rising triumph as the quarry took the paths left unguarded and avoided the villagers who let themselves be seen at carefully chosen locations.

It may have taken an hour, perhaps more, from the moment Jowan thought of Aermed's Hollow to the moment Coombe, with his valet right behind him, stumbled through a thicker-than-usual patch of mist and found pursuers close behind them and walls on either side.

"Gotcha," said Bran, in an undertone low enough that only Jowan could hear.

"I'm going to the far end," Jowan told them. "Will you keep them moving till they are too far in to climb the walls?"

"Trust me and the lads for that," Bran told him.

Jowan flashed him a smile. He could trust any of them, and Bran most of all.

He guided his horse through the tangle of rocks that marked the top of the hollow until he reached the far end. Below, he could hear Coombe and his valet bickering.

"It is a trap, Signore," the valet complained.

"The walls grow wider," Coombe snapped back.

"Twice you have said this, and each time…"

"Shut up," Coombe ordered. "Damn. Another bog. Keep to the side, Marco. It is shallower at the edges."

Not this time. In fact, from the sounds of them squelching in the mud, they had chosen the deepest side.

They were invisible in the heavy mist, but here on the heights the air was clear, and Jowan could see the villagers lined along the top of the cliffs to either side. They grinned at him, and he lifted his finger to his lips, enjoining silence, though in truth, none of them were making a noise.

"We must go back, Signore," Marco whined.

"We would like that, wouldn't we, men?" Bran replied from somewhere in the mist behind them, and a few others agreed.

"Forward," Coombe ordered, his voice grim. Only a few paces farther, and they'd be up to their thighs. Deeper, perhaps, after the persistent rain of the past few days.

"Signore, it is too deep!" Marco was panicking. "I am sinking."

The time for silence was over. "It gets deepest just under the cliff," Jowan commented. "The one in front of you. There is no way out, Coombe. My men block the only exit. The cliffs are too steep to climb, and my men are lined along the tops of them. You are trapped."

Coombe was silent for a long minute, then he yelled, "What do you want, Trethewey? Tammie? Let me out and I'll promise to leave her alone."

"Signore!" Marco sobbed.

"You cannot be trusted, Coombe," Jowan replied. "Lying and cheating are your natural behaviors."

"Signore, help me," begged Marco. "I am sunk up to my arms."

"Keep still then, you fool," Coombe replied. "Haul me out, Trethewey, and I will make you any promise you like. Money? Women? Power?"

On an impulse, Jowan said, "You alone. Not your valet. Tamsyn does not like him." He winked at the men who could see him. Was it a lie if you lied to a liar?

"Agreed," Coombe said.

"Signore!"

"It's hard enough to pull one man out of the mire, let alone two," Jowan said. Which was true. And it could not be done in the dark, but if they kept still until morning, he would try.

"One of us, then," Coombe declared.

Marco's distressed cry was wordless, but the sound of a gunshot told its own tale. Coombe must have missed, for Marco shouted his rage, and then all Jowan could hear was sloshing and squelching, followed by a scream of pain.

Jowan stepped closer to the edge to peer into the mist but could see nothing. He would swear, though, that Coombe and Marco were fighting. A gurgle was followed by silence, and then Coombe's voice.

"Trethewey. Marco is dead. The mud is up to my chin, man. Get me out of here."

"No," Jowan replied. "Nothing can be done in the dark. When the sun rises, if you are still alive, I shall try it, so you can hang for your crimes. You are a destroyer of life. It is time for you to explain yourself to your maker."

"Devil take it!" Coombe's voice dropped. He continued speaking, but not in English. If Jowan had to guess, he would say the man was swearing in one language after another. He would sink only slowly while he stood still. But eventually, he would no longer be able to stand. If the sun had not yet risen, the mire would have him.

It was a gruesome thought. Jowan had to sternly remind himself of how Tamsyn had suffered at Coombe's hands and those of his minions. Jowan was not prepared to risk the life of even one of his men to save the villain.

The head ostler from the inn came up beside him. "Quite apart from what he has done up until now, he murdered his employee in our hearing," he told Jowan. "If we could get him out of that mire, and I doubt it's possible, he will be dead anyway, when he hangs. It isn't worth risking any of us in a rescue."

That was true, too. "I will wait until dawn," Jowan announced. The ostler said that he would too, in his office as constable. Bran and several other men offered to remain with them. Jowan accepted another two, for if four of them could not get Coombe out of the bog, greater numbers would not help. He convinced Bran to return to his bride. "Look after the ladies,

Bran. Coombe might have planned something else."

Twice before dawn, Coombe tried to bargain for his life, offering money, fame, courtesans. Threatening, too, when Jowan refused to respond to his bribes. Jowan had stood, still and grim, and listened to the man bargaining, sometimes in hysterical shrieks, sometimes in a reasonable voice. With Jowan, with the other watchers, with God. Whimpering, too, and in the end, with gasps and finally, gurgling.

By the time sunlight gilded the tops of the mists, he had fallen silent.

It was late morning before the mists lifted. Neither of the villains had come out of the hollow, so they must be inside it. Jowan led the way between the ponds and the patches of unstable ground, watching for the vegetation that marked the difference between safe ground and danger, and hunting for any sign of Coombe or Marco.

But they saw only the boot marks and churned mud that marked the passage of the pair, no glimpse of either man. Not even right at the end, on the edge of the final mire, where the cliffs reared eighteen feet high around every side except that of the entrance.

In the mire, vegetation had been crushed and churned around, but the mud and the water lay still.

"They have to be under there," the ostler commented. "Might come up. Might not. Probably not. Remember the Bowithick cow." The other men nodded or murmured agreement or both. Just a few years ago, a herd of cows had panicked when their quiet amble along a moor road had been disrupted by a pair of racing curricles. One of the cows had ended up in a bog, up to its neck. Attempts to retrieve it had failed and the cow had sunk, never to rise again except in conversations such as this.

The cow, apparently, had accepted its fate with bovine grace, and sunk in silence. Not so Coombe. Jowan shuddered. He never wanted to think of it again, but he feared Coombe's dying moments would haunt him for the rest of his life. The man had deserved to die. But what a horrible death.

"I'm for St Tetha," he said. "I need to know how Miss Roskilly is after her ordeal."

⤜⤜⤜⟫⟫⟫

TAMSYN STRUGGLED FROM sleep, feeling heavy and nauseous. Before she could fully open her eyes, Evangeline was leaning over her, asking, anxiously, "How do you feel?"

"Dreadful. Have I been sick?" The words came in short phrases, with pauses between as she dredged the next few words out of her mind and forced her mouth to remember how to shape them.

She had a flash of memory. An image of Coombe forcing laudanum on her. A dream, surely?

"What do you remember?" Evangeline asked.

Evangeline was truly here. "You are home," Tamsyn said, smiling at her friend despite the truly awful headache and the equally unpleasant ache in her gut. "Welcome back, Evangeline." She frowned. "I had a bad dream, I think. About Coombe. Coombe, Marco, and Willard."

"They were here, Tamsyn," Evangeline explained, "but Patricia sounded the alarm and Jowan and the village stopped them from taking you away. You have been unconscious for hours."

Tamsyn tried to sit up, but her head reeled, and Evangeline moved quickly to support her and to shift her pillows to prop her upright. "Don't try to do anything, my friend. That horrible man gave you too much laudanum, and the doctor says you must be very careful in case your heart has been damaged."

That prompted another memory. "I told him I had not had any opium or alcohol since I left him, but he did not believe me. Willard laughed," Tamsyn said, the words flowing more easily now.

"The doctor will want to know you are awake, and so will

Bran and Patricia. I will be back in just a moment, and I shall bring you something to drink." Evangeline left the room and a moment later, Tamsyn's maid slipped inside.

"Oh, Miss. We was that worried. Do you be well now, Miss?"

"A little weak, but grateful to all the village," Tamsyn told her. She was too tired to say more, though she had, from the light, slept away the morning. The maid must have realized because she busied herself with her mending, and Tamsyn let her eyes close while she waited for Evangeline to return.

She brought Jowan with her. "I had to let him up, Tamsyn," she said. "He insisted that he needed to see you with his own eyes." She frowned at Jowan. "You can only stay a moment."

Jowan crossed the room to take Tamsyn's hand in his own. "Coombe is dead, Tamsyn. He won't trouble you ever again. Nor will Willard or Marco."

The whole room went waltzing this time. Tamsyn pressed the back of her head into the pillows and shut her eyes till the dizziness abated, and Evangeline scolded, "Jowan! You must not alarm her like that."

"No," Tamsyn insisted. "It is good. I needed to know." She smiled into Jowan's worried eyes. "I am safe. You said you would protect me, and you have."

He shook his head. "I let you get hurt. I am sorry, Tamsyn. It was my fault. I should have kept the guards on your cottage."

"Out," Evangeline ordered. "These discussions can wait until Tamsyn is well again. Go away, Jowan. Go and get some sleep. Now, Tamsyn, I have some ginger tea for you. Your stomach is probably a little sore, so nothing to eat until we see whether you can keep this down."

Tamsyn was watching Jowan leave the room, his eyes lingering on hers for as long as his head was still within her sight. It took her a moment to catch up with what Evangeline had said. "Thank you, Evangeline. I am very thirsty."

Chapter Twenty-Two

Six months later

THE DAY WAS sunny, though the wind was still bitterly cold. It was good traveling weather. Tamsyn looked up each time she heard a wheeled vehicle passing down the road outside her door, though probably Jowan, if he did come home today, would go straight to Inneford House.

He, Bran, and other witnesses had been in London since the middle of January for the hearing of a committee of the House of Lords, to decide whether the Earl of Coombe was dead—given the absence of any body.

It was just like Coombe to continue causing problems for months after he died.

Indeed, even now that the committee had accepted that Coombe and his murderer lay at the bottom of a mire and that their bodies would probably not ever be recovered, all would not be straightforward for his poor heir, a distant cousin. Coombe, according to Evangeline who had visited yesterday afternoon, had left the poor man a tarnished title, neglected estates, and more debts than assets.

Especially since the solicitor Jowan had engaged on her behalf had made a successful claim against the estate for her past two years' earnings, opening a floodgate of claims from other performers.

Evangeline had been in London with Bran, but they and others from St Tetha had been arriving back in the village for the past week. The head ostler from the inn, Lord and Lady Trentham, the mine manager, and more.

"No doubt we shall hear when Jowan arrives," Patricia commented, looking up from the schoolwork she was marking. All three women had taken up Jowan's suggestion that they involve themselves in the school, but Patricia was slowly taking over from the innkeeper's wife, and they were talking about adding an extra day of schooling for the children.

Tamsyn was teaching lessons in reading and numbers at the village school, but also music to paying pupils and talented children who could not afford the fee. She was also coaching the church choir.

When the vicar had suggested it several months ago, Tamsyn had been reluctant. "Who am I to coach a church choir?" she had asked Evangeline and Patricia. "With my background?"

"And why shouldn't you coach the choir?" Patricia had asked. "You are a brilliant singer and a good teacher. And you are a member of the parish. A faithful one, too, who never misses a Sunday."

Her past should have had her hounded from the church, but when Tamsyn said as much to the vicar, he reminded her that the entire Christian religion was founded on the principles of forgiveness and redemption. And so, Tamsyn coached the church choir.

"I daresay," Patricia added, "that we shall hear it from Jowan himself, for he shall be anxious to see you after his weeks away."

Would he? Her, especially? He was her friend. Tamsyn did not doubt that for a moment. But more than that? Months ago, she thought he was courting her. Even when autumn and then winter subjected their thrice-weekly walks to the uncertainties of the weather, he did not stop his visits, instead sitting in the cottage parlor for a couple of hours, talking about every topic under the sun.

He continued to bring her flowers and little gifts, too. But he did not speak words of love. He did not mention marriage. He did not engineer situations in which he could touch her—those possibly accidental touches with which a man initiates a seduction. He did not, not even once, attempt to kiss her, or even look as if he might be going to do so.

Oh certainly, from time to time, desire flared in his eyes. But Tamsyn did not count that. She knew she was desirable in a physical sense. She also knew, beyond a doubt, that she was not a desirable wife for a baronet. Or for anyone else, come to that. Not with her history.

It seemed Jowan had come to the same conclusion. Or, if he had not fully done so before he left St Tetha, he must have by now. Six weeks in London, revisiting the sordid details of her life with the Earl of Coombe must surely have ended any idea he might have had of taking Tamsyn, with all her unwanted baggage, to wife.

Patricia was wrong. Jowan would not be anxious to see her and would certainly not be rushing over here as soon as he arrived back home.

"I do not deserve him, Patricia, and by now he has realized that," she told her friend.

"Nonsense," said Patricia. "He would be a lucky man to have you as his wife, and from what I can see, it is just a matter of you crooking your finger. You are the one he looks for whenever he enters a room you already occupy. From what you tell me, he put his life on hold to rescue you. He has been courting you for months."

"I am not good for him. Not with the scandal of my past. His weeks in London must have convinced him of that. He will be kind, of course, for he is a kind man, but it is over, Patricia. He no longer wants me, and he has made the right decision."

"You are wrong, Tamsyn. Your friends and neighbors know

who you are, and we all love and admire you. And you are wrong about Jowan, too. He is yours for the asking."

At that moment, a knock sounded on the door, and Tamsyn jumped. But of course, it could be anyone.

A moment later, the maid opened the door to the parlor. Her words were unnecessary, for the caller stood at her shoulder, but she announced him anyway.

"Sir Jowan Trethewey for Miss Roskilly."

As Tamsyn and Jowan walked up onto the moor, signs of early spring were everywhere along the lanes. Daffodils in their clumps. Primroses under the walls and hedges. Lesser celandines, red campion, and periwinkle all in flower.

They walked under the bare branches of trees, but all around them the ground was greening, with the fresh growth of ferns, cow parsley, and fat foxglove leaves.

Tamsyn paused at the top of the lane where a few paving slabs formed a lookout over the village. "It is pretty, is it not?"

"Very," Jowan agreed, though *beautiful* was a better word. He had desired her when she was so frail, he'd feared bruising her if he touched her, but now that she glowed with health, she was stunning.

She had removed her bonnet as they walked up the lane, and her hair—escaping its hair pins as usual—formed a halo of dark curls around her head.

She pushed her hair back with her right hand, and the sunlight gleamed off her ring. He wondered if it was a good sign that Tamsyn continued to wear his ring, now on her ring finger. When he had commented on it one day, she had joked that, if she put on any more weight, the ring would have to move to the little finger.

Every time he made a comment like that, she turned it aside

with a joke or a distraction, and he let it go. He had promised to give it time, and he would keep that promise if it killed him. Some days, he thought it would.

She glanced sideways to see him watching her. "The view, Jowan."

"I am looking," he told her, without moving his eyes. He knew which view he preferred.

In the months since Coombe's attack and death, she had fully recovered from what the doctor was calling "Miss Roskilly's poisoning". More than recovered. She seemed to have lost the anxiety and lack of self-esteem that he had been conscious of even when she was otherwise happy.

Indeed, rather than arguing or becoming flustered by his obvious compliment, she chuckled. "Oh, you. But truly, Jowan, is St Tetha not the prettiest village you have ever seen?"

"Not as pretty as you, especially because I can tell—you are happy here," he said.

In answer, Tamsyn turned in a circle, her bonnet swinging from one hand, her head back and her eyes shut. "I am home here," she replied. "I have you, Patricia, Bran, and Evangeline for friends, and work that makes me happy."

Jowan bit back his response to her remark about him being a friend. He had been patient. Dear God, he had been so patient! Did she not see him as more than a friend, even now?

"You deserve every good thing," he told her.

"It is good of you to say so, Jowan," she replied, avoiding his gaze. "But I know what I am."

He had been holding his tongue through weeks of hearings in which Coombe's misdeeds had been discussed in gruesome detail—and by extension, what Tamsyn had suffered. That remark was suddenly the last straw.

"Dammit, woman. What you are is a woman of talent, courage, determination, and strength," he told her. His anger had to be expressed in movement, and he set off to march back and forth across the little lookout. "I cannot bear to hear anyone disparage you. Even you yourself. Do you not comprehend how I feel about you? Can you not understand how it hurts me to see you putting yourself down?"

She glared at him. "How do you feel about me, Jowan? You are my friend. Am I right?"

His next curse was even less fit for a lady's ears, and he apologized immediately after. "I beg your pardon. I should not have said that." The last thing he needed was for her to think he did not regard her as a lady.

"I have heard worse," she pointed out, and before he could swear again at the mere thought of being compared to Coombe and his acolytes, she added, "Remember the stable master your father used to have? I never knew what was meant by half of the words we overheard."

The unexpected memory made him chuckle. "I learned my best curse words from him," he said.

Her smile faded. "Jowan, why are you upset? Do you not wish to be my friend?"

Exasperated all over again, he snapped back, "I wish to be your husband and your lover."

Tamsyn gaped at him. "You do? Still?"

He couldn't believe she said that. "What did you think I was about? I've been courting you for months!"

"But you have never even tried to kiss me," she replied.

It was the mystified tone that shredded the last of his self-control. If it was a kiss she wanted, then a kiss is what she would have. He grabbed her by the shoulders and pulled her to him, but all his indignation eased as his lips touched hers, and he gentled the kiss, his lips firm but tender.

She opened beneath him, her tongue darting out to taste him, and his hands left her shoulders and pulled her closer. Her arms went around his waist, and she plastered her body to his, and an endless moment passed as their tongues explored one another and so did their hands.

It wasn't until he felt her hands pulling his shirt from his trousers that he remembered they were standing on a lookout above the village, where anyone could see them. Reluctantly, his lips attempting to cling, he pulled back.

"The village," he panted.

"Oh! I forgot." Tamsyn cast a glance in that direction, and Jowan's ego celebrated the fact that his kiss had made her forget their surroundings.

"I was waiting to be invited," he told her.

"I beg your pardon?"

"The kiss. You said I never even tried to kiss you, but I was waiting to be invited. Tamsyn, you couldn't control what has happened to you over the years, and you didn't need another male forcing their desires on you. If my decision to let you take the lead on anything physical gave you the impression I had stopped wanting you to be my wife, then I am sorry. But I am not sorry you were upset I didn't kiss you." Jowan was, in fact, decidedly smug about that last fact, and about how enthusiastically she had responded when he did kiss her.

"I never said I was upset," she pointed out. She had taken the hand he had offered her and was walking with him along the path into the downs. There was a spot just a few minutes' walk away that would be perfect to continue that kiss.

"You implied it," he told her.

She punched him, chuckling, and he mimed injury, pleased to clown to defuse the sensitive emotional fireworks he'd suddenly stumbled into. Tamsyn, though, tugged him directly back into the line of fire.

"Surely, Jowan, you do not still want me as your wife. Not after the hearing. The things you must have learned! I can bring only scandal to the Trethewey name."

They were there. He tugged her hand and led her onto a poorly marked and little trod path, around a small grove of trees, and into a hollow where the ruin of a cottage stood, with no roof and only two walls.

There, hidden from the path and sheltered from the wind, he

took her back into his arms. "What do I care for what they say in London? Here in St Tetha, you are the villagers' darling—their Cornish Lark. There's not a man or a woman with a word to say against you. As for the gentlefolk, Lady Trentwood accepts you, and she sets the example for everyone within a range of thirty miles."

He kissed her nose. "Your scandal, as you call it, though I say it was Coombe's scandal... Be that as it may, the scandal has nothing to do with us. I love you, Tamsyn, and if you will not have me for your husband, I shall wait until you change your mind. And yes, I know that is putting pressure on you, but what am I to do? Your claim of scandal as a bar to our match is unfair."

"But I am thinking of you!" Tamsyn objected.

He kissed her again, a quick peck on the lips. "You are thinking *for* me, which is quite a different thing. I am perfectly capable of thinking for myself, my love. Have you any other objections to the match?"

She frowned. "You do not mind about the scandal?" she asked.

"Haven't I just said so?"

"I might be barren," Tamsyn blurted. "I quickened only once in five years, and I did not carry that baby past the early stages."

Objection number two. That one was no harder than the first. "I am sorry for your loss, Tamsyn, but I will not allow that to come between us. I want you for my lover, my partner, my friend, my wife. If God sends us children, I will welcome them, but I am not looking for a broodmare."

"You are a baronet," she pointed out. "You need an heir."

"I *am* a baronet," Jowan agreed and bent to kiss her neck, just under her ear. "I undoubtedly have an heir. In fact, I do. A distant cousin over Truro way. And if he or one of his children inherit, it won't matter to me. I will have made provision for you as I have already made provision for Bran and his family. That's the only thing I care about."

She leaned back out of his reach just as he was going to see whether the other side of her neck was as delectable.

"Do you not want a son to carry on your name?"

The quick answer would not do. "That would be nice. But then, we might only have daughters. Or none, as you suggested. Either way, I will have you. And what I need, Tamsyn, is you." This time, she allowed him to kiss her neck, even tipping it to make it more accessible.

"I still crave drugs and alcohol," she said, her voice so hushed that he would not have heard it if his ear had been farther away.

"You continue to resist the craving," he pointed out. "You know what it will cost you if you surrender, and I trust in your courage and determination. But if you do have a slip, I will still love you." And that was his answer to Objection number three.

"Will you do more than kiss me?" Tamsyn asked. Demanded, it sounded like.

Aha. Objection number four. Jowan hedged. "Precisely how much more?"

She met his eyes with a glare that was also a challenge. "Everything," she insisted. "Right here, right now."

Jowan understood. She was afraid her experience would upset him, or distract him, or—perhaps—disgust him. He was sure it would not. After all, he had been dreaming of this for a long time. Close to a decade, since he first noticed his best friend was developing curves.

However, he had reservations as he looked around the rock-strewn floor. "Everything, yes. Here and now, no. It is cold and rocky. I want you in a bed, Tamsyn. How deeply does Patricia sleep?"

All her doubts showed on her face. That, in itself, spoke of how much she trusted him, for she wore the armor of calm competence for nearly everyone else. "You will come to me?" she said. "Tonight?"

She frowned and added, "Or tomorrow night. You have been traveling for a week, and have barely had time to change before coming out with me again."

"Tonight," Jowan said firmly. "I have been waiting a long time for the invitation, my dearest love. If we put it off until tomorrow night, I will not sleep a wink tonight for imagining it."

Tamsyn blushed.

"But since we are here," Jowan suggested, "I suggest we try for a little foretaste. Without taking our clothes off or impaling ourselves on the rocks." He pulled her closer for another kiss.

TAMSYN HAD NO intention of sneaking behind Patricia's back. She was, after all, an independent woman, the owner of the house, and Patricia's employer. Even so, her heart was in her mouth when she closed the door to the parlor, shortly before Jowan was due to arrive to join them for dinner.

"Patricia, may I have a private word with you?"

Patricia's face lit up. "Sir Jowan proposed!"

"No. Or, at least, yes. But that is not it." Tamsyn paused for a moment, because that was, in fact, precisely it. "At least, that is sort of it."

Patricia raised her eyebrows as she clasped her hands in front of her in what Tamsyn recognized as her "I will wait until you are ready to explain yourself" pose.

It worked on the children at the school, and Tamsyn could feel it working on her. "Jowan wishes to marry me. I wish to go to bed with him first. I fear that, when it comes to it, he will remember all he knows about me and be disgusted. Or perhaps that, when he knows he can have me without marriage, he will not feel the need to…"

She trailed off at the stern look Patricia was giving her as if she had been caught under a broken window with a ball in her hand.

"You do Jowan a disservice, my dearest Tamsyn. I understand why, but if I were a gambling woman, I would be proposing a wager that you will be betrothed by tomorrow morning. That is what you are trying to say, is it not? That Jowan is joining you in bed tonight?"

Tamsyn lifted her chin, saying defiantly, "I am sorry if you disapprove, but I need to do this."

"Dear Tamsyn, what right have I to approve or disapprove? I am your friend, not your keeper. Do what you must. I am confident, in any case, that you will be wed, soon. And you know it in your heart, I think, even if you are not prepared to admit it, yet. Even I know Jowan is one of those men who can be trusted, and you have known him for far longer than I."

After dinner, Tamsyn said she would not need her maid tonight, and that they and the cook could also have an early night once they had cleaned up after dinner. She would pour Sir Jowan a port and let him out when he had finished his drink.

She poured one for Patricia, too, and a glass of freshly made lemonade for herself. They had formed the habit of sharing a drink of an evening when Jowan came to visit. They continued a conversation begun over dinner about people and places that Jowan had seen in London. Patricia was very impressed that he was on speaking terms with a duke and duchess.

"I shall make an early night of it myself," Patricia announced when she had finished her port. "You need not worry, Jowan, that I mean to play gooseberry. But you had better stay here for another fifteen minutes to be certain the maids are in their attics."

Jowan looked startled, his eyes turning towards Tamsyn. Patricia giggled as she left the room.

"Does she know?" Jowan asked.

"That you are staying the night? Yes. I told her. She is my chaperone, after all."

"And she did not offer to unman me?" Jowan shook his head.

Tamsyn found his discomfiture endearing, but she thought she should keep that sentiment to herself. "Shall I pour you another drink?"

"A port is not what I am thirsty for," Jowan told her.

"Perhaps you would like one later," she suggested. "After." She was nervous, which was ridiculous. It was not as if she were a shy virgin. That was the problem, though. She was terrified that her obvious experience would put him off.

She was not going to pretend to be less knowledgeable than she was, though. Patricia was right about her motives, though she had not fully understood them herself until her friend outlined them. "Do you want to come up to bed?" she asked.

He shot to his feet as if released from a rubber band, and met her partway across the room, putting his arms around her.

Another compelling kiss removed all the starch in her knees, and she wilted against him. But only for a moment. The sooner they were up the stairs, the sooner he could keep the promise of those kisses.

An hour later, she lay in his arms, one hand idly stroking his chest, her mind slowly putting itself back together again after what the French called "the little death". She had always considered the phrase a Gallic exaggeration. Apparently not.

The first time had been rushed, both of them impatiently rushing through the preliminaries. It had been lovely, though. The second time had been outside of—and way beyond and above—anything she had ever experienced. She and Jowan had been so united she could not have told who was feeling what as they soared to a peak well beyond the merely physical.

"I have a license," Jowan murmured.

Tamsyn shifted so that she could see his face. "A marriage license?"

He nodded, his expression reminding her of the juvenile Jowan when he had been up to mischief, knew he had been caught, and was ready with an argument to convince the adults that he was in the right of it. A mixture of gleeful, apologetic, and determined.

She should object to his presumption, but she was too happy to bother. She settled herself back on his shoulder. "You were confident I would agree."

"Not confident, no. You told me to hold fast. The license was part of it—my gesture of hope. I got it in Plymouth on that first trip. A wedding ring, too. The one I promised you when we were sixteen. I've had to renew the license twice because they only last for ninety days. This one is good for another four sennights. I sometimes wondered if either ring or license would ever be used." He kissed the top of her head, and she moved again to stretch up and meet his lips.

His kisses were so sweet she could lose herself in them, but Jowan had not lost sight of his point. "Will you marry me, Tamsyn Roskilly?"

"I will." Tamsyn still had her doubts, but none of them were about Jowan. She certainly did not doubt his love for her. Hadn't he proved it, time after time? Hadn't she seen it in action and felt it, too, in this last hour?

He, though, seemed surprised. "You will?" The arms he had wrapped around her squeezed her in a bear hug, and his voice rose in a joyful shout. "She will!"

"That's right," Tamsyn grumbled. "Let the whole village know." She was laughing though. Not because Jowan's delight was humorous, but because happiness was bubbling up from deep within and she had to let it out.

It had been a long hard road, full of steep patches, rocks, and pitfalls. But at last, she and Jowan could fulfill the promises they made to one another when they were sixteen. Jowan had held fast, and Tamsyn had come home.

Epilogue

Sixteen years later

TAMSYN HAD THE window of the ladies' parlor open to the sunlight, so that she, her daughter, and their visiting friends could enjoy it on this sweet spring afternoon. Patricia had come up from the village, and Evangeline and her daughters from the steward's college.

They were sewing, the three girls with less enthusiasm than the adults, but the Easter festival was early this year, and they had all promised to support the school's stall.

The older two boys had gone down to the village, but Evangeline's Rick was somewhere about the estate with Bran and Jowan.

Being closest to the window, Tamsyn was the first to hear the ponies coming up the lane, and the boys shouting encouragement to the ponies and insults to one another.

"Will those boys ever grow up?" sighed Tamara, despising the two twelve-year-olds from the lofty age of fifteen. She had recently persuaded her mother Evangeline and a reluctant Bran that she was old enough to let down her skirts and had immediately given up any pursuit that might be regarded as childish.

Janet, Tamsyn's daughter, rushed to the window. "Joe is in

the lead," she reported. "He will win, for Tom has stopped to speak to Papa and Uncle Bran. Now he is off again, but too late, for Joe is already here. He is waiting for Tom, though." Jowan and Tamsyn had named their children after the hero and heroine of the folk tale that had given them one another.

Eva, who was only a year older than Janet's seven and was Janet's dearest friend, joined Janet at the window. "Now they are both waiting for Da, Uncle Jowan, and Rick."

"The boys must have heard some news in the village," Evangeline said. "I do hope it is not the king."

"Oh, I hope not," Patricia agreed. "We do not want the Duchess of Kent as regent. Or that man."

Tamsyn agreed. Everyone in the realm knew that the king was not long for the world, but they would all be better off if he lived until the princess, and his heir, Victoria, turned eighteen. But they would not have long to wait to find out. She could hear them talking as they approached the open door, the two boys cheerfully bickering.

"You got there first, Joe. You tell her." That was Tamsyn's older child, her darling Tom, bending over backward to be fair. An image of her beloved Jowan, he patterned himself on his father in all things. He could not do better, in Tamsyn's estimation.

"She is your mother, Tom. I think you should do the honors." Joe, after the triumph of victory, was prone to give away any spoils to please his friends. Jowan Artos Hughes had been born to Evangeline five days before Tamsyn gave birth to Thomas Branoc Trethewey, and they had been dearest companions ever since.

"Do it together," suggested Jowan, following the boys through the doorway, and ruffling the hair of his namesake.

Tamsyn waited, smiling as Bran and Rick entered to join the rest of the family. The little parlor where the women had been sewing and chatting seemed suddenly even smaller, but there were seats enough to go around, and Tamsyn would ring for tea and the food that the growing children seemed to need in huge quantities.

"Mama," Tom said, after a look at his cousin and best friend, "we have collected the mail and you have a letter."

He nodded to Joe, who continued, "It is from London, Auntie Tamsyn. From your publisher."

"It is a thick one," Tom commented, handing it over. "We think it must have a contract in it, Mama."

"Of course, it does," Joe said, stoutly. "Auntie Tamsyn's music is beautiful."

"Your concertos are wonderful, Mama," Tom agreed.

Tamsyn read the envelope and confirmed it was from the publisher in London who printed and distributed her music. Was it what she hoped?

"Open it, Mama," Janet said.

"Yes, Auntie Tamsyn, open it," agreed Eva.

"Girls," warned Evangeline, but her eyes said, "Open it."

Jowan came to her side and put a hand on her shoulder. "Shall I put it away and give it to you later? Or not at all?" he offered. His grin hinted that he made the offer to tease the children, who rewarded him with a groan.

Tamsyn appreciated the effort to distract her from her uncertainties. She had started writing music for her students years ago—simple but pretty tunes that a beginning pianist would find pleasurable to play. Jowan had suggested other people would enjoy them and find them useful, and his friends in London had found her a publisher and distributor.

One book after another had followed, as she wrote for more and more accomplished students. Different types of music: etudes, preludes, polonaises, nocturnes, waltzes, ballades. Music for the piano and the harpsichord. Music for instruments and for singers. Music by T. Trethewey was being used all over Britain and its foreign territories.

Then three months ago, she had finally sent the man her concertos, scored for a piano and all the other instruments of a typical orchestra. She had received a letter enclosing a draft contract and saying he was sharing them with other musicians to get their assessment. Then nothing. Until now.

"I will open it," she told her anxious family, and they all beamed, but stayed silent as she used the letter opener Jowan offered her. It took her a moment to realize what she was seeing. A covering letter. A bundle of printed copies of what proved to be her concertos. And two more documents on thick paper, folded and tied with ribbon. She opened one. It looked like a contract.

Her family were all waiting to find out what she had received. She passed out the copies of the music. "He has printed the concertos," she said.

Tom led a cheer, and even the adults joined in.

Tamsyn barely noticed. She was reading the letter. "Jowan?" She put out a hand, and her beloved husband was right there, ready to offer his support, as he always had.

"What is it, Tamsyn?"

"A contract," she told him.

"For the concertos," he said.

"Yes, but a second one." She handed him the letter.

He managed to read both pages without letting go of her hand, and he looked up, his eyes bright with pride and love. "The United States of America, Tamsyn. They have sent you a contract to have your music published in the United States of America."

Tamsyn nodded. She could hardly believe it.

Tom let out another cheer, and Joe said to Tamara, "Play us a triumphal march, Tam. Come on everyone! A march in honor of Auntie Tamsyn."

A march! In her little parlor! In moments, Tam was pounding out a march on the square piano that had once graced her cottage, and even the adults were on their feet, miming instruments or swinging their arms like soldiers as they marched in and out of furniture, shouting "Hurrah," in response to Tom's "Hip, hip," and in time to the music.

The celebration spilled over to the servants and spread

through the house, and cake and cider appeared to fuel the festivities, as all of Tamsyn's nearest and dearest took their turn to peer at the letter and admire the contract.

The visitors ended up staying for dinner, which was early in the Trethewey house so that Janet could be included. Afterward, Patricia had to go home. "I have books to mark before the morning," she insisted.

Patricia still lived in Tamsyn's cottage. Tamsyn had given her a life tenancy when Patricia agreed to take over from the innkeeper's wife as a permanent teacher. A much younger assistant teacher had moved in five years ago, and Patricia was talking about cutting back her hours, but Tamsyn would believe it when she saw it.

"I'll send you down in the gig, Patricia," Jowan said. "You shouldn't be walking in the dark." He had a word with Tom, who rushed away with Joe to organize it.

"It is time for us to be off home, too," said Evangeline. "I am so proud of you, Tamsyn, I could burst." She gave Tamsyn a hug. "Tell Joe to head home when he gets back from taking his Auntie Patricia back to Apple Cottage."

"Time for bed for you, Janet my love," Tamsyn told her youngest. "I shall be up in a few minutes to give you a kiss.

The large entry hall at Inneford House rapidly emptied, until only Tamsyn stood there, Jowan having escorted Patricia to the gig. She turned in a circle, her arms out and her head back, and so Jowan found her when he stepped back inside.

"Happy, darling?" he asked, kissing her fingers where her wedding ring nestled next to the signet ring he had given her so long ago.

"Happy. I am the most fortunate of women, beloved, and that is even without contracts from America. You, our two beautiful children. Work that I love. Wonderful friends. A village full of neighbors."

"We have been greatly blessed," Jowan agreed. "Tamsyn, Tom asked if he could stay with Joe tonight, and I said he could go straight there after they return the gig to the stable."

"Let us say goodnight to Janet and go to bed ourselves," Tamsyn suggested.

As always, her husband's gaze heated. "Two minds with but a single thought," he said.

Sometime later they lay, as they often did after physical loving, in one another's arms. "I am," said Tamsyn, "perfectly happy." Even as she said it, she realized she had given her husband the opening line for one of his favorite jokes, and sure enough, he pasted on a mournful look.

"I have just one niggling fly in the perfect ointment of my bliss," he told her, sadly.

She rolled her eyes, but said, "And what was that, my love?"

"Who is Mac?" Jowan asked. "And what does he know?"

THE END

The story of Tam Lin, True Thomas, Tamlaine, Thomas the Rhymer
The story that inspired *Hold Me Fast* is "Tam Lin" (and all its variants), in which a faithful sweetheart is determined to rescue her beloved from the Faery.

I say "story" rather than "stories" because they are, in essence, the same tale told in different ways by different bards, poets, or storytellers. The Queen of the Faeries steals away a human to entertain her and her court. He is sometimes a musician, sometimes a poet, and sometimes both. He is always called some variant of the name Thomas. He becomes the Queen's lover and remains with her for seven years. (In some stories, it is seven years in faery time, but much longer passes in the everyday world.)

In the tale of True Thomas, the Queen sends him home at the end of his time, with the "gift" that he cannot tell a lie.

In other versions, she plans to offer him to hell to pay a tax owed by the faeries. Shortly before the tax falls due, he meets Janet (Margaret in some versions), who decides to rescue him. This involves pulling him from his horse during a midnight ride of the faery court and holding him while the Queen turns him into all sorts of dangerous and dire things.

When the Queen realizes she has lost her pet, she loses her temper still further, but her threats and ranting cannot now keep the two lovers apart. Tam (Tom) is saved from his fate and is back in the human world.

This is one of my favorite folk tales, and I wanted to do it justice. As soon as I began to think about the mechanics of Regency-era people with the underlying viciousness and cold-hearted hedonism of the faeries in the oldest tales, I knew I had a group of selfish entitled aristocratic men with too much money and too little conscience. And what is more likely than that a person in withdrawal from drug addiction is going to be changeable, near mindless, and dangerous?

By the way, I use the spelling faery, for the Fae of the old tales do not at all resemble the sweet creatures of more modern stories, with their butterfly wings, and their human-like lives and morals.

Cornwall and Cornish

This story is at least partially set in Cornwall, so I thought a few notes about that county might be in order. Tin has been mined in Cornwall for four thousand years, right to the end of the twentieth century. Other metals, too. By the mid-nineteenth century, overseas competition made the Cornish mines less profitable, and so many miners and their families emigrated that the Cornish have a saying: "A mine is a hole in the ground with a Cornishman at the bottom".

In my research, I discovered that Cornish (Kernewek) is one of those languages that has been brought back from extinction in the past fifty years. It is still classified as critically endangered. In the sixteenth century, many people in Cornwall spoke only Kernewek and objected strongly to the English Book of Common Prayer becoming the sole legal form of worship in England.

The so-called Prayer Book Rebellion was harshly put down. The language declined in the next two centuries, for several reasons, but at least in part because the local gentry adopted English so that they would not be considered disloyal and rebellious.

By the end of the eighteenth century, very few people (and perhaps no young people) spoke Kernewek.

Names are a different matter. Both first names and surnames are passed down through the generations. My hero and heroine have Cornish first names, as do several of the other Cornish characters.

As to the bogs and mires that play an important part in the story, Bodmin Moor has numerous peat deposits, as well as spectacular granite outcrops. Blanket bogs are peatlands that cover crests, slopes, flats, and hollows of a gently undulating terrain. Valley mires are areas of water-logged deep peat in valley bottoms or channels.

Good advice to walkers is to test the depth of any wet or shaky ground before they step on it.

Drugs, sex, and music

What drugs might have been accessible to my villain?

Laudanum was legal and easily available. It was sold as the answer to all sorts of things, from sleeplessness and sorrow to toothache in babies. Laudanum is a mix of opium and alcohol. It mightn't fix what ails you, but you won't care anymore. It is brutally addictive, as many users found at their cost.

The market also contained other "medicines" that contained opium. Dover powder was a mix of opium and ipecacuanha, to be taken in a sweet drink such as a white wine posset. Godfrey's cordial combined opium with treacle and spices in water.

Opium itself was also readily available, to smoke, chew, or otherwise consume.

In all those forms, the benefit was a euphoric "rush" followed by relaxation. And in all these forms, people became addicted with regular use.

Ether was a new toy for the idle in search of a thrill, too. Sold as a medicine called Anodyne, liquid diethyl ether gave users dissociative effects and a sensation of happiness. Warming it and smelling the vapors worked faster, but ether is highly flammable, which could be problematic in the hands of those high on the effects. Burns were common.

Cannabis and its derivatives weren't readily available from the neighborhood apothecary, but it's likely that my villain could have found *majoun* or *char* as—blocks of cannabis resin—in the docklands, where sailors might well have imported such products for their own use and for sale.

Nitrous oxide parties also fall within my time period, with gatherings to inhale the product held as early as 1799. The idea that laughing gas might have medical applications wasn't picked up for another forty-five years.

Spanish fly, a preparation made from blister beetles, was used as an aphrodisiac. It caused a rush of blood to the sexual organs and was highly toxic. As was Fowler's preparation, a solution using arsenic for the same purpose.

Were psychotropic mushrooms in use in England at the time? We know that in 1799 a family picked mushrooms in Green Park, cooked them up, and ate them. The father and four sons experienced spontaneous laughter followed by delirium. This was in the news at the time. You can, if you wish, take the view that idle dilettantes like my heroine's patrons would read about such an event and decide that mushrooms were a step too far. But I'd be willing to bet that some of them had a go. Certainly, my rotten lot did so.

And when all else fails, there's always alcohol. I've written before about the huge quantities consumed as a matter of course at all levels of society. Yes, glasses were much smaller than they are today, and so were bottles. And alcohol content was probably lower than it is today. But still, the reported volumes downed in a night are astounding. It was by no means unusual for a man to down seven or eight glasses of wine at a meal followed by several bottles of port or brandy over the evening. A three-bottle man was nothing surprising. A six-bottle man set an example to be admired.

Those were men, though. Wealthy influential men. Women also tippled but were not admired for it. And the drinking of the poor was accounted to their shame. Ah, me.

The idea that it might be desirable to abstain from alcohol and other drugs was still a highly unpopular one. It was not until the 1830s that the earliest temperance advocates began to set their sights on the elimination of spirits, and opium continued to be part of a home medical kit in the United Kingdom until well into the twentieth century.

Humanity continues to seek easy ways to escape from troubles, not counting the cost. I believe—I hope that my stories show—that true happiness can be found in the love and support of our friends and family.

About the Author

Have you ever wanted something so much you were afraid to even try? That was Jude ten years ago.

For as long as she can remember, she's wanted to be a novelist. She even started dozens of stories, over the years.

But life kept getting in the way. A seriously ill child who required years of therapy; a rising mortgage that led to a full-time job; six children, her own chronic illness... the writing took a back seat.

As the years passed, the fear grew. If she didn't put her stories out there in the market, she wouldn't risk making a fool of herself. She could keep the dream alive if she never put it to the test.

Then her mother died. That great lady had waited her whole life to read a novel of Jude's, and now it would never happen.

So Jude faced her fear and changed it—told everyone she knew she was writing a novel. Now she'd make a fool of herself for certain if she didn't finish.

Her first book came out to excellent reviews in December 2014, and the rest is history. Many books, lots of positive reviews, and a few awards later, she feels foolish for not starting earlier.

Jude write historical fiction with a large helping of romance, a splash of Regency, and a twist of suspense. She then tries to figure out how to slot the story into a genre category. She's mad keen on history, enjoys what happens to people in the crucible of a passionate relationship, and loves to use a good mystery and some real danger as mechanisms to torture her characters.

Dip your toe into her world with one of her lunch-time reads collections or a novella, or dive into a novel. And let her know what you think.

Website and blog:
judeknightauthor.com

Subscribe to newsletter:
judeknightauthor.com/newsletter

Bookshop:
judeknight.selz.com

Facebook:
facebook.com/JudeKnightAuthor

Twitter:
twitter.com/JudeKnightBooks

Pinterest:
nz.pinterest.com/jknight1033

Bookbub:
bookbub.com/profile/jude-knight

Books + Main Bites:
bookandmainbites.com/JudeKnightAuthor

Amazon author page:
amazon.com/Jude-Knight/e/B00RG3SG7I

Goodreads:
goodreads.com/author/show/8603586.Jude_Knight

LinkedIn:
linkedin.com/in/jude-knight-465557166